NAMPA PUBLIC
LIBRARY

In memory of
George B. Amundson
from
family and friends

Crow
in
Stolen Colors

Crow
in
Stolen Colors

Marcia Simpson

Poisoned Pen Press
Scottsdale, Arizona

Poisoned Pen Press
6962 E. First Ave. Ste 103
Scottsdale, AZ 85251
www.poisonedpenpress.com
sales@poisonedpenpress.com

Printed in the United States of America

For David
who shares the Great Adventure

Acknowledgments

My profound gratitude to the following people:

Dave Jack, former lieutenant, Wrangell Police Department, then harbor master; the Lopez Writers' Group: Marcia Barthelow, Kip Greenthal, Georgie Muska, John Sangster, and Alie Smaalders, for all their encouragement; Jane Chelius, Natalee Rosenstein, and Barbara Peters, for wonderful support; my husband, David, who read the manuscript over and over and over; Sheila Simpson-Creps and Dave Simpson, superb readers; and most of all, Shirley Hake, who gave me the hero of this story.

The village of Kashevarof and the Marten House people exist only in the author's imagination, and there is, as yet, no logging operation at Steamer Bay. Otherwise, Wrangell and the waters west of Wrangell are as accurate as charts and memory can make them.

...For them the stone lamp flickered
and the drafty cave
was walled with visions.

The stories they told us were true,
we should have believed them:...

John Haines:
Watching the Fire

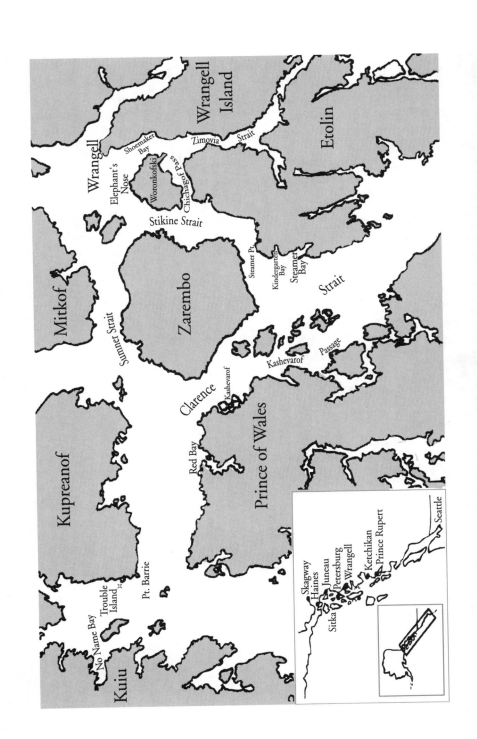

Prologue

From the troller's bow, the man watched wind write across Steamer Bay. The bay was poked like an arrow into the side of the island; the tide had barely turned to flood. He favored low tide in strange waters. At low tide you could see more dangers. And for this Raven man, Elder of a dwindling, ragtag village, dangers were everywhere.

He could see a little notch of sandy beach over there. Odd the way those black boulders lined up. He knew the ocean did some funny things with rocks, nudged them up in rows, threw them over logs and ledges. But the tide line curved with the shore, while that rock line was straight.

"The tide's coming in over those rocks," he said to his nephew, pointing at the shore. "Another hour and they'll all be hidden. We'll row in. There's something wrong over there."

He took the little inflatable down from the wheelhouse roof and dropped it over the rail, steadying it while the boy climbed over. Then the man climbed down and took the oars.

"Tell a story," he told the boy. The boy looked back at him, no smile except his eyes.

"One time," the boy said, "the Grandmother is chasing her son through the forest to catch back from him the fish pole he stole, and the fish pole, it's shouting and catching trees..."

"Only seven winters on this earth and already sassing," the man said. "You'd better watch yourself, or you'll be the bait on the hook of that fish pole. Now, tell one of those I taught you."

The boy nodded but his eyes laughed still. "In long ago when Man came, First People hid theirselves in Water and Stone, Fog and Wind..."

The man stared over the boy's shoulder, and the words flowed past like the green water. Could he hold this child long enough to teach him all the stories, all the ways of living kindly with Earth? Most of the others had left, gone to make some life in that world where Time moved fast and all one way, no circle for keeping honor with Past or Place. Only twenty-six left in the village, most old, only three children now, and not likely they'd care. Not likely they'd stay.

He looked at the boy, worried, and tried to put the worry from his head. He tried to catch in on the story, but it had slipped by like the wake of the raft. "Did you tell about First People turning into Bear and Beaver?" he asked.

"You don't even listen so good as Listening Stone," the boy said, scowling. "I said all that and I told how Bear led First People up the mountain in the flood."

"Tell another," the man said, but the boy folded his arms across his chest and turned his head away, and the man laughed to himself.

When they heard the raft grind itself on gravel, the boy climbed out and led the bow line up the beach, knotting it around a boulder. The man stayed sitting there on the seat, staring up at the snow-covered rocks on the island's backbone. Mid-March now, day and night almost the same length. A thousand streams slip-sliding down from snowfields—he could hear the water rushing, see it dig its tracks across the gravel beach.

Out there by the Point, the spruce poles on his old hand troller, *Sarah Moon*, dipped and rose in a sudden gust. When they got home from fishing, he and the boy would give it a coat of paint. Not much of a boat, old twenty-five-foot double-ender, cramped little wheelhouse. Still, with the hand-troll permit, they'd caught enough salmon and halibut to keep alive, some to smoke and some to sell. But he better stop this looking. He hadn't come over here to stare.

He pulled himself to his feet, swung a leg over and climbed out. The boy had trotted along the beach to the farthest point.

The man watched and the boy circled his arms and shouted against the wind. A flock of gulls rose screaming.

The man walked along the line of black boulders. They were set below the last high tide line, the water coming back now to cover them. He went over to the smallest one and got down on his knees, ran his hand over the top of the rock, then the sides. He knew already what he would find. He dug his fingers into the sand and pried. The rock levered itself over and Raven's round eye stared out at him.

A petroglyph. A rock carved by his ancestors. Eight thousand years ago. Ten, maybe. By every stream and river, the petroglyphs had called to the salmon: "Come home, come home." Those rocks were missing now, stolen and sold, hidden in warehouses and back corners at down south art galleries. One time, not long back, those men had come around, talking, asking, wanting. He didn't listen. The things they wanted didn't belong to him. The things they wanted belonged to no one and everyone.

His finger followed the outline of Raven's eye and beak. First People. Raven had tricked First People out of the Sun and Moon; had created a new people from Leaf. But Raven hadn't changed since someone spent years—years—carving his picture into this rock with a stone tool. Raven was Always.

His ancestors had carved rocks and totem poles so they would remember how Raven stole the Box of Daylight, how Grizzly Bear saved the people from the glacier floods, how Eagle was avenged against the great hunter. In case they would forget, they made masks and rattles and bowls to tell those stories with songs and feasts.

Then the missionaries came. Jealous for their own god, they were. Thought the totem poles and masks and rattles were worshipped, so they'd ordered them burned. Not many stories had escaped those missionary fires.

He didn't know how long he crouched there looking at Raven. Anyway, till his nephew came back.

"These rocks lived somewhere," he told the boy. "Each rock lived at one special stream or beach or ledge. Now they can't ever go home."

He felt tears coming and looked away at the sea bending over the reef. "Raven," he said, "this Raven right here looking at us..."

But the boy wasn't looking at Raven, he was looking at the man, so the man tried to hide away his tears. "It wasn't stolen," the man said. "It was kidnapped."

Some time in the night, the man woke up. It was so dark below deck that he had no eyes. He lay there listening to the boy's whispering breath and the water trickling along the hull as the boat swung slowly on her anchor. Then, far in the distance, he heard the sound of another boat. Not many boats this time of year—they'd traveled all the day before, seen only a tug pulling a fuel barge out in Sumner Strait and a few fishing boats. This boat sounded large, the heavy, water-muffled drum-drum of an engine coming near.

He felt around for the child and put his arm across him. The boy sighed and turned over. The man whispered, "Where White Bird flies up and Raven waits for Salmon..."

"High above is Listening Stone," the boy said, yawning and pushing his legs out straight. Then he told the rest of the story in quiet words while the man waited.

"Always remember it," the man said. "You remember even when you are old and I am gone and there is another boy to tell. You say it so much you will never forget."

Now the man heard water boil past and slosh against the hull next to his head and he was afraid. He felt a shadow passing over, darker even than the pitch blackness in front of his eyes. Something bumped the rail and lines snaked along the deck above their heads. The troller listed sharply as somebody climbed over the rail. The man threw the sleeping bag back and stood up.

"Somebody aboard," he said. "You stay here." He poked the cover tight around the boy to keep him safe. Then he mounted the ladder and slid the wheelhouse door open. A boat towered next to the troller, a black shape painted on paler sky.

"Hello?" he said to the person facing him, someone standing right there, only a few feet away. Then, in the smallest slit of time, he knew that his voice made him a perfect target.

Chapter 1

Shivering inside her black rain gear, Liza Romero stomped her feet and muttered to herself while she waited for the anchor to come up.

Say it's black, Liza. Say everything's black: sky, sea, nightmares. The color of your true love's hair. Your life. Say you're crazy? Say your brain lists to port?

When she heard the anchor clank against the bow, she slammed the brake over on the windlass. She'd been having trouble with slippage on the big winch that hauls in the anchor chain, but today when she threw herself hard on the brake, the anchor chain didn't slip at all.

Thrusting her way past the crates of Leghorn pullets, she shouted, "Sky's falling, Chicken Little." The chickens, ruffled and sulky under their green tarp, made gulping noises deep in their throats.

No one yells at chickens, Liza. One oar short, lady. But good lord, who would try to raise chickens in the bush? Nothing but a bear cafeteria.

Lashed along the rails next to the chickens were eight cases of motor oil, a boxed refrigerator, a small gasoline generator, and twelve rolls of barbed wire, the day's freight for Kashevarof. And in the former captain's stateroom, books. "You're the librarian, ain'cha?" they'd said, when she announced her delivery service to the roadless villages and logging camps. "Bring us some books."

Liza kicked the door of the wheelhouse shut before Sam could pry his way past her. Sam, product of a yellow Lab and a lanky red hound, had a retriever's swimming ability but a hound's sleek russet coat and ground-covering speed. Clearly a much improved product. She peered through the window at his sorrowing brown eyes and stuck her tongue out. Improved product, yes, but very very wet.

In the fierce gray dawn, she eased the *Salmon Eye* through the shallows of Kindergarten Bay. She chewed her lip, watching the numbers on the depth finder bounce around—ninety-four, thirty-one, sixty-seven, seventeen. The ancient boat, sixty feet long at the water line, drew almost nine feet.

"Mariners with local knowledge," the *Coast Pilot* recommended. Well, she'd been acquiring "local knowledge" the hard way. A steep learning curve. Alaska's rock-strewn waters were no place to make a mistake.

The *Salmon Eye* was an old wooden halibut schooner turned salmon packer turned delivery boat, with the wheelhouse aft and a crane on the foredeck for hoisting fish or freight. Yesterday, in heavy seas, the hydraulic lines to the crane had broken, spraying the deck with an oily film. Liza had turned in to make repairs. Maybe she should have gone on around the corner into Steamer Bay, which was deeper.

In the wheelhouse, the green cat's eye of the radar circled and the radio was waking up, fishermen making first contacts of the day, the Coast Guard weather report…"trough of low pressure…Sumner and Clarence Straits, gale warning, southeast winds to forty-five knots….'"

She cranked the wheel to starboard to avoid the rocky island in the center of the bay and flexed her fingers, realizing how tightly she'd been holding on. Holding on was all she did anymore.

The *Salmon Eye* was passing Steamer Point when Sam raced to the bow. Propping his front paws on the rail, ears streaming like a windsock, he pointed his nose at the sky and bayed. Liza's neck prickled. Even whales or sea lions didn't make Sam sound like that. She throttled down and put the gears in neutral.

Grabbing the binoculars, she scanned the ocean, then the shore, and almost missed it, the thing that was lying there. All one color with the rocks. When she did see it, she said, "Seal, Sam—it's just a seal, for pete's sake." But a second look told her it was no seal. Someone human huddled in fetal position, the tide rising so fast it was going to be a race to get to the rocks ahead of the water. No one else in sight, no boat, no sign of debris, nothing floating at all except a flock of murres beyond the Point.

"Wretched dog," she muttered, heading for the wheelhouse. "We didn't need this." Sam wagged in disagreement. Salvage rights. Whatever was on that rock belonged to him.

Liza put the *Salmon Eye* back in gear. When the depth sounder showed ten fathoms, she dropped the anchor and hurled the inflatable raft off the stern. She grabbed a couple of life jackets out of the locker and tossed them into the raft. On top of Sam. "No," she shouted. "You're not going."

He shrank down against the raft's floorboards, his eyes pleading. She looked across at the lump on the rocks. The water had risen till it was almost lapping whoever it was. Cursing, she dropped over the rail and shoved Sam out of the way while she jammed the oars into the oarlocks.

The current carried the raft to the rocks so fast she needed the oars only to stay on course. The water had just covered the ledge beyond the body; the raft bumped and scraped over great clumps of blue-brown mussels.

A small boy, curled on his side, lay motionless an arm's length beyond reach. The rock was flat and low in the water. Liza tried to hang on, but the rock was slippery. Barnacles razored her palms. A wave exploded into needles and drenched her with spray.

Lean out—hook the oar under the boy's leg. But the raft slammed into the rocks, and Liza clung to the upper side of it, shouting, "Wake up...hey! Wake up!" while Sam clawed frantically at the floorboards.

Now the waves were lapping the boy's legs. Liza fought the raft around, bringing it stern to, and wrestled Sam into the bow. On the next surge she leaned all the way over, one ripple from disaster, and grabbed the boy's foot. The boy slid across the rock on his back, clothes catching in cracks and barnacles. The trough sucked the raft away from the rock and the boy came streaming along behind it.

Liza struggled to lift his face out of the water. He was carried up on the next crest. She threw herself backward, and the boy came hurtling over the stern to the floor. Instantly she felt his neck for a pulse, thought she caught it, the faintest tick in all the thunderous commotion of the sea.

Clear the airway. Victims of near-drowning often vomit. She tried to turn him on his side, but Sam, in an extremity of joy, began licking his face. Liza knocked Sam away, but he squeezed under her arm, falling heavily across the child, licking frantically as though his tongue could rough the life back into this small person. And it did.

The boy raised one shoulder and ducked his head, trying to protect his face. They were all in the stern now, the raft nearly vertical from their weight. Liza slid her parka off to wrap around the child. Then she crawled to the center, jammed the loose oar back into the oarlock, and pulled hard against the current for the *Salmon Eye.*

The boy struggled to shove Sam away from him. Liza didn't interfere. Hypothermia consumes the sleepers—the more he fought, the more he'd keep the blood coursing his veins. He opened his eyes an instant, glanced at Sam, and squeezed them tight as though the dog was part of some unbearable nightmare.

Strands of straight black hair clung wetly to his face and neck; the skin of his face had a withered look from cold and water—how long could he possibly have survived those temperatures? His coloring, despite the drained pallor of his face, made her think he must be a Tlingit Native. Maybe seven or eight years old?

From the corner of her eye now, Liza could see the *Salmon Eye* swinging on her anchor, long gray hull barely outlined against the shore. An iron lid had clapped down over the water, rain hammered the washboard surface, and a gust of wind drove them the final few yards.

The child was too groggy to protest when Liza stripped off his soaked clothes and rubbed him vigorously with a rough towel before thrusting him into a sleeping bag by the stove.

His shoes or boots were missing—his feet bare and scratched. He had a blackening bruise under one eye, and the palms of his hands were gouged.

Except for the swollen bruise, he seemed remarkably unscathed. Questions, questions, but things to do first. She felt his pulse again—fast but regular—and watched his breathing another moment.

The diesel stove was still warm. She turned it up, filled the kettle, and set it on top. While she waited for the water to heat, Sam turned three times in ancient ritual and settled down on top of the sleeping bag, arranging himself so he could lick the boy's face as needed. Liza filled two mason jars, squatted and thrust them into the sleeping bag—armpit and groin, she thought, trying to remember the instructions from a long-ago first aid course. And not too hot at first. Warm tea.

She made tea, put lots of sugar in it, and sat down beside the boy, propping him across her knee. Sam sat up to watch, his head lowered like an anxious nanny. "Can you drink some of this?" she asked.

He dipped his chin and swallowed, made a face and shook his head. She held the mug there, pressing it to his lower lip, and in a minute he took another swallow, then shuddered.

"Tea," she said. "Drink some more. It'll help you warm up."

He rolled his eyes to look up at her. Then he took one more sip and pushed the mug away decisively.

"I'm Liza Romero. What's your name?"

"James."

"What's the rest of your name?" Liza rubbed her hand gently over his salt-sticky hair. "James what?"

"Why is that dog sitting on me?"

"He likes you. He found you, so he thinks you belong to him. His name is Sam. Sam Romero," she said, trying to prompt him.

"He keeps licking me. He's wet."

"Do you want me to put him out?"

James shook his head and touched one of Sam's velvet ears, provoking a sigh.

"How old are you?"

"Eight next time."

"James, listen. I'm going to call on the radio and get help. Tell me your mom's name, or your dad's.

"No." He slid down in the sleeping bag till only the top of his head was visible. Another "no" was muffled by the down filling.

Liza climbed the three steps into the wheelhouse and unhooked the transmitter. "U.S. Coast Guard, Ketchikan Group, this is *Salmon Eye.*"

When they answered, she switched to Channel two-two alpha, their official "talk" channel. After the usual preliminaries— *"what is your present location—how many aboard—do you need medical assistance at this time?"* she launched into what little she knew.

"He's seven or eight years old, black hair and eyes, Native American, I think, first name is James. I picked him up about zero seven hundred on the rocks just southeast of Steamer Point. He seems to be doing all right at the moment—strong pulse and respiration. Over."

"Roger, Salmon Eye. We have no reports of anyone missing off a vessel. Any sign of another boat, or debris from a boat? Over."

"I can't see anything like that from here."

"We'll check it out. Have you questioned him?"

"I've tried, but so far he's given me almost no information."

"Roger, Salmon Eye. We'll send someone out. What's your destination?"

"I was on my way to Kashevarof, but I'll head back to Wrangell now."

"Your ETA, Wrangell?"

"Approximately twelve hundred if the weather doesn't get worse."

"We'll put out a description and call you if we get anything. And we'll check the area—no distress calls in the last twenty-four, but we'll look. Please stand by on sixteen, Salmon Eye. This is U.S. Coast Guard, Ketchikan Group, out."

"Roger. *Salmon Eye*, standing by on sixteen."

She grabbed a sweatshirt off a hook by the door, got out a pair of sweatpants and some wool socks and helped James into them, then replaced the water bottles in the sleeping bag.

"Why do you have that dog?"

"Because I get lonesome if nobody's around."

James looked directly at her for the first time. "You do?" he said. "You like to have a dog so you don't get lonesome?"

"Sure. We keep each other company—he's a good friend."

"Yeah," he said. "He's a Sam dog, isn't he, a friend, isn't he—like, maybe I could be his friend, too." Suddenly his eyes were brimming. "Was somebody by me? Like, in the water?"

"No," Liza said, with a surge of panic. "Were you with someone? Is somebody else out there in the water?"

"No. There's not somebody." He looked away, biting his lower lip fiercely. "Not *anybody*." He started to sob.

She hugged him to her a moment, then rolled him off her lap. From the deck, she scanned the shore and the broken surface of the ocean. The rock where James was lying had vanished except for a spin of spray where each wave fractured as it passed. She could see no one else.

Her stomach clenched. This whole damned coast was a magnificent frigid lie. Had she missed someone? Someone too cold to swim anymore? A moment was all it would take, one fleeting instant.

Liza shoved a reluctant Sam, her lookout, onto the spraysoaked deck, and raised the anchor. Edging the shoreline, she tried to scan the rocks and arcs of gravel beach, but rain draped the forest and melted the shore to gray mush.

As they rounded the wooded islet holding Steamer Point light, Sam threw his head back and bayed. Five bald eagles rose and perched in the trees. Swirls of ravens lifted silently, then descended to the rocks again, picking stiffly along the edge, regal in their irritation.

Through the binoculars, Liza could see the ocean pounding itself into shards on a series of ledges that rose like Neptune's ladder. Protruding from the back of one of the ledges were two human legs.

Chapter 2

"Hello? Yes...speaking."

"Did you get it?"

"What we have right now are seventy-three spruce root baskets, some bentwood boxes, several amulets, six Chilkat blankets..."

"Yeah, but I mean the..."

"...three fine examples of early Shaman masks. A Marten House crest headdress. And the best preserved..."

"This is a terrible connection. Can you hear me? I asked if you got the..."

"...the best preserved group of totem poles so far. Original paint. Also a superb box drum, and a carved salmon trap stake."

"A what?"

"A salmon trap stake. They were set on the weirs to show respect for the salmon. Nice little knickknack, worth maybe a couple thousand."

"All right. Whatever. Is this stuff already shipped?"

"We never ship C.O.D."

"I just deposited a bank draft to the Alaska West account in the amount we agreed on."

"Good. Excellent. So, we're crating up the small things and you'll have them by the end of next week. And the large items, the petroglyphs from Tuxekan and Porcupine Creek and the totem poles, are stored where they won't be noticed till the barge can pick them up."

"Okay, now answer my question, goddammit. Did you find the Stone?"

"You mean the Listening Stone? No, we don't have the Listening Stone."

"I want it. It's the heart of a lost culture. Priceless, till we put a number on it. And according to all the stories, it marks something else of enormous value."

"If it exists—a big 'if,' I'd say—there was only one man who knew its location. And we never did persuade him."

"Remember I'm talking seven figures. Nobody'd ignore that."

"This man lived in a remote village—leftover band of people devoted to the old ways—nothing to spend money on—and he was their respected Elder. Their Chief. The only chance, the one we were going for, was his nephew, who would have been the next..."

"Hey—hey, listen to this—they've found the kid."

"Hang on—something's coming in on the radio."

"They've got the kid."

"Alive?"

"Catch this call—someone talking to the Coast Guard."

"...be doing all right at the moment—strong pulse and respiration. Over."

"Roger, Salmon Eye. We'll send someone out. What's your destination?"

"Salmon Eye! Shit, why'd it have to be her? Goddammit. Hello? Listen...something's come up...I have to go. But on the Listening Stone: it's possible we can track it down. Seven figures, right? I'll get back to you in a couple days."

"Well, stay on it."

"Right. Right, we sure will. So long, now."

"A million plus?"

"Yup. That's what the man said. So when that kid jumped over and didn't show up in the floodlights, it was megabucks on the bottom. We're maybe in luck, though, for once. Are you absolutely sure you scuttled the boat? Opened all the sea cocks?"

"Yeah, yeah, sure...she was half under before we even left the bay."

"Okay. So long as it's down. And maybe the kid won't remember who we are. It was really dark."

"We gotta get him again, is all."

"You think she'll leave him by himself one single second? Not her, man. No way."

"He's spilling already—they're blasting his name all over Southeast Alaska."

"Shit. Now we'll have to get them both."

Chapter 3

"Wrangell Police Department. Sure, sure, I'll tell him. He'll get back to you right away. Have a good day, now."

Lieutenant Paul Howard bolted through the door of his cubicle before the extension could ring. Who'd hired that lousy woman with the sweetie-pie voice? He couldn't stand to listen to her.

From the back of the outer office he could hear chatter over the VHF. He walked back and stood with his hands in his pockets, shoulders hunched, while he listened.

"...*seven or eight years old, black hair and eyes, Native American, I think. I picked him up about zero seven hundred on the rocks just southeast of Steamer Point.*"

Native kid. Hunh. What would some Indian kid be doing out there by Steamer Point? Little guy, too. Must have fallen off a boat. Paul hitched his shoulders up and down in nervous irritation. Seven or eight. Same age as Joey when Carolyn took him off to Texas.

"*Roger*, Salmon Eye..."

The *Salmon Eye*. That Romero woman.

"...ETA, Wrangell?"

"*Approximately twelve hundred if the weather doesn't get worse.*"

He listened to them sign off, then went back to his office. He sank down in the swivel chair and leaned back, bracing one foot on an open desk drawer. The phone rang. Norma from the front desk. "You pick up that radio bulletin on the *Salmon Eye?*"

"Got it. Lemme know if there's anything more on it."

"Sure. You bet. Have a good day, Paul."

Shoot that woman sometime. "Paauulll." "Have a good day, Paauulll." Sheesh.

He thought about the report. They'd be coming in around noon. Sure to check in at the police station. Before then, he'd call down to Ketchikan and see if they'd turned anything up. If not, he'd have to get hold of Community Services, find somebody to take the kid till they located his family.

Romero. Tex-Mex kind of name. What was her first name? Lizzie? Something like that. Long bones strung together on a tight wire was how he always thought of her. Strange face— bony, hooded black eyes almost like an Indian herself. Likely Mexican, though—name like that. He kind of liked her face, actually—wide mouth that turned down when she smiled, like she was mostly laughing at herself.

He grinned sourly. A pistol, according to some of the Library Board members he knew—most of them grateful when she set up the *Salmon Eye* as a freighter and left the front desk. He'd seen her around town some since then—she was Larry Hayden's babe. Oh, excuuuse him. Significant Other.

Thought it was about two years since she bought that boat from Hayden and started up her freight service. Funny guy, Hayden. He and Lizzie always seemed to be arguing about something or other—funny what made people stick with each other when they couldn't act happy together five minutes.

Well, it wasn't his problem. The Indian kid with Lizzie Romero was his problem. He picked up the phone and dialed the number for U.S. Coast Guard Ketchikan Group.

"Nothing so far. Yeah, yeah, it's odd, all right. We're checking the area—sent a helicopter out. No reports of a kid missing, no boat overdue. We'll keep checking. We've got a bulletin out, but so far, not a word."

"Okay, keep in touch."

"Right. We'll let you know if we get anything. Ciao."

Next he dialed the harbor master's office and actually reached the man. Usually he was out on the docks anticipating the next complaint. It seemed to Paul that harbor masters in Alaska had replaced lightning rods for attracting troubles.

"You catch that message from the *Salmon Eye*?" Paul asked.

"Sure did. Lucky she found him."

"Where's that boat berthed now?"

"Keeps it out at Shoemaker."

"Kind of an old tub, isn't it?"

"Hey, man, that's the old Lituya Bay. *I mean she is one old boat, built for a halibut schooner when the Indians were still paddling around out there in their war canoes. Hayden changed her name from* Lituya Bay *to* Salmon Eye *and packed salmon from the boats to the cannery, but after he took up flying he kinda let it go. Romero's fixed it up a little, but I dunno how much."*

"What slip's she in out at Shoemaker?"

"Outside finger—third in from the end. I'm looking right here on the chart."

"Okay. I'll take a run out there when she's due. We'll have to figure out something on that kid. Thanks a lot."

"Sure. You bet. Curious myself. Lemme know what happens."

"Right. I'll do that."

Paul hung up and stared at the stack of folders on his desk. He ought to do some work. She wouldn't be in for another couple hours. He glanced down the day's report:

4:10 A.M.—Disturbance/Disorderly Conduct: Three people yelling on Grief Street. Removed by friends before police arrival.

7:20 A.M.—Possible Fish and Game Violations: Buck deer in the back of a pickup. Turned out to be a decoy.

7:48 A.M.—Bear Complaint: Citizen reported a mama bear and 2 cubs in the back of the Forest Service parking lot.

A *mama* bear? Sheesh. Goldilocks for mayor?

He flipped through the file on Gordy Patrick—they'd transferred him up to the penitentiary at Lemon Creek yesterday. He'd have to go up to Juneau and testify when the case came up.

He'd accompanied the Federal Marshal and the Troopers out to the logging camp over there near Virginia Lake to pick him up. Recognized him when they took him. Been in Wrangell year before last. Couldn't miss that wide scar splitting his face down one side, beard didn't grow over it. Ugly bastard. Wanted on homicide/armed robbery in five states. Seven-Eleven clerk and three customers smeared in the potato chip aisle.

Norma again. "Can you take a call, Paul? Line two-ooo."

His hands clenched involuntarily.

"Yeah, hey, hello there, Myrtle. Long time no see. They what? Took all the totem poles? Yeah, I know where they were, that storage shed next to the old Wrangell Institute. Thought it was emptied when they moved the museum. Anything except the poles? Oh, they were just pieces of poles? You sure somebody hasn't put them away for safe-keeping till the museum's done?"

He pulled a yellow pad over and scratched, "Myrtle Joseph— pieces of poles, storage shed. Missing."

"I bet somebody from the museum put them some place else," he said, trying to reassure her. Myrtle must be eighty plus—one of the Elders—still had a finger in every pie and two if it was a Tlingit recipe.

"Sure," he said, "you bet I'll check it out. I gotta get out to Shoemaker later this morning anyhow, and I'll take a look at the shed." He drew a circle around the word 'missing' and made arrows from it like a sun. "But likely somebody just forgot to tell you they were putting them someplace else."

He listened to the negative grunt on the other end. Nobody would forget to tell Myrtle something as important as that. Even Paul knew nobody would forget to tell Myrtle if they were fooling around with tribal stuff.

"I'll get back to you soon as I check it out, Myrtle. You sit tight and don't worry. Yeah, yeah, I know a lot of old stuff has gone missing the last few years, but those things were locked up and hardly anybody knew they were there. It'll be somebody from the museum. That shed's damp, you know. Somebody thought, 'these things are gonna rot before the new place is done—let's clean 'em out and put 'em somewhere else till we move.'"

He connected the arrows around the sun and "missing" and boxed them in with bolts of lightning. "I'll call you back. Yeah, today—maybe early afternoon. Yeah, yeah, by one o'clock, no later. Okay, bye now."

Man, what a tiger that old lady was. One o'clock or she'd send Raven to steal his glasses. He snatched them off and threw them down on the desk. So take 'em, Raven. Shame the way his eyes were going. Jesus, *old* was like day after tomorrow.

He leaned back and rubbed his eyes wearily, staring at the wall. Chart of Wrangell Island, shaped like the dove of peace flying north, the least peaceable place he knew of, always factions and infighting, only pulled together when somebody was in trouble.

Bulletin board layered in notices from the state of Alaska, Wanted picture uglies. And snapshots, dozens of them, Joey at two on his kiddie car, Joey at five with the bug-eyed Irish Lord rockfish he'd pulled in off city dock, a five-by-seven enlargement of Joey laughing up at Carolyn only a month before she'd packed up and headed back to Texas with him. Paul had cut out the smiling, curly-haired blonde woman. Now all he ever saw was the hole.

"Line two, Paul."

Tasha George, a longtime worker in the drug abuse program in the building next door. *"You catch that radio report from the* Salmon Eye?" she said. *"Trust Liza to get into something every time she heads out of here."*

He sighed. Never mind the Romero woman—it was the Indian kid that worried him. "I heard it—Coast Guard hasn't got anything yet. She'll probably be in before long—I'll take a run out to Shoemaker and check."

"Pretty weird deal, isn't it? Kid just hanging out on a rock? Well, I just wanted to let you know in case you hadn't picked it up."

"Yeah, thanks. I better call the Tlingit council—the kid'll have to go someplace till we find his parents."

"Oh, someone's bound to turn up. Kids don't just float around like driftwood."

"Yeah, but she says he's an Indian kid, and the council won't want him put just any place."

"Oh, come on, Paul. You don't have to turn this into Wounded Knee, you know. I'll take him if it's all that important. My folks were down there on the beach carving petroglyphs—as far-back-Tlingit as they go."

"Well, we'll see. They oughta be here before long. I'll take a run out and see."

"Let me know—always room at Tasha's B and B. See ya."

He hung up and rocked back in the swivel chair, tapping his fingers on the blotter. Five years ago he wouldn't have cared that an Indian kid might go to white foster care. Carolyn, though...wrecked his life, stole his kid...

Shit. Why was he letting himself think this kind of junk? Paranoid, that's what it was. Any little thing came along, it pushed him into one of his black moods. Fifty-one. Maybe he was menopausal. He grunted and smacked the desktop with one hand. Get going. He reached up and grabbed his cap off the hook at the end of the desk.

The police chief was standing in the doorway, staring at him. "You pick up that radio on the Indian kid Romero found out at Steamer Point?"

Paul nodded.

"Lucky she saw him. Afraid the other news isn't so great. Gordy Patrick made a break up in Petersburg. Sounds like a comedy series the way they did that transfer. They think a boat picked him up—of course, no idea what kind of boat—fishing boat, skiff, barge? Oh no, just, 'probably on a boat.'"

Paul snapped his cap against the desk. "Patrick's one they shoulda chained to the plane prop. How'd they ever lose him?"

"Stopped in Petersburg to pick up a Trooper who was headed back to Juneau. Would you believe they let Patrick use the can? You gotta wonder if criminal brains evolve faster than normal ones do."

"So why do they think he's on a boat?"

"Somebody reported seeing him climbing down the ladder at the gridiron. If there was water over the grid, probably somebody picked him up—a skiff could get in on the end of it at most tides."

"Planned, you mean."

"Looks like it."

"I thought Patrick was a loner."

"He's been around here a while—maybe took up with someone."

"At least we'll recognize him if he shows up. I saw him once year before last and never put his face with the APB. Think I'd be smart enough to notice that scar."

Woods shrugged, gave him a thumbs up, and crossed the outer office in three strides.

Paul launched himself to his feet, yanked his cap on, grabbed his jacket, and fished in the pocket for his keys. He'd be on the dock waiting when that Tex-Mex white woman came in with her Indian boy.

Chapter 4

Liza pulled the throttle back and felt the current press against the hull. She tried to hold the glasses perfectly still—was there movement in those legs? She reached over and pulled the cord on the ship's bell, clanged it three times, and watched. Nothing.

"Why are you doing that?" James said, from under her elbow. His dark little face poked turtlelike from the huge neck of the sweatshirt. His eyes squinted anxiously, as though he already feared the answer to his question.

"See all those birds?" she said, not giving him the binoculars. "See the eagles in the trees there? You can spot them by their white heads against the dark branches."

He turned to look through the window, holding onto the binnacle that held the compass and bracing his feet wide against the roll. "Yeah, I see them. They get the fish guts, hunh? You gonna throw them fish guts?"

"I don't have any today," she said. "I guess you must fish a lot, though. You throw the fish guts out to the birds?"

He looked quickly at her, then away, seeing through her ploy with the wisdom of an adult. "No," he said, with the same finality he had used to turn off her other inquiries.

They had drifted much closer. Even through the curtains of rain Liza could see clearly that somebody was lying motionless on that ledge. She tried to quell a rising panic as she pushed the throttle up again and headed back around Steamer Point, running just far enough toward shore to drop the hook again, close to the now-invisible rock where James had been. Sam raced back and forth on deck, whining anxiously.

What to do with James while she checked on the legs? She should call the Coast Guard, too. She'd already listened twice to their broadcast—*Pan Pan, Pan Pan, Pan Pan, all stations, all stations, all stations, this is United States Coast Guard, Ketchikan Group*, followed by a description of James and the position where she'd found him. *Anyone with information about a missing boy please call this station.*

As far as she knew, there'd been no answer. The Coast Guard hadn't called her back. Now she needed to call them about the legs. *(Oh, right, lady. Another body. Seen any UFOs lately?)* But how could she call with James standing next to her?

"I have to take Sam ashore to do his business," she told James. "Can you stay by yourself a few minutes? We'll be right back."

He nodded. "Are you going in that red boat?" he asked. "That one?" He pointed at the inflatable, which she'd left tied to the stern. It had drifted toward the bow in the slack current. The tide would ebb soon.

"That one. Maybe you could take a nap. You must be a little tired, sitting so long on that rock."

"How can Sam get in that boat?" he said.

"You watch out the window and you'll see. Sam's a very good jumper. He's a good swimmer, too."

"I'm a good swimmer," he said. "I can beat even Emerson, and he's way a lot older than me. He's eleven next time."

"Is Emerson your brother?"

"Can Sam swim super really fast?"

She sighed. "Don't touch things around the steering wheel, okay? I don't want you heading out of here without us."

He looked at her with a little twitch of a smile. "I won't do it, because you couldn't swim so fast, could you? Even Sam, he couldn't swim so fast as this boat goes, could he?"

"No, he couldn't. So don't leave us, James. We'll be right back."

Liza hauled the inflatable into a narrow streambed cut in the rock, and looped the line over an outcropping, not bothering to drag it up since the tide would be receding. The rocks were covered with olive-yellow rockweed; the tiny balloon ends snapped like Rice Krispies under her feet, wafting the smell of sulfur into the wet air. She cursed as she lost her footing on the slippery surface. Sam nosed through the tide pools and lifted his leg at every boulder, zigzagging ahead of her, then lagging as he crunched and ate a dead crab.

She tried to stay along the ridge. The legs had protruded from behind a ledge near the western tip of the islet; she didn't want to stumble over someone lying in the crease behind the rocks. Her breathing seemed unnatural; she was panting, like Sam. Rain drove in fierce blasts against her face.

At the highest place, the rocks banked away steeply on both sides. She stood there, looking north and west. A tug hove into view heading northeast. Just south of the Point Nesbitt reef, a gillnetter was turning into Stikine Strait. The string of small islands, the Blashkes and Shrubby, seemed close across the stormy water. She took a deep breath, turned around and looked down.

A man lay on a ledge a few feet below her, sprawled on his back, limbs jumbled loosely where the tide had abandoned them. Before she jumped down beside him, she knew he was dead.

Sam jumped onto the rocks above her, shaking himself in the rain, a shard of crab shell dangling from his lip. He sank to his belly, his tail clutched tightly to his rump, his head almost touching the ground. He reported death in every line.

Liza crouched beside the body. The man's face was almost covered with his scraggly black hair glued to his skin by the sticky salt water. She swallowed hard, then gingerly peeled the hair back, holding it while she bent closer. His face was as cold as the stones under him. The eye she could see was half open, blank, a tiny scar at the corner angling upward like a laugh line. He could have been forty or sixty, his face weathered and waxen.

All at once, she thought she'd seen the man before. Seen him with Crow, one of Wrangell's local celebrities. A cousin, maybe? A drinking buddy? Anyway, somebody who hung out with Crow. But not often. She thought this man wasn't in town very often—he came from somewhere else.

She could call the Coast Guard or the Wrangell Police Department and tell them, "Find Crow and find out who this man is." Was. And Crow would give them the key to James, because this man must surely have something to do with James. Two people washed up within a few hundred yards of each other had to be more than coincidence.

And then, turning his head to the other side, she saw it. Behind his ear there was a ragged, star-shaped hole. In her mind she began paging in horrified fascination through Efren's police manuals and forensic guides. Her own weight became too much to hold up, and she sank to the rocks beside the man, pulling her knees up under her chin, her mind swirling with ugly pictures.

This man's head was cradled on rock—her husband's on cold cement. She'd known everything the night Sergeant Reynolds came and stood on the other side of the screen door, known before he said words as jumbled now as they were four years ago—"heat-blasted junkie got him...died instantly, never knew what hit him..."

Say he did know though—say he thought of you. Efren Romero knew before he hit the pavement, Liza. She shuddered with a grief that four years had only deepened.

Fighting back her need to get away from there, she tried to observe details. The man was lying just above the last tide line, deposited there by the higher of the high tides during the night, undoubtedly the one that had carried James to safety on the rocks. Tonight's higher high tide would come back to claim him. She couldn't leave him there.

She rose, got her hands under his arms, and backed up the ledge. His boots thumped, and water poured from the tops of them as she dragged him through a small cleft in the rock. She got him as high as the brush line under the trees and let him down gently, as though he might bruise.

Sam stood on the rocks above her, his head drooped so low his ears veiled his whole face. Were they the only mourners?

She felt a wave of loneliness; this dark that was gaining on them all.

Wait—wait: could James have seen the murder? She'd blasted his presence all over the air waves, given out their position. If he was a witness, she'd set him up like a hunting decoy. She had to get back.

She stepped forward and a rifle cracked. Sam yelped and tumbled off the rocks, sandwiching Liza between a body and a bloody dog. Her heart hammered so hard she barely heard the next shot.

Chapter 5

James had watched them go. Liza was facing him, rowing, Sam sitting in the bow. She'd said, "Take a nap—you must be tired," but he hadn't *promised* to take a nap. He wanted to go home, but if he told her take me home, maybe those men would find out and come where he lived. Maybe they would get his grandmother and throw her away like they threw Goran away. When he sneaked up on deck, he saw Goran floating in the water. He tried to swim to him but he couldn't—it was too cold. And too dark. He couldn't remember anymore where Goran went that he couldn't find him.

He walked around the deck to the bow. This boat was different from the *Sarah Moon*. The *Sarah Moon* was a troller. This was pretty nice of a boat, the *Salmon Eye*. He wouldn't mind having a boat like this. And a dog, too. Like Sam.

He couldn't see Liza and Sam anymore. They went around the other side of the Point probably. He wondered why they didn't just go straight in there to the beach where it was gravel for Sam to do his business.

Quite a lot of boats were going by out there past the Point. He watched till they were most of them out of sight. And then he saw the other one. The boat those men were on. The one that came and those men got on board of the *Sarah Moon* and shouted and next thing his uncle was floating in the water.

He got down on his hands and knees behind the rail, but trying to see over it to watch that boat. It was too cold to swim to the beach even though it was pretty close. He could swim that far, but it was too cold. He was already shivering. The rain had got his sweatshirt soaking wet, and the wool socks, too.

"Remember this," his uncle had told him.

"Where White Bird flies up," James said out loud, to see if he still remembered. Tears came in his eyes, though—he couldn't think about Goran, think how his voice was, whispering the stories. Anyway…"Where Raven waits…That which is Nameless can never be found. Listening Stone. Listening Stone hears Wind's story."

The boat wasn't turning like it was coming in here. It was heading around the Point. The *Salmon Eye* was swinging sideways now, the tide going slack, the boat swinging a little farther, back again, farther and farther and back…The men's boat was clear out of sight now.

He heard a shot. Then another shot. Like somebody was hunting in the woods back of where he lived. And then he remembered something else. Before those angry voices were shouting on the *Sarah Moon*, he heard a gunshot. He tried not to cry, but tears kept on coming in his eyes.

Chapter 6

"Shit, how could you miss? She was a bull's-eye."

"I dunno—she moved or something."

"Had the original lock on it and got the dog instead. We coulda got her out of the way, gone back and picked the kid up. God damn it. Now she'll head for Wrangell as fast as that thing will go."

"Bet we could beat her back to the *Salmon Eye* right now and take the kid before she gets there. The skiff's real fast."

"Sure we could. But if she saw us, she'd know us a mile away."

"So? You said we're gonna do her anyway."

"Yeah, right. But she's one smart bitch, believe me. She'd never leave the boat without a hand-held radio. So we can't take a chance on her seeing us before we get her—she'd have our names out there in a flash. Anyway, the Coast Guard'll be there any minute after her call about finding the kid."

"So...we'll just do the job in Wrangell, like you said."

"Shit, man. How could you miss?"

Chapter 7

Liza rolled out from under Sam, trying to see where he'd been hit without raising her head. He struggled to stand up, and she had to lie across him to keep him down. Blood was pouring down his right hind leg, high up, but not, it seemed to her, from any vital organ.

She whispered to him with what little breath she could muster, "Sam, good dog, good dog, stay down, Sam, stay," a litany that slowed her own pulse not at all.

A rifle—the shots must have come from the water—there wasn't any other place to stand. By tipping her head back as far as she could, she could see across Clarence Strait, but trees obstructed her view of Stikine Strait to the northeast.

The tug had disappeared beyond the Steamer Point light now; the log boom was just passing the ledge where she lay. A gillnetter went by. Its blue filament net that the salmon gills catch in and the white cork floats attached to it were still wound on the stern reel. Its sleek topsides and cabin were startlingly white against the somber background. It had crossed behind the boom to pass on the south side, closest to her. Both boats, tug and gillnetter, would have been in range when those shots zipped past.

Suddenly she caught a glint from a shiny surface. A double-end troller, its old spruce trolling poles barely visible, was dawdling along above the Point, camouflaged by its flaking wooden planks, grayed to the same weathered antiquity as the rocky shore. Another possibility.

She was trying to hold the flesh of Sam's leg tight over the blood—she couldn't see the wound without turning him around and raising her head, but her fingers seemed small for the job. His leg was quivering uncontrollably. She needed to get back to the boat and the first aid kit. And James. Could he have heard those shots? Too far away, she hoped. Oh, hell, what if someone had already gone after James?

Behind her, toward the inflatable, there was a cut in the rocks carved out by the stream. She thought they'd be out of sight in it if she could just get over there. How did you get an injured dog to crawl?

Her solution was painful, but it worked. She lay on her back and pulled Sam on top of her so that he was lying bloody side up. Then she slid herself like sled runners under him, scraping over the sharp edges and small pools of water. The slope of the ravine was covered with the olive-yellow rockweed she'd just cursed when she'd lost her footing. They had a quick, soft ride down. Hereafter she'd hold her tongue when she climbed around on that yellow treachery.

From the water's edge, the tug was invisible, past her now up Stikine Strait, the log boom a long perforated line behind it. With a little help from Sam, she managed to maneuver his eighty-some pounds over the side of the raft. The tide was running out of the bay already. She had to row hard to keep from being carried out into the Strait but finally got the Point between her and anyone lurking in a boat.

The *Salmon Eye* had swung her stern out with the tide. Liza rowed in and grabbed the stern cleat, then dragged the inflatable along the side to the lowest place opposite the wheelhouse.

"Did that Sam dog do his business?" James was standing at the rail under the tender. "He's got blood on him. Why does he got all that blood all over?"

Liza thought his voice sounded teary and glanced up at him as she fastened the painter. He'd been crying. His eyes were red, and he wiped his face with the sleeve of the sweatshirt. She shouldn't have left him—should have ignored those legs, reported them by radio and headed home. Now she could only try to reassure him. Then again, the situation wasn't very reassuring. She'd been shot at, and here they were like ducks in a row. No way to hide a boat like the *Salmon Eye*. Move. Get James off the deck. Hurry up and get out of here.

"He hurt himself a little," she said. "I'll have to lift him up on deck. You stand inside so there's room for Sam."

James shuffled back a few inches but didn't go in. Liza propped Sam's shoulders and head against the side of the boat, then got herself under him. Straining with her back and arms, she lifted his hind quarters, sliding him upward along the smooth planking till she could push him over onto the deck. He scrabbled at the deck with his front paws, trying to help, but blood spurted freshly from the wound and covered her arms and chest.

"He's got a bad hurt, hunh?" James said. He crouched by Sam's head and stroked his ears. "Poor Sam. I got my knees skinned on the rocks. Mine got all a little bloody too. And my hands, too. See my hands?" He held his palms out for Sam's inspection. Sam tried to lick them, but he didn't raise his head, and Liza was suddenly in an even bigger hurry.

"James," she said, "open that cupboard over there and get out the metal box with the handle. No, first give me that blanket, there on the bunk. Then get the box."

Somewhere she had read about tests of child development— "Follows two-step directions." "Follows two-step directions with information interposed." How about, "Follows two-step directions from woman who changes her mind and panics easily"?

He was back with the blanket before she could stand up. He was there again, laboring under the heavy metal emergency kit, before she had spread the blanket beside Sam. "Eight next time" could follow directions, no matter how confused they sounded.

She rolled Sam onto the blanket and slid him toward the door. She would have to drag him over the six-inch threshold designed to keep the seas out of the cabin. She bent to lift his shoulders, but James slipped past her and lifted on the other end of the blanket. Together they slid Sam over the step and lowered him onto the cabin floor.

"Eight next time" sees a problem and solves it without assistance.

The bullet had carved a ravine across the upper part of Sam's leg but somehow missed the deep chest ahead of it. He'd bled a lot, but even that was slowing. Liza cleaned the blood away while Sam struggled against the sting of the alcohol. James watched closely, his hands restraining, then caressing as Liza shaved the fur and covered the wound with antibiotic ointment.

While she wrapped the leg tightly, James said, "He got shot, didn't he?" He didn't look up, asking the question very quietly. "I heard somebody shooting two times. I was scared."

What was he picturing? What had he seen? Murder? "I'm afraid somebody thought Sam was a deer," Liza said. "I think that's what happened. But he's going to be fine."

Sam's thick tail signalled his pleasure in all the attention. "Tough beast, you old hounddog," Liza said to him.

"Sam's a hounddog?" James asked.

"He is," she said. "In a manner of speaking."

"He's a good old Sam dog. Good old Sam in a manner of speaking. In a manner of speaking, in a manner of speaking," he chanted, rubbing his cheek with one of Sam's coppery silk ears.

Liza's rain jacket was covered with drying blood. She took it off and hung it on a hook like an ugly reminder. She needed to call somebody, get help. She grabbed the transmitter, thought about it, and replaced it. Somebody had tried to kill her. Was she going to announce, "Here we are, right here at Steamer Point?"

She started the engine and raised the anchor. When she went back to the cabin to check, James was stretched out full length on the floor next to Sam, one hand gripping Sam's ear. They were both asleep. She threw the sleeping bag over them and hoped they'd sleep till Wrangell.

She herself was sleepwalking the *Salmon Eye* along Stikine Strait before her knees let her down. When reaction struck, she had to lean against the bulkhead, put the steering on auto, cover her face with ice-cold hands. Sam had caught a bullet meant for Liza Romero.

None of it could be real, and at the same time, every detail was clear: the sound of the shots, the face of the dead man, his black hair stiffly glued to his cheeks; the sulfur smell of the crushed rockweed and the rain driving against her face. If it weren't for that bloody crease carved across Sam's leg, she could believe she'd been hallucinating.

At last her knees steadied. She checked directions on the autopilot, then walked back to the cabin. Sam's nose was so close to James's ear that each breath lifted a wisp of hair. She looked carefully at James. The bruise on his cheekbone was dark and sharply defined—it would get no larger before turning blue, then yellow. The creamy, café au lait of his skin had returned. He was deeply asleep, the anxious lines around his eyes erased, his breathing so quiet she had to watch the corner of the sleeping bag by his chin for any sign of life.

It was already four o'clock, hours later than she had given as her Wrangell ETA. The shores of the Strait had a cloud line halfway down them, here and there pierced by a spruce sword. Hundreds of small streams combed the misty forests. The metal surface of the sea was scarcely rippled in this protected passage.

She crossed over and went through Chichagof Pass, a shortcut around Woronkofski Island to Shoemaker Bay. Shoemaker Bay was home to the *Salmon Eye*, home to Liza. Five miles south of Wrangell along Zimovia Highway, a narrow two-lane road, Shoemaker Bay was totally isolated, no stores, no houses across the "highway," a muddy, pot-holed parking lot at the top of the ramp, woods on both sides of it. The trail to Rainbow Falls across the road went steeply up the mountain through dense forest. In winter, there were only two liveaboards, Liza and the man across from her who lived on his gillnetter.

The milky silt from the Stikine River turned the water to jade as she made the turn. The Stikine River, one of the great watersheds of the North Pacific Slope, trading highway from Canada, path of explorers, fur traders, and gold prospectors, had gradually extended its territory, filling the sea bed around Wrangell to a treacherous shallows.

Ahead, Liza could see the bright lights of the lumber mill spattered along the shore as day slid imperceptibly into night. Her mind went back to the dead man, the image too indelible to put aside for long. A friend of Crow's. A relative, maybe. She groped for the memory—she was sure she'd seen him sitting with Crow at the bar, walking along the street with Crow. Why did she think he might be a relative—she didn't actually know the man. But she certainly did know Crow.

Crow had come to her attention her first year in Wrangell when she'd heard the custodian swearing loudly in the rest room at the library, late one winter afternoon. The crash and moan that followed her string of obscenities had brought Liza to her feet. By the time she reached the bathroom, Millie was grappling with the limp body of a man fallen sideways off the toilet.

"You shit," Millie shouted, "coming in here, drinking where it's warm. Look at that," she hollered at Liza, pointing at the floor. "Look there—he gets that free coffee you put out there in the lobby, he pours his damn rotgut in it, sits in here where it's warm...look at him." She gave him a fierce kick on the shin. "Dead would look *good* on him, you ask me."

The man was far gone—"dead," as Millie put it, was indeed going to look good on him soon, if not that instant. Liza bent to feel for a pulse, but Millie pushed her away, grabbed his legs, and dragged him. She thumped him against the sink and door, gathered momentum on the floor of the reading room, kicked the front door open and literally threw him onto the front walk. Millie was a short woman, not more than five feet, and she carried her whole history in girth, most of it, apparently, as muscle.

"You can't just throw him out here," Liza protested, bending over him while Millie stood there panting. "This man's near death. It's half snowing. He'll die of cold."

"Wouldn't die of falling in the ocean, that one. He'd wash back up good as ever." She slapped her hands together, ridding them of Crow's taint. "Not that he's ever any good," she snarled.

"I'm calling the police," Liza told her. "I can't let a man die on our doorstep, good or not."

"Hunh," she said. "Go ahead. Crow, he ain't even gonna be here by the time they come. He may be passed out, but he ain't *dumb* passed out."

"That's his name? Crow? Is that his first name or his last?"

"All of it, far's I know. He don't answer to nothin' else, anyway."

Liza grabbed the phone. "Millie says his name's Crow," she reported to the Wrangell Police Department.

"Yeah?" the dispatcher said. "Crow drinking too much coffee again?"

"Too much mixing."

"Yeah, well, call us if he's there in an hour."

"Listen, it's starting to snow. It's cold as Paul Bunyan's barn. You get him out of here."

"Yeah, okay, somebody'll check it out. Don't get your tail in a knot."

"Thank you very much," Liza said, slamming the phone down. No respect, those guys. Pigs. Her campus vocabulary still came in handy.

She went back to see if "dead" was already looking good on Crow and found him walking toward the center of the street. Although his head was thrust forward, and his feet surveyed each step before he put his weight down, his upright position seemed incredible in one so recently moribund.

The headlights of a car swept around the corner. Crow glanced over his shoulder, stepped high over the curb, and faded between two houses diagonally across from the library entrance. The police car slowed and the driver shone his spotlight over the walk, flashing it upward till it blinded Liza. He switched it off, grinned, and lifted his hand at her before he drove away.

Liza saw less of Crow after the Library Board decided it could no longer afford to offer free coffee to library patrons. Now and then he'd return from a spell in detox and come to the library in his sober guise. He had the garrulous but precise speech of one who needed to practice, not eye-hand coordination, but brain-tongue.

"Liza, lemme tell you," he'd begin, and she'd put aside what she was doing because there was no denying Crow when he wanted to talk.

"My family, you know, out there...my family, it goes back a lot of years, a long time ago when they built the racing canoes—had their potlatches, all that. You got those pictures around?"

The library had a number of books with old photographs—Angoon before the American warships came. Wrangell in the days before the Russians sold the "icebox" to Secretary Seward and the Thirteenth Amendment freed Tlingit slaves, too.

Crow would spread the books out on the table and write down names of people he knew whose fathers and grandfathers were shown in ceremonial robes, lined up holding drums and masks; in some of the photos, children were seated with the women, the men standing in back, stern in their spruce-root hats and blankets.

"See that?" Crow would say, pointing to the background in one picture or another. "Gone now. Nothing left there—see that Chief's house—see that painting on those poles there? Gone. Somebody liked it, see? Pretty things, they were, those poles and bent box things, carved pretty they were, masks, those things..."

He'd run his finger back and forth over the pictures, as though he could feel the indentations of the adze.

"Somebody always likes things if hardly anybody else has 'em. That's the way of it, eh? If there's just a few of 'em, everybody wants some. Never enough of some things, is there?"

Getting to run the streetsweeper when he came home from detox was always Crow's graduation present. After work, he'd come to the library and run his hands over the beautiful pictures.

"Liza, lemme tell you..." His red-rimmed eyes would stare past the books of photographs, seeing that which was never enough.

Chapter 8

For the second time that day, Paul Howard climbed back up the ramp at Shoemaker Bay. Getting some exercise at least. He could use it—he'd run all to belly lately—gravity seemed to be getting stronger. Tides lower, ramp steeper, belly droopier. Better than belly up, anyway.

He slammed the door on the Blazer and patched out of the parking area. Where was she? Something had happened. Weather was blowing up, too. Maybe she'd pulled in some place to wait it out. Naah, the pass from Steamer was so protected it wouldn't be a problem getting back. Long ago, too. She'd said noon and it was close to five.

Back in the office, he drummed his fingers on the phone, wanting to call the Coast Guard again but embarrassed to do so. They'd said they'd call him. Let him know if anything turned up on the kid. He'd heard their Pan Pan bulletins, but no responses. She hadn't called them again, either. And she hadn't turned up.

He'd stopped on his way back at noon to look in the shed at the Institute. The Wrangell Institute had been a school for Native children. They were sent from all over Alaska to Wrangell for their education, little children even, like Joey. Strange, sending your child off like that, some city-way—foreign culture kind of thing. The school had been abandoned for a long time now since oil money had brought education to the tiniest village. The buildings were falling down, the roofs collapsing.

Inside the shed there were piles of old, rotting newspapers and some shelving stacked on one side. The place smelled of rotting wood and mildew. He noticed that one corner of the floor had a hole in it, and moss was beginning to take the sagging board. There were no totem poles, or pieces of poles, and no containers that might hold them.

From the office he'd called all the Wrangell museum board members—no one knew anything. Frank Mackenzie was pretty sure everything had been moved out of the shed years ago— "maybe Myrtle forgot—she's getting on, you know."

Paul had called Myrtle—twelve forty-three when he called, barely saved from Raven's curse. Unfortunately there'd been no memory failure. Myrtle had checked on those things every month since they were stored there, and they'd been there in February and she'd had to dig the snow away to get the door open so there wasn't any mistake that it had been February, and now it was March and they were gone.

"I'm setting up a file on it right this minute, Myrtle. Seems like a lot of stuff has gone this year. Got a report in the fall that there's only twenty-five or thirty petroglyphs left on the beach."

He drew Raven carrying a pair of glasses in his beak. "Yeah, yeah, I know. Used to be hundreds. Maybe thousands. People just walk away with 'em. Lucky some of 'em are too big to move. What? Yeah, I remember when the dredgers hauled off the ones from Cemetery Point. We never got 'em back."

He drew a rock with a spiral petroglyph underneath Raven. "Well, listen, Myrtle, I'll do all I can. Sure, I'll let you know what I find. Thanks for letting us know about it."

Police report:
9:23 A.M.—Missing Dog: from Pelican, German shepherd female, black, 3" scar left rear leg, 1/2" scar side of muzzle. Caution: does not like men wearing baseball caps.
11:10 A.M.—Bear presence on First Street.
1:30 P.M.—Suspicious Person: a shop owner reported a person off the ferry came into the store with a dog. The dog wet on two postcards. The owner said that will be $4. The man left without the dog.
2:53 P.M.—Bear presence at Golf Course.

4:17 P.M.—Suspicious Circumstances: Citizen reported person yelling on beach at 3.5 mile Zimovia. Investigation: person doing normal talking to self.

He glanced through the glass divider that separated his office from the outer one. Lizzie Romero was there, standing at the counter, rain jacket open over a gray sweater, black hair pulled back in a rubber band under a faded red cap. Not a young woman the way he'd been thinking of her—at least forty, he'd guess, no disguising the lines around her eyes, fatigue dragging at her shoulders.

Don't rush it, he thought. Slow down, take it easy. He turned his back to the glass and riffled through the file drawer. He couldn't tell if she had the kid with her, but he wouldn't be able to see a seven-year-old over the counter. Did she look like she was talking to someone on the other side of the desk?

He stole a glance and found her looking gravely at him as though she read his delay for exactly the subterfuge it was. He nodded once at her, slammed the drawer with his foot, and walked to the counter.

For some reason, when he'd thought about her after hearing the radio report, he'd forgotten how still she was. Now, as in the past, it was his strongest impression. Everything about her seemed absolutely quiet. Other people must move all the time for him to be so struck by this. But a charged stillness, like the high voltage wires that ran down the Back Channel.

"Liza Romero," she said. "I've got a little problem."

"You run that delivery boat thing?"

"That's me. The *Salmon Eye.*"

She was alone. He opened the gate in the counter and led her through the outer office, pulling a chair out for her in front of his desk.

"What'n I do for you?" He leaned his shoulders back and swung his swivel chair sideways.

"I found this little boy out by Steamer Point. James, his name is. Then I found a dead man on the island that has the light. And then somebody shot at me. Twice. They hit my dog."

Shot at her? She was speaking so calmly. How could she be so calm?

"He lost a lot of blood, but he's doing pretty well now."

Not so calm. He noticed her blink fiercely and turn her head away from his gaze.

"Shot at you. Didn't report that, did you?"

"No, I decided I'd already given out too much information over the air. Someone knew exactly where we were."

"I heard on the radio you found a kid. Where is he?"

"I left him in the truck with the dog."

"Shouldn't leave a kid in a vehicle, you know."

"I do know, Lieutenant. He's scared, though. And I had to talk to you about the dead man. I couldn't do that in front of him. I locked the doors, and Sam would kill anyone who tried to take him away." She smiled that strange, downturned smile that didn't reach her hooded eyes. "Sam thinks he's got salvage rights."

"Well, nothing's come in about a missing kid—Coast Guard doesn't have a report of anyone missing." He stared at her. "It's weird. You'd think someone would be going nuts looking for him. What's the kid say? He old enough to know what's going on?"

"He seems too scared to say anything. He's seven, I think—'eight next time,' he says—but he seems older in some ways. I don't think he's lying—he just changes the subject. He must have something to do with the dead man, though, since they were so close to each other."

He listened without interrupting while she told him about seeing the legs, going to look, thinking the man had something to do with Crow. "Then somebody shot at me. The shots had to come from the water—nothing else around to stand on."

"Okay, gimme that location exactly," he said. "Steamer Point?"

He dug around in the lefthand desk drawer and took out a yellow pad, scribbling Steamer Point on the second line. Then back on the top line, he printed LIZZIE ROMERO.

"Liza," she said. "L-I-Z-A."

He nodded, circling the name a few times with the pen. "So are you absolutely sure about where those shots came from—couldn't be from someplace on shore?"

"I don't see how. Sam was hit from the back, and there wasn't any land behind us except the other side of Clarence strait."

He went over to the filing cabinet and got out a chart. "Show me," he said. "Where were you standing—where's the body?"

She made a little X with a pencil. "Right about there. The island with the light is steep to, you know—deep water right up to it on the strait side. Nobody standing behind us. Couldn't have been."

"What about the rocks east of where the light is?"

"I just don't see how anyone could have gotten that angle on us from there," she said, "but I suppose it's possible. Maybe it could have been like that. But I can't quite see it."

"What about boats?"

"I saw a gillnetter—fancy white fiberglass job, and an old wooden double-end troller just behind it. There was a tug pulling a log boom, too."

"Identify them?"

She laughed unexpectedly. "I was upside down holding a bloody dog on top of a dead man."

Paul had a sudden image of her on her back, struggling to quiet the injured dog. How could she find that funny? It made his skin crawl. "Okay, how about somebody moving close in beyond the island after shooting at you? You wouldn't see them, lying behind the rock. They could duck in a lot of places along there—look here—here's a little island right beyond, and here's Quiet Harbor. See, they could have gone in a lot of places. Or just kept going. They would have been way ahead by the time you started back."

She followed his finger outlining the shore. "You're right. It could have been like that. The only boats I actually saw, though, were the tug and the two fishing boats. No one passed us, either direction, on the way home."

"Don't even know which tug?"

"Couldn't see the name. Red and black. Probably over at the mill now. But I'm sure no tugboat crew would...I mean, whoever it was, Lieutenant, they weren't kidding."

"They could have seen something, though, *if* something was going on...a shooting...maybe they could identify those fishing boats."

Without blinking, her eyes bored into his. He hadn't meant 'if,' exactly—not to imply she was making it up...but it was such a weird story. "You recognized the dead guy? Crow's buddy? He smell like booze? Sure he wasn't just passed out?"

"He wasn't just passed out. He was stone cold. No pulse. Bullet wound behind his left ear. Sam knew too. You know how animals are—they tell you when something's wrong."

"You recognize a bullet wound?"

"My husband was a policeman. I used to have this awful fascination for the pictures in his manuals. And he talked to me a lot. I was the only one he..." She stopped abruptly and shrugged away the end of the sentence.

Paul waited. Finally he said, "Was?"

"He was killed in a drug bust."

"Sorry," he said, irritated by the sudden wave of sympathy he felt. Junkies with guns—could be Paul Howard any day now—plenty of junk in this town.

"All right," he said, "we'll run out and check around. It's not our jurisdiction, but we'll either get authorization from the state troopers, or turn the whole mess over to them. We'll pick up Crow and get some ID."

He stood up and followed her out. "I'll talk to the kid," he said. "Kids like that can be real clams once they're scared."

They walked out to her pickup, a lime-green '64 Chevy with a crown of moss growing out of the roof trim. A heavy-boned, copper-colored dog hung over the tailgate and Paul rubbed his ears, noting the professional-looking bandage on the dog's hind leg. He walked around the truck and looked through the driver's side window. His son Joe was sitting there, pressed against the far door.

Paul stared at him in stunned silence. But of course it wasn't Joey, couldn't possibly be. Joe was thirteen years old now; the snapshot Paul had gotten at Christmas showed him with long hair, unlaced high-tops, and a camouflage vest. He was holding a guitar across his knee. A cool dude.

This boy was wearing a large black rain jacket with the sleeves rolled back and gray sweatpants stuffed into the tops of huge wool socks. And this child's face, now that he studied it a moment, was a little longer, his eyes tilted up a little more at the outer corners. Otherwise, Paul would have called them dead ringers. Same enormous front teeth, serrated from recently sawing through gum, same black silk hair hanging like a curtain over their eyes. He knotted his hands against the door to keep from flinging it open and sweeping the child into his arms.

When Lizzie opened it, he leaned in and said, "Hey there, I'm Paul Howard." He held his hand out, and after a minute, James touched it, then snatched his hand away, watching Lizzie anxiously as he did so.

"You Lizzie's son?" Paul asked.

James said, "No," turning away from him and pressing his forehead against the opposite window.

"What's your name, then?"

"I'm just visiting," James mumbled.

"Oh, sure. I get it. You came on the ferry."

"No," James said, turning to look at him. "I came on the *Salmon Eye*. Me and Sam…" Suddenly a little smile appeared. "Sam and *I* came on the *Salmon Eye*," he said.

Paul tilted his head back and looked across the roof of the truck at Lizzie. "No dummy," he said to her, quietly. "Knows exactly what he's doing."

He poked his head back into the truck. "Well, you have a good time, you and Sam. What did you say your name was? I didn't quite catch it."

"James. J-A-M-E-S."

"Wow, you're old enough to spell already? Betcha can't spell your last name, though."

"K-I-T-A-I," James said. Then he covered his face with his hands. "No," he said. "It's not. I mean, that's just only my middle name."

Paul nodded, accepting James's fear. "Well, James Kitai Whoever, come see me again. Lizzie here's a friend of mine, so I'll see y'around."

He withdrew his head and grinned at her.

"Slick," she said. "I have to hand you that one."

"I'll get hold of the Tlingit council. They'll get him off your hands."

"I'll keep him till we sort out where he's from."

"Hunh unh," he said. "Can't do that. You gotta be licensed—stuff they gotta check out for a foster home."

"Well, it's not a foster home, Lieutenant. I'm just keeping him till you find his folks."

"Same thing. You still living on that boat out at Shoemaker?"

"Yes, I am. The phone number's in the book under Romero."

"So, I'll get back to you tonight maybe. Don't think we can leave him overnight."

"Lieutenant Howard. I am not trying to adopt this child." Her fists clenched, and she shoved them in the pockets of her jeans.

He'd breached that calm. For an instant he wondered why he'd wanted to. But he knew he had, knew he'd done it deliberately.

"I'll get back to you soon as we get a report. But listen, Lizzie...there's no way you're keeping him." He rocked back on his heels and stuck his hands in his back pockets. "None at all."

She slammed the truck door so hard a large wad of moss was ejected from the roof trim onto the windshield. He bit his lip, trying not to grin. He watched her pull out onto the highway and turn south. Sheesh. Why couldn't he get a grip? Maybe it wasn't the kid. Maybe it was something else.

Chapter 9

Liza watched him in the rearview mirror. An enormous man, must be more than six inches taller than her own five-eight. Thick shoulders like a brown bear's. Black hair clipped close to his head, eyes full of pain. Pushing fifty, he must be, plaid shirt stretching tight above his belt when he reared back in his chair to listen; the populist Wrangell Police Department had never run to uniforms.

Something wrong with that man. He'd scarcely reacted when she'd told him about the shots, but when they went out to the car, his face became a gross wound. She'd thought he was going to grab James and run.

She headed south along Zimovia highway, her hands gripping the wheel so tightly she had to flex her fingers one at a time. Her conversation with Howard had aroused memories of Efren.

After his death, shocked and agitated, she had taken a job in the library in Darrington, Washington, Then, restlessly, she'd moved to another in Ellensburg. Months later, still desperate and grief-stricken, she had seen an ad in the *Library Journal* for a job in Wrangell, Alaska. She read it as an invitation to leave her terrible first life behind. Read in it, "Escape."

She had flown in on a clear green day, water and forests every possible shade of alive, snowcaps ranging toward infinity. A greenhouse warmed by the Japanese Current and perpetual rain. She had reached the ragged north edge of the continent and finally discovered the truth: "Wherever you go, there you are."

Now the wind was whipping Zimovia Strait into horsetails, and the clouds had lowered till the islands on the other side were almost invisible. The temperature was dropping; rain exploded into icy stars on the windshield. The wet pavement seemed covered in paste and the one-speed wipers scissored and clacked.

Paul Howard's words kept rhythm with the wipers: "No-way/no-way/you-are/you-are/keep/ing/keep/ing—no-way/no-way..." The words changed to: "So-what/so-what..."

She looked down at James and knew "what." He was slumped against the seat back, his eyes drooping, dark lashes sweeping ice-cream cheeks. Round black eyes and polished skin—he could be her own child—the child of Efren Romero—they were planning to start a family before...

You're not James's mother, Liza. You'll never be anyone's mother. She would never relinquish him to anyone but his real mother, though. Paul Howard be damned. She turned in the drive at Tasha's house and slammed on the brakes to avoid flattening a bicycle.

When Wrangell was dug up by future archeologists, the yard at Tasha's would raise many interesting questions. A classic '47 Ford truck on blocks awaited a new engine. The paint had been lovingly and artistically removed and the burnished doors and hood sported bolts of lightning and a dragon rampant. A '71 Datsun had been stripped of every usable part, including the seats, which graced the sides of the truck bed under a blue plastic tarp. The plan, Liza had learned, was to carry the soon-to-be-famous rock band RipRap to its frequent gigs and eventual national spotlight.

Surrounding the vehicles were assorted crab traps, coils of line, blue oil buckets, gallon paint cans, their tints proclaimed down the sides, handlebars of a motorbike, twenty-three tires (she'd counted), three on rims, a doghouse with half the roof missing, a lumber pile of lengths needed by all carpenters, three old rabbit hutches, several lengths of rusted stove pipe as well as the sawdust burner that had once heated the whole ancient house.

Liza told Sam to stay. He sat down and hung his head.

"Poor Sam," James said. "He wants to come, doesn't he? Maybe he could get lifted out."

"No," she said, "they have four cats, for starters. Sam goes nuts trying to chase the cats. And he might make his leg hurt, start to bleed again."

They waded through the boots, kindling, buckets and fishgear on the back porch. Liza knocked on the kitchen door, listened a minute to steel strings amplified, knocked louder and then opened the door, shouting, "Anybody home?"

They stepped inside and let the door slam shut behind them. The cooking smells made Liza's mouth water, and James rubbed one hand over his face. Simi, a stocky yellow Lab, came whirling through from the other room, her tail wagging all the way to her ears. James bent and grabbed her by the neck and pressed his face against hers.

"That's Simi," Liza said. "She's Sam's mom. Hellooo..." she bellowed, trying to be heard over the pounding percussion. In a minute, Tasha appeared in the doorway. She barely reached Liza's shoulder. Her fine black hair was cut little-boy short, and she constantly raked her fingers through it in exasperation so it stood straight up, giving her a perpetually startled look. Despite five kids, she could be mistaken for a twelve-year-old, but her voice was Authority, her vocal cords tuned like a double bass amplified by a bullhorn.

"Who the fuckin' hell's making all that noise?" she said. Then she noticed James and bit her lip. "Sorry," she said. "Didn't know you had a friend with you." She gave Liza a one-armed hug and held her other hand out to James. "Pleased to meet you," she said. "I'm Tasha. What's your name?"

"James."

"Why don't you go meet the rest of the family?" Liza suggested.

James looked up at her, worry flitting across his face.

"I'll stay right here," she said. "Promise. If you need me, come back."

"Do you got any kids?" he asked Tasha.

"A whole army," Tasha said. "The one about your age, that's Andy. The other one's Margie. They're in the sunroom watching

TV. The rest of them are upstairs, in case you can't tell from the noise."

She watched as James shuffled toward the other room, casting one more anxious look over his shoulder at Liza. "Nice clothes," she said. "You kidnap him? He looks like he hasn't eaten this month."

"Beach boy," Liza said. "It's more than a story. I really came to bum some clothes for him. We gotta go eat—the story'll have to keep till we fuel up."

Tasha went to the door. "Erin," she screamed. "Come here a sec. Leftover deer stew," she said, turning back to Liza. "You aren't too proud, are you?"

Liza smiled and lowered herself gratefully but cautiously onto one of the ancient dinette chairs, its plastic seat more duct tape than upholstery. The table had gradually been lengthened with assorted wood planks as the kids took up more space, and odd chairs seized from curbside rubbish piles tilted around it at rakish angles. She watched as Tasha took a kettle from the refrigerator, set it on the stove and turned the heat on under it.

Her name, Natasha Annie George, was a history of Alaska, but Tasha herself was pure Tlingit. Finding the Tlingit names too gutteral for their tongues, settlers and missionaries had simplified them. Dan Jim, Violet Gamble, Simon Jack—the throaty, oboe music of their Tlingit names had been drowned out in the promised land.

Tasha had spent, or misspent, some early years crewing on a seiner, helping to feed out the huge net that the seine skiff used to encircle the salmon. After that, she worked as a cook in a logging camp. Her memories were surprisingly vivid considering that most of the time she was wasted on assorted drugs with letter names, washed down or rubbed down with some variety of ethanol. But her roommate died on a burning boat, and two other bodies from the boat washed up with bullets in their skulls. Tasha's roommate and three others were never found. Tasha recognized the professional victim circuit and signed herself in at the local tank.

Recovered, she went to Anchorage, lived on student loans, and got a degree in social work, reliving now an earlier life inside the glazed-over faces that visited her office every day.

Erin, twelve years old and broomstick thin, dashed into the kitchen and threw her arms around Liza. "You've been gone years—who's that kid in there with Andy and Marge?"

"He followed me home, Mom. Can we keep him?"

Erin shook her head. "He didn't really. Honest, Liza, who is he?"

"She'll tell us, she'll tell us, don't bug her," Tasha said. "Go get some of Andy's jeans and shirts and underwear—out of his drawers, not off the floor, please, and bring them down here. And a couple sweatshirts."

"Socks," Erin said. "Shoes, too? Andy's shoes are awful, Mom. He doesn't have any that have laces and no holes."

"Look in the boot box," Tasha said. "Be creative, my darling artist."

Erin went off, then reappeared in the doorway. "Don't tell till I get back, Liza," she said, warning her with raised fist.

"Food first," Tasha said. She ladled up the stew and got out a loaf of bread and the butter dish, which looked like it had been in a duel. She went to the door and shouted, "James, supper. We ate already," she said to Liza, "but there's enough left over to feed a mighty horde. There's them 'round these parts too proud to eat deer meat seven nights a week, and we're all but out of fish."

James and Andy came in, Andy talking about his teacher at school. Liza thought James was only half listening. The plate of stew pulled him like a magnet. He put his hand out for the fork, then dropped it and looked up at Tasha for an invitation.

"Dive in," Tasha said.

"Yuck," Andy said. "Deer meat. I'm sick of deer meat."

"Good," James mumbled, his mouth full. "It's pretty good," he said, when he'd swallowed. "I like it," he told Tasha.

"Nice to have somebody appreciate it," she said. She spread a slice of bread for James and put some more stew in his nearly empty plate. "Hollow leg, here," she said to Liza.

"He's only had peanut butter, and I think Sam ate most of that."

"Sam," Andy said. "Where is he?"

"Part of the story," Liza said.

Andy's eyes widened. "He's okay, isn't he? There didn't anything bad happen to him did it?"

"He's okay. He's in the truck."

"He got hurt bad, but Liza made him be all right," James said. "He was all over blood," he said, wringing all he could from Andy.

Tasha turned around from the stove and raised an eyebrow. Liza shook her head slightly, wanting to wait till they were alone.

While they ate, Tasha said, "Tom came by right after I got home from work to find out if I'd heard from you. Gets his shorts in a bundle if you're late getting back. And Larry called just a few minutes ago. Couldn't reach you at Shoemaker—he's got some Japanese charter group."

Liza sighed. Too many guardians—it made her want to run away, but how much farther could she go than the edge of the earth?

Tom Morrison managed a team of timber cruisers that surveyed for the logging companies, moving around by helicopter from one section of forest to another, bushwhacking their way into the woods to calculate the board feet of usable timber. Morrison had become Liza's guardian whenever Larry Hayden was out of town, which was often, now that he flew his own charter plane.

A few months after she came to Wrangell she had seen the *Salmon Eye* turning along the edge of Zimovia Strait, noticed its lovely old schooner lines, the painted trim she knew should be uncovered and varnished. Months later she'd discovered it tied up in Shoemaker Bay. She'd gone out to look at it so many times that the skipper had finally caught her at it.

"Wanna buy it?" Larry Hayden asked. "Gorgeous boat, isn't she? I'll give you a great deal."

And on impulse she'd done it. There weren't many takers for an ancient wooden halibut schooner, so it did seem like a fairly good price. It turned out, though, that Larry considered himself part of the package.

Larry took her out on the *Salmon Eye*—she had to learn to maneuver a big power boat, didn't she? And a few hours here and there turned into longer passages and night anchorages, and somehow he'd captured her with that high-voltage current that surged between them.

She had moved onto the *Salmon Eye*, and then, on a wakeful night in the fall, the idea of a freight service/book-mo-boat came to her. She could use her librarian skills to select a permanent collection and perhaps the Wrangell library would provide her with a rotating selection of books that were no longer quite on the best-seller list.

Three months later she resigned from the library staff and began her freight and book services, setting up a regular schedule to the roadless villages, a schedule that, in winter, had to be continually revised.

Erin came in with Andy's clothes and set them on the table. Andy immediately went through the pile—each garment had a history—"this one's the one I was wearing when I fell off the roof chasing the cat. And these jeans you can't button the top button and those ones were Arnie's before he got too fat for them. They aren't any good, actually. So he can even keep them."

"Very magnanimous of you, my dear," Tasha said. "James— more stew? No? You guys can watch TV then, till Liza and I have a chance to talk a little." The boys vanished. "Okay, now, tell."

Tasha, for all her rough talk, was a trained listener. She watched Liza intently, nodding now and then as Liza struggled to describe everything exactly, staring impassively when Liza repeated a half-dozen times about two bullets and the blood streaming down Sam's leg.

When Liza finally ran down, Tasha got up and went over to the door. "Ken," she bellowed. "Willy—you guys get down here."

Eventually came the sound of herds crossing the tundra and the boys appeared, jostling and punching, filling the kitchen with animal presence.

"Get Sam out of the truck," Tasha said. "He got hurt. Liza's going to stay a while longer—he shouldn't be out there freezing up."

Ken drummed the top of Liza's head lovingly as he passed, and Willy gave her a high five. A minute later they were back, grunting over Sam's struggling length stretched between them. When they lowered him to the floor, Simi flew at him, growling and snapping and wagging until Sam shrank back. The dogs went through this ritual every time—Simi was the only female in the world who could exact respect from Sam.

"Is she looking a bit matronly?" Liza asked Tasha.

"I don't care to discuss it," Tasha said. "Mind your own business."

The boys stormed out, jamming through the door at the same time in bruising thuds. Simi examined Sam's bandage thoroughly, then settled down next to him, her head between her paws.

"Liza, sheeee—it. What a horrendous tale."

"I've become an instant mother, Tash. Which of course simply grinds in memories of my own. I keep hearing my mother's voice. 'You're whining, Elizabeth.' Scolding me for feeling sorry for myself. And I argue with her. No one forty years old argues with a mother who vanished twenty-some years ago. Is that crazy or what?"

Tasha shook her head. "Naah, we all hear our mothers' voices—that's what keeps us on the straight and narrow."

The voice in Liza's head also warned her not to give way to temper or grief. Liza's mother, a tiny woman of the Lummi Nation in Washington State, had been an advocate for abandoned and abused children. Liza remembered her as having a fierce sense of justice and utter compassion for the underdog. Was it her mother's devotion to uncovering truth that had caused her to disappear when Liza was twelve? She's dead, Liza. She never never would have left you. Black wolf on your shoulder.

"You're still angry at your mom for dying. And Efren, too."

Liza stared at the rain beating itself into frozen flowers on the window. Yes. Yes, I am angry. The people I loved more than anyone in my whole life went away and left me.

Finally Liza hunched her shoulders forward and went back to the story. "Well, I'm a mother till Paul Howard grabs James away. There's something wrong with that man, you know."

"Howard, you mean?"

"Yeah. Lieutenant Paul Howard, Heap Big Indian Warrior. He acts like I kidnapped James. 'No way you're keeping him,' he says, like I'd even think of it if we could find his family. What's the matter with the guy?"

Tasha laughed. "I told him he turns every little thing into Wounded Knee. His wife left him a few years ago. He married her off the boat, so to speak—white tourist—from Texas, I think she was, years younger than Paul. Had a little boy, Joey. Light of Paul's life, that little guy. So when Carolyn went south and took Joe with her, Paul took her to court. Unfortunately the judge leaned toward motherhood and Caucasian. Turned Paul totally bitter. Too bad—he's a great guy underneath the warpaint."

"I wouldn't know—he's so hostile he can't even write my name right. But it explains why he was so nice to James. I thought he was going to bleed to death when he looked in the truck and saw James."

"He's never gotten over it. I don't think he's ever had a clue why Carolyn left him. We've never talked about it—Paul keeps to himself—we're good friends, but I don't pry. Only now and then something comes up, like James, and you can see the pain."

"He really got my back up."

"I'll talk to him. But something's wrong with this picture. Nobody's reported James missing, right? And he isn't talking?"

"I figure you'll get the story out of him. That's your biz, after all—filling in the cracks."

"He won't talk to me—I stink of authority—kids like that, they've been raised never to speak to anyone who looks official. He might talk to Andy, though. Give that kid some time, he can find out God's middle name."

They went to look for the kids. Erin, Margie, and Andy were sitting on the sofa watching *Jeopardy.* James was fast asleep, his head in Erin's lap. Erin's fingers combed his hair absently as she stared at the screen. He sighed when Liza scooped him up against her shoulder but didn't wake.

She drove back to the Shoemaker parking lot, lurching through the rain-filled potholes into a space opposite the Dumpster. A man was walking quickly behind the line of cars facing the harbor. In the yellow light he was only a silhouette, a large man, thick in the middle, the hood of his rain jacket pulled low over the brim of a cap. She watched him till he went behind a van and she heard a car door open and slam.

Probably Jake off the *Aquila*—Jake was heavyset—a euphemism for his beer-keg shape.

The ramp was steep at low tide, and she inched down it, James's head and legs dangling over her arms. As she passed the *Aquila*, she thought she caught a movement behind the dark glass. Must be a reflection. She'd just seen Jake in the parking lot.

Her hand hesitated on the padlock. She didn't remember leaving it open. It was looped through the hasp—had she just hooked it through and not snapped it shut?

She braced James's weight with one knee and flashed her little penlight over the lock. An old one, bronze, not easily pried open. She'd been in a hurry to get to the police—she must have left it that way.

The phone was ringing—at least she'd remembered to plug in the power and phone lines before she left. She pulled the sleeping bag over James and grabbed the phone on the fourth ring.

"*My god, where have you been? I've been frantic.*" Larry's voice. She eased into the sound of it.

"It's such a long story. I got delayed—had to turn around and come back. Have you been calling a while?"

"*I called Mink at the Velvet Moose—I thought you were headed for Kashevarof. Didn't find you, so I called Tasha, but she didn't know where you were, either. So where have you been?*"

"In a stupid mess. But I'm home safe and sound, and so tired I'm going to hang up and go to bed and tell you all about it tomorrow. Where are *you*?"

"*Sitka. Got a bunch of Japs that want to tour logging sites. Listen, Liza, just give me a clue—weather...engine trouble?*"

"None of the above. Too complicated a tale for this late at night, and I'm exhausted. Call me tomorrow, okay?"

"*Liiize...*"

"Please?"

"*Okay, I'll call you tomorrow—might be late—I gotta fly these guys all over. Hey? Love you, woman.*"

"Take care of yourself." She hesitated a moment. "Larry? Come home soon."

She was too weary to fall asleep easily. Her blood felt carbonated. Strobe lights streaked behind her eyes: water exploding on rocks, a dead man's face. Finally she began to drift. The last flash was a man walking behind the cars in the parking lot, his black hood catching the harbor lights. A pinprick of recognition before sleep. Not Jake. Lieutenant Paul Howard.

Chapter 10

They were awakened before seven by a sudden warning growl from Sam, followed by heavy footsteps on deck and a shout, "Ahoy, *Salmon Eye*—anyone aboard?"

Sam got to a sitting position, then lowered himself from James's bunk, his bandaged leg held away from the floor. He scrambled clumsily up the companionway ladder, tail waving hello, his teeth bared in a ridiculous smile. From the top of the ladder, Liza could see Tom Morrison's tall silhouette through the curtain on the door.

"Wait a second," she called. "I'll be right there."

James was sitting up in the other bunk. He looked over and said, "Who's that?" Before she could answer, he said, "Don't let him come in here."

He pulled the blankets up around his shoulders. She could see only his eyes and the top of his head. His eyes were wide with fear, as they'd been when Lieutenant Howard had offered his hand.

"It's okay, James," she said. "It's just a friend of mine. Tom Morrison. He's an old friend, somebody you'll like."

"A friend of yours?" He looked back at the door. Tom had gone around to sit on the bow while he waited. "I don't want to see him. Why did he come here?"

"Because he's a friend. You'll like him, James. He's very nice. And he's a great ballplayer—he used to be a pitcher on a baseball team. He coaches kids just your age. Do you know how to play baseball?"

James shrugged, then threw himself down and pulled the blankets over his head. "I don't want him to come here," he said, a protest muffled by a pillow.

Liza took her clothes to the head and got dressed, opened the door and called to Tom. Sam limped out and they greeted each other noisily, then Sam stood at the rail till Tom boosted him over onto the dock.

"Been beating him?" Tom said.

"It's a long story. It'll have to wait, though. I'm a mama now."

"Say what?"

"Sam found this little boy out on the rocks by Steamer Point and adopted him."

Tom stared. "You're kidding. Sam *found* him? Come *on*. Lemme see him."

"Later. James has had a pretty rough twenty-four hours. He's scared of something—he isn't ready to meet strangers. And he won't tell me how he got out there on those rocks."

"Maybe he doesn't remember. Like it was a car accident and afterwards you don't remember anything, even being in the car."

"He acts more like he doesn't want to talk about it, than not remembering. The Lieutenant pried his last name out, although afterwards James insisted it was his middle name. James spelled it, K-i-t-a-i, and Lieutenant Howard pronounced it Kee-tye. I assume he must know that name—James never pronounced it for him."

"Kitai," Tom said, repeating it slowly.

"Ever heard it?" Liza asked. "I skimmed through the Southeast phone book at Tasha's last night and didn't see it."

"You went to Tasha's? How come you didn't give me a call? I was worried—didn't Tash tell you I'd stopped by?"

"I'm sorry, Tom. I just stopped to pick up some of Andy's clothes for James. We were exhausted. I was going to call first thing this morning." Either Larry or Tom was always checking up on her, fretting if she was even an hour late. She couldn't muster the energy any more to dodge either the lover or his appointed guardian.

Say you run away again, Liza. Where you gonna go this time?

Rain was making its opening salute, a brisk tattoo on the deck and cabin roof. They pulled their hoods up and shrugged against the onslaught. The wind had picked up from the southeast, slicing through the mountains and straight across Shoemaker Bay. Gusts alternated with ominous silences, the rising swells beginning to pitch the boats and rattle the rigging.

"Blowin' up," Tom said. "Team's supposed to do a job out at Labouchere Bay—take a week, probably—some kind of litigation over holdings. Probably get weathered in, though."

"I listened last night—supposed to slack off later. I've got to get rid of those chickens—I'm going to run over to Kashevarof this morning. Maybe somebody over there will recognize James." She thought of Lieutenant Howard's warning to stay in town. Would he bring kidnapping charges? Probably.

Tom frowned. "Don't go. Listen, don't be a fool, Liza. This'll take time to blow itself out. It'll leave big seas even when the wind dies."

"Oh, I can handle it."

"Well what about that little boy? You gonna risk him, too? What about Sam?"

She laughed. "Is Sam your ace in the hole?"

Tom grasped her arm. "This is no place for a woman to be out on the water by herself—look at this blow—what if you get caught out there, can't get in before you're hit with twenty foot seas—Liza, it's just stupid to run around all by yourself out there. Please!"

"I suppose it's okay for a man to be out alone in these waters?"

"Hell, you know what I mean. Okay. Yes. Yes, at least a man's strong enough to handle things if it gets bad—enough guys get lost as it is, and you do such dumb things—shit—I can't believe the dumb stuff you do." He was clutching her arm so tightly she had to pull it away.

"Sorry," he said. "I didn't mean to do that." He shook his head and frowned at his hands.

"Give me one example of dumb stuff I do. Like what, Tom?"

"Like going out to rescue those guys that capsized their kayaks last fall in that nor'easter. Running all the way to Wrangell on fumes—*fumes*—because there wasn't any fuel left on the barge at Kashevarof." He held up his hands, enumerating her stupidities on his fingers. "Hiking that nontrail above McHenry without a gun for bears."

Liza stared at the sailboat next to the *Salmon Eye*, the masts swinging like metronomes. A bald eagle was hunched on top of a piling beyond it, its feathers blown into a dark ruff around its white head. "Whenever you're through...I hope you have enough fingers to get it all."

"I'll take off my shoes. You Will Not Leave Wrangell," he said, beating the words out on the rail.

She burst out laughing. "'Are you my mother?' Verbatim quote from a well-known piece of literature: 'No, the Snort was not the baby bird's mother. It was a big, big Snort!'"

"You are going to get into big big *trouble*, Liza."

"You sound like you're reading my horoscope. Do you have a crystal ball, now?" Why the hell was Tom so angry all of a sudden? She stifled an impulse to tell him she'd been shot at. Don't tell anyone. You don't know who did it.

How silly, though—you're just being silly. It couldn't be Tom. He's trying to take care of you.

She had a sudden chaotic desire to flee—kidnap James and run away south. "Sorry," she said finally, "but I have to get going. It's a fair piece to Kashevarof in this wind."

He stamped across the deck, swung over the rail and started along the dock. In sudden rage—he had no right—no right at all to talk that way—she reached into a crate of book returns standing inside the door, grabbed the heaviest volume, and flung it at Tom's back. It landed on the dock far behind him, but the resounding thud made him turn and look.

They stood there glaring across Harold Brodkey's lifework until she started to snicker. In a minute, Tom grinned, walked back and lifted the book off the damp cement. He read the title aloud: *The Runaway Soul*.

"Me or you?" he asked. He grinned at her. "I'm gonna sue you for hurling a vicious weapon."

She watched him jog along the dock, his shoulders hunched against the rain. What had all that been about? Why had her plan to go to Kashevarof made him so angry? Oh *well*. Too bad, though, she'd picked Harold Brodkey. Sue Grafton would have soared much farther.

Chapter 11

After Tom stormed away, she had second thoughts. Maybe she shouldn't head out in that wind. She was willing to take the risk for herself, but what about James?

"Mothering isn't always easy, Elizabeth," her mother's voice said.

She thought about that. Had Emma Wells found mothering very difficult? Maybe it was running interference between Liza and Liza's father that made mothering so hard. Her dad was an extremely successful attorney with a regal bearing that served him well in the courtroom. But his stern demands kept a distance between Liza and him, a distance that eventually became a chasm.

The fickle wind dropped abruptly and the forecast for the afternoon was winds to fifteen knots. She decided to go—the wind had piled the seas up, but by the time she reached Clarence Strait it would be nothing but a chop, and if it was worse than that, she could always anchor back in Kindergarten Bay.

Out in Zimovia Strait, the brilliant green light in the water reminded her of the day she'd arrived in Wrangell almost three years ago. She switched on the radar and Global Positioning System. The GPS went through its warm-up patterns and James stood in front of it, watching as it acquired its satellites. When it had settled down, she punched in the coordinates and got the distance to Kashevarof, thirty-seven nautical miles, crow's flight route. More, since they couldn't become airborne over the south tip of Zarembo, but not a lot—it was a pretty direct run.

"What are you doing?" James asked. "Is that a computer?"

"Sort of. It's called a Global Positioning System. Do you know how to use a computer?" she asked him.

"No, I've only just saw one."

"Where did you see a computer?"

"Emerson's dad. He's got one but he doesn't let me and Emerson play with it. Can you show me how to work that computer?"

"Well, this is a very special computer that tells us where we are, even in the dark and fog. When you switch this knob it shows you the latitude, where we are north and south, and next to it, the longitude, where we are east and west. So I can look at the chart and tell where we are even when I can't see. Or if we had some trouble, I could call over the radio and tell somebody where to find us."

"Like you'd just say those numbers on the radio?"

"Right, I'd just read them right off, and they'd know exactly where we are. Are you a good number reader? Can you read those?"

"Sure. Five six dot dot two six dot one two, one three two dot dot two nine dot one five."

"Terrific, James. If we ever get in trouble, you just pick up this transmitter, push this button, and say, 'This is the *Salmon Eye*. We need help. This is our position' and then you'd read the numbers."

"I could do that okay. I know about boats pretty much."

"From fishing?"

"Well, I just know."

Like an eagle carrying a salmon, a helicopter appeared over the northern ridge of Etolin Island, logs dangling beneath it. "Look, see that helicopter?" Liza said. "It's going to take those logs to a landing place and drop them, and go back for more."

She wasn't a tree hugger, but she'd long ago embraced Crow's philosophy, "Never enough of some things." Even the Tongass National Forest with its sixteen million acres of trees would never be enough to replace air destroyed in L.A.

James watched the helicopter begin its descent. It finally crossed a low ridge and disappeared from view. The southeasterly was still blowing a bit. Liza was surprised they'd be doing helicopter logging, but it was possible there was barely a breeze over there. The islands created strange microclimates.

She reached to set the compass direction on the autopilot and noticed the red warning indicator blinking on the temperature gauge. The engine was overheating. In fact, it was very close to boiling. Instantly she scanned the horizon. There were no other boats in sight.

Must be a belt. But she'd changed all the belts in the fall. Maybe one had loosened up. She turned away from shore, getting as far from any obstacle as possible. Then she shut down the engine. Immediately the *Salmon Eye* rolled sideways into the trough, rose and surfed down the next wave.

"We've got a little problem," she said to James. "The engine's too hot. I'm going down to check it. I want you to stay inside, and hang on, because the boat's rolling badly."

"Do I gotta call on the radio and say five six dot dot three one?"

She stared at him an instant before making up her mind. Had she been alone, she wouldn't have hesitated, but she'd become a parent suddenly, and parents, she was finding, were a different species. All at once she could hear Tom listing her stupidities. In your face, Morrison.

"No," she said, "not yet. I don't think it's big trouble, just nuisance trouble." She opened the locker and dragged out some life jackets.

"Put this on." She pulled the strap tight around his waist and hooked it. Then she reeled down the ladder, clutching at the handholds. When she opened the door behind the ladder, the engine room was hot as hell.

She checked the belts. All intact. The water pump? She'd have to run the engine again to check the pump. A last resort, restarting that overheated engine. And dismantling the pump would take much too long.

Gingerly she released the pressure cap on the heat exchanger, but there wasn't any pressure. The fresh water was gone, and right there, right under the heat exchanger, was a little pool of water on the engine block.

She felt along the hose and found a hole under her fingers. She lay flat and looked up. Just before the molded right angle of the hose was a round puncture wound, high enough that water could not run out until the pump started, small enough so they would get well off shore before the engine went dry. A hole that could only be made by a sharp object driven with great force through the tough rubber and mesh casing. An ice pick would do it, or a Phillips screwdriver, or a huge nail hammered in. She remembered the loose padlock. Somebody had been in this engine room.

James was climbing over her feet now, and Sam was licking her ear. Decide, Liza: repair the hose, or try to get back to Wrangell by filling and refilling the heat exchanger. Hard trip, wind against current—she'd try to fix it first.

"You can help," she told James. "First, get Sam out of here—he's totally in the way. Put him in my cabin and shut the door."

She lunged up the ladder and looked out. With no way on, the boat was taking the seas on her beam, rising sideways on the crests and dropping like an elevator into the troughs. Islands loomed and vanished. Though the boat was drifting rapidly toward shore in the tidal current, the depths were still too great to show on the depth sounder.

She couldn't anchor in such depths. She could wait till they were carried down to the north side of Woronkofski Island, but the shelf there, sixty to eighty feet, shallow enough for anchoring, was extremely close to shore. On this side of the shelf, a sheer underwater cliff, the depth was more like four hundred. Maybe she could make a repair before they got there, despite the heavy seas.

But say you can't, Liza. What then?

James crawled up the ladder and sat on the floor of the wheelhouse, bracing his back against the roll. "Sam didn't like to stay by hisself," he said, "so I stayed a little bit so he wouldn't get scared."

"Fine. Now I want you to stand right here and read off the depths. Numbers will start showing on that screen as soon as we get a little closer to shore. If we get shallow enough, we'll drop the anchor."

"I can do that," James said, looking at the blank screen on the depth finder. "I can read numbers." He set his feet wide against the steep roll of the boat and leaned forward, his arms around the binnacle to hold himself in place.

"You're great," Liza said, taking out the toolbox. "Shout when you start seeing numbers."

In the engine room she braced her feet and back against the bulkhead while she mixed up some quick-set epoxy in a jar lid. The boat was shuddering as it took the waves over the rail, the noise like Grand Coulee Dam.

"Three eight nine," James shouted.

With the bolt cutters, Liza cut a six-penny nail off about an inch past the head.

"Three nine four."

She covered the edges of the hole and the underside of the nail head with glue, stuck the nail into the hole, and pressed it hard.

"Three four three."

It would take five minutes for the glue to get tacky, twenty to get hard. They wouldn't be carried ashore in five, but twenty...?

"Three seven seven."

Taking the roll of duct tape—she figured you could repair the San Andreas fault given enough epoxy and duct tape—she began wrapping.

"Zero six three."

In two jumps she was up the ladder. The boat had drifted south, and the current was setting it straight onto the reef at Wedge Point. As the boat leveled out between rolls, Liza shoved the door open and moved hand over hand along the swamped foredeck, kicking loose the brake on the anchor windlass. The chain rattled out to its twelve-fathom mark before she slammed the brake down.

She couldn't back to set the anchor so it would certainly drag, but at least it should slow them down. A wave broke over the rail and the *Salmon Eye* dropped sideways in the hissing green water. Liza clawed her way back to the wheelhouse and through to the galley. She grabbed a large bucket and filled it to the top. Dropping down the ladder, she filled the heat exchanger.

Climbing back to the wheelhouse, she looked out at the reef. Close now, but still a margin. She said to James, "Go down and tell me if you see water running out of the hose when I start the engine." Immediately he vanished down the ladder.

While she held in the glow plug button, she glanced at the depth. Twenty-two. Plenty of water under them. Not so much ahead of them, though. She pressed the starter button. The cooled engine choked, grumbled and stalled. Don't panic, don't panic. Give it a moment—we aren't aground yet.

She tried to count to ten while she held in the glow plug button again. Suddenly the boat shuddered and swung hard to starboard, yanking the wheel from Liza's hands. Now the panic: she looked at the depth. Twenty-four. They couldn't be aground—the boat wasn't listing—maybe jammed sideways against a submerged rock? But the boat was swinging sideways now, and she knew. The anchor had finally dug in. There wasn't remotely enough swinging room—unless she got the engine going, the *Salmon Eye* would be driven straight onto the reef.

She jammed her finger on the starter button. Slowly the grumble changed to a deeper sound, and the engine roared to life. Name this boat *Lady Luck*.

Throwing the gears into reverse, Liza inched the *Salmon Eye* back on the anchor chain. "James, get up here!" she shouted.

His eyes, when he appeared on the ladder, were enormous black pools.

"I have to raise the anchor," she told him, trying to speak calmly. "You've got to hold the wheel steady. It's hard. Put your hands on it like this, and try to hold it straight. Can you do it?"

He nodded and she crouched beside him, trying to see what he could see. Wind-carved trees loomed crazily beyond the bow. Waves exploded fifty feet in the air and spume poured down the windshield in coiling runnels. The boat was still swinging to starboard. The depth read thirteen feet. Liza throttled up, trying to get enough way to stern to hold the boat back.

"Can you see?" she asked James.

"A little bit—those trees there."

"Okay, try to keep the middle of the window aimed at those trees. Are you all right?"

"Sure. Sure, I can do it."

Leaving the engine running hard to stern, Liza crawled past the chickens, the coils of wire and crates of motor oil, her hands and knees in icy water that swamped the deck. The boat bucked against the chain like a bronco.

Kneeling beside the windlass, the winch that hauls the anchor chain, Liza reached for the brake but saw she'd made a terrible mistake. With the engine in reverse, the anchor chain was pulled out tight, strumming under thousands of pounds of pressure. If she released the brake, the chain would go racing out and the anchor would stay where it was. They were too close to shore though, so if she let the boat go forward to slack off the chain, the current would slam them onto the rocks before she could crawl out here again to release the brake and start the windlass.

The chain's vibration ran up her arm to a brain that had frozen. Goddammit, what had made her think she could do any of this? Larry? Tell me what to *do*.

Another wave broke and dashed across the coamings. Liza went to all fours, her breath yanked from her lungs. They'd have to abandon ship—no—wait—she wasn't thinking clearly—she could just back further and run the chain out to its splice with the nylon line, then cut the line, leaving the chain and anchor on the bottom—that was it, that's how she'd do it. She reached for the brake, but at that moment felt, rather than heard, the engine's beat change.

The *Salmon Eye* stopped her bucking motion and the current carried her rapidly forward over the anchor. James. James had put the gears in neutral. As soon as Liza felt the chain go slack, she jammed her foot against the brake and started the windlass. Then she lunged for the wheelhouse. As the chain came taut, the bow of the boat dipped and rose, its weight lifting the anchor from the bottom of the sea.

As Liza hurled herself through the door, the *Salmon Eye*'s new skipper, standing squarely behind the wheel, shoved the gearshift into reverse. Once more, *Lady Luck* backed away from the reef at Wedge Point.

Chapter 12

"Shit—that was so close!"

"Yeah, well, nice try. Too bad it didn't work."

"Guess we're gonna have to wait."

"She never leaves him alone, see. Just like I told you. But she'll go out again."

"With the kid?"

"She might leave him in town after this. She musta been scared. But she may try to take him home. Then we'll just have to try again."

"Gotta make it look like chance, right?"

"Can't look planned. No metal. We can play it like this: a split second—she isn't paying attention—she looks away and it's over. Happens a lot. Fishermen get caught in their own nets, yanked over. So maybe the crane'll catch her off balance, or the loader...whatever. Just chance."

"Too bad we messed the first one up with a bullet."

"That's why this one's gotta be different."

"So that'll leave us where? Shit, we still won't know anything."

"But we'll have the kid. Take her out first, then get the kid."

"So why don't we just grab him at Shoemaker and head out? Take the skiff and the big outboard—she'd never catch up with us."

"Can't take the risk. She'd know us a mile away if she happened to see us. That's the one thing we can't do."

"You think *she* knows where the Listening Stone is? Then we could just grab 'em both."

"I doubt it. The kid's real young, so you never know what he's told her, but these Indians, they don't talk. And anyway, he'll be a lot easier to persuade if she isn't around. If we'd got him the first time, after we did the uncle, we'd be there by now."

"So why does the kid know where it's at, if nobody talks?"

"They're raised knowing. That tribal line goes back and back, uncles raising nephews to take over. If you're in line, Chief to nephew, then you know how to find the Listening Stone."

Chapter 13

Dizzy from the moments of terror, Liza sagged against the wheel, her breath coming in painful sobs. At long last, gripping the wheel with one hand, she threw an arm around James and hugged him to her side.

"You saved us," she murmured against his cheek.

He nodded and turned his head away to hide his smile.

Liza looked down at him. "You knew exactly what to do. You've handled a steering wheel before, haven't you? And gears too."

"Well, I steer when Gor..." He broke off and moved away from her. "When we're fishing. I steer so the lines can get pulled in and everything. I better get Sam. He could be scared from how the boat was rolling so bad." He sped to the top of the ladder and disappeared.

None of this, she knew now—the shooting, the hole in the hose, the break-in—she *had* left that padlock locked—none of it had anything to do with her. Somebody didn't want James to go home.

Well, by god, we'll get there anyway. We'll get there on glue and duct tape and tough shit, buddy.

"*Way to go, Elizabeth.*" She had a sudden flash of her mother's small figure standing there on the foredeck, her arms raised in a victory sign. Yes indeed, Liza, you are definitely getting crazier.

Despite the prediction, the weather was turning uglier—the green light on the water had changed to a bruised yellow-black, the wind was blowing horsetails off the waves, and sheets of rain flailed the windows, obscuring even the closest land. Liza decided to go back to Wrangell. With a taped-together rig she wouldn't try crossing Clarence Strait in a blow like this. I do know when to quit, see, Morrison?

But don't, she warned herself, do not mention even one word of this to Lieutenant Howard. He'll have James away in a nanosecond if you add engine damage to rifle fire. He'll accuse you of kidnapping and you'll wind up in the slammer. Picture that, Liza: transported to Lemon Creek in leg irons.

Rounding Reef Point, her hands still white-knuckled on the wheel, she headed into Chichagof Pass. Immediately the wind dropped to near zero, the narrow passage blanketed by the ridges on both sides. A tug without tow was coming through Chichagof from Shoemaker. When it got closer, the skipper changed course and headed toward the *Salmon Eye*. When he'd straightened out, he opened the door to the bridge and leaned out, wearing his best Ross Elliot grin.

Ross Elliot was Tasha's ex-husband. In the early days, Ross fished when the weather suited him and worked at the mill when the weather got bad. Then he quit his job at the mill to go moose hunting for three days. When he got back, everything he owned was sitting in an enormous tent like an army barrack, planted in the front yard.

The shock seemed to jolt Ross back to reality, much as her roommate's death had galvanized Tasha. He folded his tent, moved to an apartment in town, went to work for North Pacific Towing, studied for his skipper's license and finally worked his way up to assignment to the *Albert M. Thomas*. Tasha had sworn off him, though. "I worked way too hard to get this place, get the kids' heads back together—he isn't gonna mess us up again."

Ross was leaning over the rail, now, pointing at James, who was disappearing into the cabin with Sam in hot pursuit. "You got a new first mate?"

"Yup." Inventing on the spot, she said, "He's Efren's nephew. Great crew. Just helped me repair my engine."

Ross dashed into the wheelhouse and put the tug in reverse, setting her against the current so he could stay alongside. "You got something wrong with that engine?" he shouted.

"Just a leaky hose. Engine overheated. It's all fixed, now."

"Rot out?"

"More Roto-rooter than rot. Where you headed?"

"Pick-up sticks. It's a game we play." He went back into the wheelhouse and waved as the *Albert M. Thomas* pulled away.

"Who was that?" James asked, trying to look back at the receding tugboat.

"Ross Elliot. Andy's dad."

"Does he live in Andy's house?"

"No, actually he doesn't anymore. He just visits. He drives that big tugboat called the *Albert M. Thomas*. And he goes to see Andy and the others when he's in town."

Damn. She'd forgotten to ask Ross if he'd been passing Steamer Point yesterday morning and seen anyone else. Anyone with a rifle. Sabotage on the *Salmon Eye* has totally blown your brain, Liza.

And then they were back at Shoemaker Bay, safe and sound. Except Liza didn't feel safe and sound. She was still breathing too rapidly, her pulse tripping away in her throat. Everything looked sharper to her, as though the boats, the dock and ramp, were outlined in pen and ink.

She knew she should go straight to the police station—she should put James in the care of someone else—someone who could protect him till he was taken home.

Do it, Liza—do it. You can't take care of this kid. What a terrible mother you are.

She looked down at him and he smiled a little, his eyes still excited behind the curtain of black silk hair.

Not now, not quite yet...

"This is lots of boats, isn't it?" James said, as they walked along the dock. Liza was carrying a bag of laundry containing James's salt-stiffened clothes and an accumulation of her own. James had his hand through Sam's collar. "We don't got this many boats." He pointed at the boat opposite the *Salmon Eye*. "That one's a gillnetter, hunh? Like, it runs out that net behind it the salmon can't see and they get caught in it?"

"Yup," she said. "That's a gillnetter."

A gillnetter was always moored opposite the *Salmon Eye*, a modern, fiberglass boat, Liza realized, that would glow stark white as it passed Steamer Point. But she knew the *Aquila*'s owner, Jake Fremantle. Jake, consumed by rage at the United States Government, the State of Alaska, and the Harbor Master of the City of Wrangell, would never waste a bullet on anyone who didn't wear a badge of officialdom.

They had already reached the corner of the dock when Sam pulled away from James, turned back and put his front paws up on the stern of the *Aquila*, his weight all on his left hind leg. Jake had come out on deck to clean a red snapper. Gulls boiled around Jake's head like surf, their Day-Glo beaks open in screams of anticipation. Jake leaned over the bow and rubbed Sam's ears, glancing darkly from beneath the bill of his cap. Jake was not a social animal.

James stood behind Liza, peering under her arm. Jake glanced at him, then suddenly jumped to his feet. "That dog's gonna scratch up the side. Keep him home, hear?" He slammed the cabin door hard.

Liza was startled by his rudeness. He'd always seemed rather fond of Sam. She found herself staring at the *Aquila*, trying to remember the gillnetter that had passed Steamer Point. The *Aquila*'s name was on her bow, not at the stern on her transom. Had she seen lettering on the transom of that gillnetter? The *Aquila* had a curved, blue-tinted Plexi glas windscreen on the bridge. Had she seen anything blue on that white, white boat?

The outline was etched in her memory, but the details had not been recorded. The *Aquila* must have been out, though, if Jake had caught that snapper. No, he'd caught it off the dock— he'd clean it right away.

James lagged as they walked toward the truck, squatting to pick up a set of keys, slightly bent and badly scratched where they'd been run over by all the cars that had driven through.

"Look, Liza, keys. Maybe somebody could be looking for these keys, hunh?"

She turned them over in her hand—ordinary keys, two house keys and a post office box key.

"We can turn them in at the post office," she told him. "See this key? It's for somebody's post office box. The people at the post office will know who it belongs to from the number on it."

There'd been fierce arguments when the citizens of Wrangell had been offered the opportunity to have their mail delivered. They had voted down the proposition as antisocial. The marble edifice was where you met your neighbors—an active traders' market in gossip and junk mail.

"Can I hold the keys?" James asked. "See, I got this pocket, and it has sticky on top so they can't fall out. And then I can give them back, whoever is wanting to get them."

She handed the keys back to him, and he dropped them into his pocket, twisting sideways to peer into it, then carefully rubbing his hand to seal the Velcro flap over them.

"Sam can ride inside with us," James said.

"Sam does not ride inside. When Sam is wet, his fur smells like landfill."

"He stinks?" James said, refining Liza's meaning. He laughed. "Oh, that's okay, Sam. We don't care if you stink."

"I do." She grabbed a newspaper out of the Dumpster as they passed. She boosted Sam into the truck and forced him to sit on the paper, then helped James up the high step to the front seat.

Why had James seemed to startle Jake? Jake would never shoot at her, though. She stared at her car keys without seeing them. Jake? A killer? All right, Liza, how many people do you know that you think of as killers?

James sat forward on the edge of his seat, tense with anticipation.

"Fasten your seat belt," Liza said.

"What seat belt?"

"Here. I guess you didn't notice yesterday that I buckled you in." She reached around him and grabbed the buckle. "We have to wear our seat belts so we don't get hurt if something bumps into us." She snapped the ends, then scooted him back on the seat so she could pull the belt tight. He looked down at it and fingered it, opened the buckle and popped the end in and out.

The truck jolted through the deep ruts of the parking lot beyond the Dumpster. The sanitation truck had just emptied it and two ravens were picking over the leavings. Shoemaker Bay was a recent Wrangell harbor development, an effort to relieve the crowding of Reliance Harbor in downtown Wrangell, but, as Crow would say, "never enough of some things."

On the way in to town, Liza thought about James's careful examination of the seat belt. She asked James if he'd ridden in a car before yesterday.

"Not this kind of a car," he said.

Today he sat forward as far as he could to see out. Wrangell must seem as big as Seattle to a child who'd never ridden in a car, Liza thought. "Not this kind," he'd said, but slyly. A Jesuitical answer.

The road along Zimovia Strait crossed Cemetery Point, dividing in half the cemetery with its graves of British colonists, Russian Orthodox, and the low white fences identifying Tlingit remains. The ballfield and picnic grounds adjoined the cemetery, a continuum of past and present edging the tide. Beyond Cemetery Point, the road passed a cove with log storage, then the fish dock, then turned up the hill away from the water. James's eyes were wide, taking in everything without comment.

Liza swung the truck slowly along Outer Drive and stopped so James could watch the cranes unload the Alaska Marine Lines barge. He got up on his knees and propped himself on the dashboard, silent in awe of so many people and machines.

Men in orange wet gear and hard hats dodged in and out of towers of pallets and crates. Cranes swung giant containers onto the rock fill that once was the water side of Front Street, until a series of fires decimated Wrangell's commercial blocks. Everything used on the island, appliances and automobiles, linoleum and brick, engine parts, canned tomatoes and nails, was "value-added" goods, crossing a wide moat of salt water by barge.

Of course, if you were in a mad rush, Alaska Airlines's *Gold Streak*, would get it there faster. But "fast" was a relative term. Liza had learned the words "overheading" and "weathered-in" when she returned from her first vacation and wound up in Anchorage, every one of Southeast's airports buried in mile-deep fog.

"Overheading" meant you were putting your seat back and tray table into their upright and locked positions while the pilot circled blindly through jagged, glacier-ridden mountains. "Weathered-in," meant looking up at a leaden sky, listening to the rumble of an invisible plane's engines passing above you.

Before the police, the laundry. Let's keep the priorities straight here, Liza.

There was only one other person in the laundromat, a fisherman named Rob Hendel who had a wooden leg and immediately had to show it to James. Rob was a good fisherman, fished alone, claimed his wooden leg gave him better balance on a rolling deck.

James hung back at first, standing behind Liza till his curiosity got the better of him. He felt the leg and then looked at Rob's hands. "You anyway got both hands," he said.

"You know somebody that can fish without two hands?" Rob asked him.

"Yeah," James said. "It can be you can fish with one hand, sometimes. I know somebody can fish with just only one hand."

"Yeah?" Rob said. "Who's that? Maybe I know him."

James stared at Rob's face a minute, then dropped the curtain between them. "No," he said. "You don't."

"How d'you know? I know everyone that fishes around here. Just tell me his boat name—I bet I know him."

"No," James said. "You don't know him. Not anybody knows him except me." He ran out of the laundromat and across to the truck, climbing in on the driver's side to rub Sam's ears. Liza signalled him to lock the doors. Better watch him every minute now—somebody was certainly determined.

"James is my late husband's nephew. His dad's a fisherman," she said, compounding her lie.

Rob hauled himself to his feet and walked over to the dryer to take out his clothes. "You know, I think there is some guy that has one hand, runs a troller. Seems to me I've heard of him—fishes out west, I think, Coronation Island, that area—can't think of his name. You still tied up in Shoemaker?"

"Still home. So long, Rob."

She checked the truck again, wishing she knew who that one-armed fisherman was, but not wanting to tell Rob about her mystery child. She finished sorting and loaded one washer with white things, one with colored stuff. She picked up James's dilapidated jacket and automatically felt in the pockets. There were some small stones and bits of metal in one, and a piece of wood in another. Obviously a beachcomber. She stuck his treasures in her pocket, put quarters in the slots and started the washers.

Liza went back to the truck. Time to face the music, she supposed, though no way was she confessing the morning's troubles to Paul Howard. *Lieutenant* Paul Howard.

Sam was resting his chin on the steering wheel, and James was looking at the *Wrangell Sentinel* that Sam was supposed to be sitting on. "Look," James said, pointing at the Sentinel's logo of three frogs topping a totem pole. "This is a shame pole, hunh?"

"Right. These three frogs sit crosswise on the top of our ridicule pole, for three Kiksadi sisters who owed a debt. You know about ridicule poles?" Liza asked.

"Ours is got a beaver," James said. "A beaver with very huge-huge teeth and a crisscross tail."

"So one of the Beaver People owes a debt to your people?"

"And a Marten, too. We got a Marten shame pole and everybody doesn't like it because nobody that's a Marten should shame us because of we're Marten People."

"So a Beaver and a Marten have to repay their debts a hundredfold to the Marten people, right?"

"Did the Frog people pay a hundred times?"

"You know, I don't even know what happened. Maybe they did. But it was a long time ago, and we keep the pole because it's such beautiful carving. I doubt if anyone who owed the debt is still alive."

"Ours is. The Marten is, anyway. He's still alive and he's shamed, so we got the pole up till he pays. The Marten has a bird in its teeth. Like a black bird. A crow, I guess it is."

Chapter 14

Paul let her wait at the counter again, watching her surreptitiously. He thought she looked even more fine drawn than on her previous visit. As though every nerve was vibrating. He didn't understand what made him so nervous around her—that charged feeling got under his skin, was all.

He finally gave in and greeted her with a nod, led her through the outer office to the smaller one, passing the Police Chief, who was standing by Jerry's desk talking on the phone. Woods gave them a little wave but didn't interrupt his conversation to speak to her.

Paul watched as she hung her dripping jacket on the back of her chair. Her face looked exhausted, the skin stretched tight over those high cheekbones. She was perched at the very edge of the chair as though she might take flight at any moment.

"Where's James?" he asked, trying not to sound challenging but hearing the gruffness in his own voice.

"James insisted on staying in the truck with Sam. I waited while he locked the doors." She jammed her hands into her pockets. "I've started telling people he's my late husband's nephew."

"He hasn't come up with anything else?"

"He told Rob Hendel that he knows someone who fishes with one hand. Maybe that'd help locate his relatives—there can't be too many one-armed fishermen around—I mean, people would recognize someone like that, wouldn't they?"

"We'll check it out. Nothing else?"

"No, nothing of any use. Won't say a word about his family—it's obviously become a game to see how close-mouthed he can be. He even laughs a little now, when he says, 'no...no...nobody...' Did you find the dead man?"

"Nobody there, either. Not a trace. Searched the whole of the little island where the light is, *and* Steamer Point, found one old boot that'd been there at least a year. You sure where you saw this guy?"

"I can't believe you didn't find anything. Not even blood? Not even a bullet stuck in a tree? I mean, I was *not* dreaming. Look at Sam's leg. I can't believe there was nothing there." She stared fixedly at Paul. "It's crazy."

"Didn't find a thing. Only thing clear, actually, was the smashed-down rockweed where you said you'd slid with Sam."

"That was the spot—right there behind that shelf of rock, right there on the island with the light. I dragged the body all the way up to the tree line. So somebody went back. Whoever was shooting at us must have hidden like you said and gone back. Did you talk to the tugboat crew?"

"We checked the mill office—the *Albert M. Thomas* came in around one P.M. yesterday, and the *Clara M.* about two-thirty. Tied up their booms, went in and fueled up, took off sometime early this morning. Ross Elliot'll be back with the *Albert M. Thomas* on the 26th. Eric Sendhoven won't be back with the *Clara* till after the 29th sometime—moving one of the camps over to Steamer Bay from the other side of the island."

"But I saw Ross in Chichagof Pass this morning, so he couldn't have gone all that early." She bit her lip and waved her hand as if she wanted to brush away her words, but Paul was receiving loud and clear.

"Yeah? What were you doing in Chichagof this morning? Thought I told you to stick around."

He watched her intently. This woman took no leads from anyone, apparently.

She shrugged and stared at the bottom drawer of his file cabinet. "I had to run out to Kashevarof to get rid of some chickens. And I thought maybe somebody over there might recognize James."

He glanced at the clock in the main office. One-forty. "You got back quick—that some kinda speed record?"

"We didn't get there. We turned around. You know...with the weather and everything."

She still wouldn't meet his eyes. Something funny here. "You mean you just set out, found out the weather report was right, and came back?"

"Well...yeah." She shrugged again and turned to look through the glass at the outer office. "We had a little engine trouble, actually."

"Engine trouble?"

"The engine overheated." She was chewing her lower lip now. Then she straightened and looked right at him for the first time. "Somebody punctured the hose from the heat exchanger. Drove a hole into it with something very sharp."

"You fixed it?"

"With James's help. He's an amazing little boy. He seems to know a great deal about boats for one so young."

Paul leaned back in his chair and took a deep breath. "You got trouble, ma'am. Somebody's after you. You got a past I oughta know about?"

"Nothing."

She turned her head away from him, but not before he saw her blinking back tears. There was something there—had to be. He waited.

"And anyway," she said, still not looking at him, "it isn't me, it's James. Somebody doesn't want James to go home."

"So say somebody wants to get rid of him. That's exactly what I've..."

"But why?" She sat forward on her chair, her still-teary eyes frightened. "Why would anybody need to get rid of him? He's just a little boy. What could make him dangerous?"

"Maybe he can identify the killers. Maybe that's why he isn't talking. Scared out of his mind. Whatever. But that kid's in trouble. Or maybe it's you." He stared her down, pushing her, driving at her, wanting what? Some sort of confession? Some plea for help?

"It's not me," she said, setting her jaw. Her hands in her lap were twisting together, turning some object over and over. Looked like an old wooden halibut hook.

"Nice hook you got there. Looks like an old one. Where'd you find that?"

"What?" She looked down at her own hands. "James." She looked startled. "It was in James's pocket—I took everything out of his pockets when I threw his clothes in the wash."

"Native hook," Paul said. "Indian halibut hooks were carved to fit the fisherman—a fist-sized hook would catch the size fish that the fist's owner could pull in. That hook's small, a James-sized hook."

He reached out for it and when she handed it to him, turned it gently in his fingers. It was old and superbly wrought. "A sea wolf," he said, showing her the hook arched like an index finger above the glaring eyes and fierce grin, the wood polished by a workman as well as the sea.

She felt in her pocket. "There were some rocks—I just thought he'd picked them up on the beach—you know how kids are—pretty stones, bits of driftwood with animal shapes, stuff like that."

She spread the stones on the desk in front of him. Not stones, charms. Pendants. A nose ring.

Paul turned them over in his hands, examining the fine carving—one pendant inlaid with abalone, the nose ring tarnished blue-green. He rubbed at it with his finger and scraped away some of the tarnish with his nail, uncovering a glint of bright copper.

He showed her the spot. "Old," he said. "The later ones were silver, not copper. Don't see things like this just lying around. Who wears a nose ring now? Where'd he get 'em? Somebody's collection, must be. Probably why he isn't talking. Stole them—thinks he'll get in trouble if we find out."

"No," Lizzie said, shaking her head. "I don't think so. He doesn't act like that. He isn't afraid of getting found *out*, he's afraid of getting *found*. But I'll do some more asking."

The phone on his desk rang. "The chief wants you—line one, Paul."

"Hello…Steve? Yeah…Where? Steamer Bay? Why would they put Patrick ashore in such a public spot? Log operation over there has people all over the place. Who actually saw him? I better talk to them. It doesn't sound real likely. Probably somebody else. On the other hand, they've been damn casual with him. What the hell's he up to, anyway?

"Yeah, yeah, I'll get on it as quick as I can. Lizzie's still here. We gotta find a way to take care of that kid—he may be in danger. Right. Right—it's next on my list."

He banged the receiver down, then pushed a button and spoke to Norma. "See if they can get Crow up here," he said.

"Sure, I'll go down and check, Paul." He winced. "Pauulll." The corners of Lizzie's mouth turned down in that wry smile. "Get James," he ordered her in irritation. "We'll see if he recognizes Crow."

In a few minutes, Crow, supported by a police sergeant, lurched through the doorway. He slumped down in the chair at the end of the desk, his eyes like red onion rings. Lizzie came back leading a worried-looking James by the hand. She sat down facing Paul again and James leaned against her shoulder. The tiny office seemed jammed with people, the air consumed by the smell of ancient clothing and used booze.

James stepped to one side and stared at Crow. Then he simply went to ground like a fox to the hole. Crow was as impassive as James, and yet Paul felt that he, too, had made some imperceptible response. Without a recognizable signal, there had been recognition. Paul looked at Lizzie and saw that she had seen it, too.

He waded in. "James Kitai, this is Crow. You two already know each other, though. Probably been a long time, right? You come from the same place. Haven't seen each other in a while, right? Not since Crow was visiting you, I bet."

James moved away from the arm of Lizzie's chair toward the desk, reaching for a whale's tooth lying on the desk, when he saw the halibut hook and nose ring. His hand hung poised above the desk an instant, his eyes suddenly shuttered. Then he dropped his hand and picked up the whale's tooth. "What's this?" he said. "It's a tooth, hunh?"

"You ever caught a halibut with this hook?" Paul asked, holding it up."

"I been halibut fishing."

"What d'ya bait with?"

"Ahhh, herring, is all. Jig with herring. *You* know," James glanced at him suspiciously.

"I don't fish much. I gotta work here most of the time. Use a pretty good-sized hook, hunh? These carved hooks, a fella once told me he could catch a two-hundred pounder with one of 'em."

James nodded. "Well, you could, only you don't use those kind, you only use gavel...gavelnized hooks, really. You should go fishing where there's good holes, is all, like me and Goran."

"Oh, sure, Goran Kitai, you mean. He's your cousin, right?"

"Uncle," James said. Then he turned his head away. "No. I mean, he's not my uncle, just only a guy I know. A fisherman, is all." He jammed his hands into his pockets and hunched his shoulders, a study in resistance.

"Well, listen, James," Paul said. "Crow wants to talk to you, right? Find out how your folks are. Maybe the two of you can go in the other room and have a little chat. He hasn't seen you for a pretty long time."

Crow shifted in his chair, braced himself and opened his eyes enough to show dark rims below the lids.

"Liza," he said, his tongue barely clearing her name, "know those pichurs? See, better we don' say nothin', hey, Liza?" He wiped the saliva from his lips with the ragged cuff of his wool shirt.

"Pictures? You mean the old photograph books? Do they tell something about..."

He interrupted her. "Nothin'. Don't tell nothin', 'cept...aaah, no, nothin'. And you can' tell no stories that don't belong to ya." Crow half-rose in his seat, one arm gesturing at James, who stood motionless in front of the desk, the whale's tooth rising between two fingers like the beak of an eagle. Everything in James's face concentrated on the tooth while everything in his posture listened to Crow's words.

"Kid won't get nothin' for a story—he ain't trading for shit—ain' no Kitai trades for shit." Crow slumped down in his chair again, closed his eyes, dropped his hands at his sides.

"You can talk to him alone, Crow," Paul said. "See, you and James own the same stories, don't you? So you both got the right to tell them. You give him permission." He leaned forward in his chair. "Crow?"

Crow looked like a man spun dry, not detoxified. Energy had been expended. The rest was entropy.

The tension ran from James then, his fingers beginning to smooth the whale's tooth, his eyes casting around for other objects of interest. Ignoring the inert Crow, he walked over to look at the snapshots on the wall.

Paul shrugged, blew out his lips in frustration. "It's all there, isn't it?" he said. "It's all right there. But we maybe won't get it. What a pair, eh? 'Fraid I'll have do a little threatening with our saturated friend, here."

"What did you mean about 'they own the same stories'?" Lizzie asked, "and Crow could 'give James permission'?" She looked over at the sleeping man.

"Old Indian notion of property. Stories belong to a clan or a family—nobody else has the right to tell that story even if they know it. Or if they tell it, they have to change it so they aren't into someone else's rights. That's why there's so many different versions."

"Like copyright?"

"Yeah. Exactly like copyrights."

"It's good, it seems to me. I mean, it seems as though it gives people ownership over their own history."

"Yeah, but when only certain people have the right to a story, the stories get lost. Disappear like smoke through the hole in the ceiling."

"Runs in your family, too, does it?"

"Sure. There's Howards all over the place, over there around Baranof and up north." He gestured at the pictures James was still examining. "I been thinking lately my son shoulda known more about his family. I never bothered. Then I see James, and it seems like he's a tough little kid, mostly because he's been brought up thinking family's important. Like, he's got this loyalty."

"Maybe you're the one who can get the story. You know the rules."

He glanced sideways at her. Sure. He knew the rules, but what good had it done him? Dumb Indian, was all that judge had thought—dumb Indian guy wants to take a little kid away from his mother.

"It's totally dumb," he said, "me letting the two of you run around this place, when somebody wants to make fish fodder outa the witnesses."

"I hear you, Lieutenant. But believe me, I'm watching out. I'm still dreaming in body counts. Especially after the problem this morning."

"Yeah, well…we'll be checking on that. And I'll lean on Crow a little—he's kinda marginal today. He knows something, though."

He looked over at Crow and caught a glimpse of dark eye under sagging lid. He was listening to them. Not just listening. Plotting. Crow already knew James's story. Paul was sure of it, just the way he was certain that Crow and James had recognized each other.

"I'll work on him," he said. "Bribe a little—trades, Crow will call it. Too bad though, to use his weakness against him. Maybe I can find another way."

"Odd guy, Crow. He has such dignity when he's sober."

"Yeah. That's the tragedy. He's dug his hole too deep. What can you do? It isn't Crow—it's a way of life."

Her head came up at that, her eyes snapping. "Don't tell me he's a victim of society, please. You're right, he dug his hole deep, but the world doesn't owe him just for being born. And he knows something true. He had to fight for that—for what he knows."

"His world got screwed long before he was born," Paul retorted. Then he shrugged. He wasn't about to engage in that debate. "I called the Council." All at once he felt deeply reluctant to tell her their decision. "Like I told you, you can't just pick up an Indian kid and keep him."

"Well I'm Indian. Half, anyway. My mother was a Lummi— you know—they were the ones that won the *Boldt* decision— giving the Natives fifty percent of the fish caught. And she was a child caseworker for the Washington State Department of

Social and Health Services. So I also know the rules, Lieutenant."

"And your dad...wasn't Indian." Paul watched her out of the corner of his eye. He shouldn't be bothering with her background—Lummi weren't Tlingit, and she'd said "half."

"My dad's an attorney."

"White man."

"Yes."

"They live around here?"

"My mother's gone. My dad lives in Seattle."

"And your husband? The cop? What's his background?" Why was he asking all this—it didn't make any difference.

She was speaking, though: "...migrant workers from Yakima—first one in his family who ever went to college. First Chicano policeman in Bellingham."

He stared at her a while. He'd lost his son to a white woman—he'd never lost his rage. He did not want any white woman to have an Indian child. Not ever. "Kid's a Tlingit, Lizzie. Not Lummi or Mex or white."

"Liza. L-I-Z-A. How come it makes you so mad that I have him? Sam found him. We've got salvage rights. Finders-keepers. That's naval law."

"Yeah? Well, listen up, Lizzie." He sat forward and leaned across the desk. "You don't have *any* rights. It's just one of those things. Like you probably know, an Indian's always got a family, even if they're spread out different places. He's got family, okay? Right here in town, he's got family. Me, even. I'm family."

"So then, why don't you take him?"

He tattooed the desk in a drum roll of fingers. "Uhhh...oh, well...Council's found somebody to take him. He's going tomorrow." He couldn't look at her. "Sorry," he said again, further annoyed that he was apologizing for things he couldn't control.

She jumped to her feet and leaned across the desk, her voice strained through clenched jaws. "I'm another end-of-the-roader, right? Living all alone on that old tub...a crazy...could never take care of a child, right? Right, right, right."

She pounded her fist on the desk right in front of him. "Listen, *Mister* Indian, *Mister* Lieutenant Paul Howard, I'm keeping James till I find his real family."

Paul waved his hand, trying to brush aside her anger, but right before his eyes she crouched and shuffled sideways, shaking her fists like rattles, chanting, "I'm an Indian, I'm an Indian toooo. Woo wooo." Then she stood straight as an arrow and raised her arms over her head. "I'm the Warrior for the Defense."

They were gone before he could get out of his chair.

Chapter 15

She put a sleepy James to bed and crowded into the bunk next to him and Sam to recite:

"James James Morrison Morrison Weatherby George Dupree / Took great / Care of his Mother / Though he was only three."

"Three," James said. "That's pretty silly, I guess. Three is really little, like just a baby, isn't it?"

"James James / Said to his Mother / Mother, he said, said he:"

James slid down flat in the sleeping bag, and Sam sighed and rolled onto his back. She finished to a sound asleep audience.

"You must never go down to the end of the town / if you don't go down with ME!"

Sleep had erased an old man and left a fragile child in her care. "James James Morrison Morrison / whoever you are / you're fine," she whispered, and laid her face against his cheek.

She went up to the cabin, sat on the bench next to the table, stretched her legs out and opened her book. But she couldn't read—her mind was a jumble of confused ideas, of James, how he'd gotten onto that rock, of Crow, of the dead man. She brushed her hand over the ancient tabletop, fingering the scars that were left after all the many, many years of use. She longed for Larry, needing him here right now so she could tell him her lengthy and awful story.

And there he was. There was a light tap on the door, and she shoved the curtain back before opening it, the lieutenant having persuaded her to caution. Larry stood there, not a monster with a knife in his teeth.

He ducked through the door, his tall frame not well designed for boat life. She hugged him tight; his arms around her were comforting, his mouth was sealed to hers—she was safe. Finally she stepped back and beckoned to him, slipped down the ladder and pointed at the sleepers. Sam's tail thumped but he didn't raise his head. Larry bent to look carefully at James, smiling as he straightened up.

"Far out," he whispered. "Gone for the night."

They went back up the ladder and sat side by side at the table.

"Where in the world did he come from?"

"It's such a complicated story—I'll try to make it short: the other day, Sam and I found him on the rocks out by Steamer Point, and then we found the body of a man around on the other side. And somebody shot at me. Maybe you didn't notice the bandage on Sam's leg, but they got him instead."

"Shot at you?" He turned and stared at her in horror. "My god, Liza. You *have* called the police."

"Sure—first thing. But the lieutenant doesn't have a clue why the boy was there, or how he's related to the dead man, or where his family is. And no idea why anyone would shoot at me, except maybe to keep me from telling about the dead man."

"Where's the kid's home?"

"That's the thing—he won't tell us. Scared somebody'll get his family."

"How old, did you say?"

"Seven, I think."

"Old enough to understand. What's his name?"

"James. James Kitai. Nephew of Goran Kitai, the dead man."

"Kitai." Larry nodded, stroking her neck as he thought about the name. "Never heard the name before, but we'll find it." He put his arm around her and rocked her gently. "At least you're safe. Better Sam than you, my dear."

Liza said, "How come you're here? I thought you were away all week?"

"Ahhh, those guys. Don't know what they want. Gotta see everything. Fly here, fly there. They're staying at the inn—

money is no object—dollar's cheap compared to yen. And I'm making a bundle just taking them around at their whim. Like I always say, 'richer's better.'" He pulled her tighter against him. "Listen, when I get back from flying these guys all over Alaska, we're gonna get married. We need each other. We're two of a kind, Miz Lize."

"Your mouth's not hooked up to your brain," she muttered. "You don't want a numb, dumb broad with a history like mine."

"I do, I do, it's what you have to say," he hummed in her ear.

It was time to put away her grief for Efren. She had to move on. Did she love Larry Hayden?

"Better than a hole in the ground, Elizabeth.'" Her mother's voice, teasing.

She started to laugh and they argued their way to bed. "Bed without board," she mumbled, before his hands worked their magic. Electric shock therapy, it was. This man could fill up all the empty spaces. Admit it now: "Alone" will never be enough.

After Larry left at dawn, she lay awake, feeling the warmth next to her slowly leak away. She seemed to be having a major meltdown. Finally she dozed, then woke after a chaotic dream that featured Crow's face. All she could recover was a sense of brooding sorrow and his hooded eyes watching her from below a steel surface. The sadness was so profound that her face was wet with tears.

She lay there thinking of the tragedy of Crow. Somewhere in Crow's drowned pride lay the key to James. She thought about Crow's pleasure in the old pictures, how he knew so many people by name, knew which Eagle had married which Raven; the dispersal of the clans, Kiksadi and Kogwonton, Nanyaayi, Decitan; who belonged to the old houses of Salmon and Grizzly Bear, Killer Whale, Frog.

Those old picture books: one book of Wrangell and Old Wrangell, one of Angoon. She wondered if James could have come from Angoon. Too far away, though, if his uncle came often to Wrangell. Angoon was clear up on the west side of Admiralty. No reason Goran would come down to Wrangell— she had to look closer to home.

It must be in the book about Old Wrangell that she'd find the ancestors Kitai. If they were there at all.

The next morning, the wind had dropped to a stiff breeze. The clouds overhead were volcanic, tearing past in a fierce jet stream, but on the western horizon, a line of transparent sky promised a calmer day.

You'd better have a calmer day, too, Liza. What on earth possessed you? You made a total fool of yourself in Paul Howard's office.

"It's your temper, Elizabeth." Scolding, scolding... *"Really, you're quite bad tempered sometimes, you know."*

She pictured Paul Howard's huge hands fumbling the papers on his desk, face strained, eyes shadowed, black, like Efren's eyes. You wanted to tell him you were sorry he lost his son, didn't you, Liza? That you know how he must feel? And especially how his son must feel, torn away from his father? You're a sucker, Liza—you get suckered in by everyone.

"You hurt too much, Elizabeth. You wear your heart on your sleeve."

"Shut up, Mother," she said in exasperation. "So did you."

By ten o'clock, James had fed and watered the chickens and Liza was ready to go. She warmed up the engine, checking to make sure the new hose she'd picked up at the hardware store was tightly clamped—no holes.

James took the bow line off the cleat. While he was unfastening it, Liza glanced along the dock. Coming down the ramp was a large and all-too-familiar figure, followed by an extremely fat woman who clung to the rail and let herself down hand over hand. Vivian Fredericks. Foster mother to a substantial percentage of Wrangell's neediest children.

Lieutenant Howard stopped at the foot of the ramp to wait for her, exasperation in every line of his twitching shoulders. Liza tumbled James aboard, let the stern line go, and hurled herself over the rail. As the *Salmon Eye* drifted back, she watched the lieutenant run toward the slip, Vivian panting along in his wake.

He shouted, reaching out as though he could hold the boat back. He managed to grab the tarp covering the chickens, dragging it loose. It caught on the wire and flapped in the breeze. The chickens erupted into shrieking white feather dusters.

Liza jogged the boat up. The lieutenant shouted again and she leaned from the wheelhouse, twiddling her fingers graciously like the queen.

The *Salmon Eye* tore along the west edge of town, past the log booms and cannery dock above Cemetery Point, to the main harbor, doubling back through the channel to the fuel dock. While Liza waited impatiently for the nozzle to click off, she stared across at the boats lined up in the transient moorage and the ramp behind them to the harbor master's office.

A man was walking down the ramp. Even from that distance, Liza could tell from his height and the downward angle of his cap that it was Larry. He headed along toward the floatplane dock. A large part of Liza would be overjoyed to have him back when he'd finished flying those men around—a tiny part still needed to grieve.

The nozzle snapped off, interrupting her reverie. She paid the man at the fuel dock and swung the *Salmon Eye* in an arc in the inner harbor. At the channel entrance, the tugs for Pacific Towing were rafted up. Look-alikes. She tried to see some identifying characteristic that would tell her from a distance which one she was passing.

Rounding the breakwater, she headed west before realizing that the *Clara M.* had been one of those rafted there. What did she know about Eric Sendhoven, skipper of the *Clara M.*? A lot of tragedy—a son lost on a crabber off Kodiak, a wife who died of pancreatic cancer, a daughter mixed up with a junkie. A bitter man, she'd heard, with much to be bitter about.

Why was Sendhoven in town? The lieutenant had said he'd be out for a couple weeks or more. Nobody keeps to schedule around here. That's island time for you.

Out in Zimovia Strait, a thin ray of sunlight pierced each wave and suspended it a long shining moment before it burst and the next one crowded in. To the north, the clouds had lifted and the high peaks above Le Conte glacier glittered against the sky.

Crossing Clarence Strait in a choppy sea, Liza worked the *Salmon Eye* cautiously through the Kashevarof Islands, "beset with rocks and reefs," according to the *U.S. Coast Pilot*. As they headed out of Ossipee Channel, a fountain of spray was silhouetted against the dark shore of Prince of Wales Island, then another and another.

"James, look out there ahead of us. Whales."

He ran into the wheelhouse and pressed his face to the glass.

"See? Watch for their fins when they break the surface." In a moment, three tall dorsal fins arced up and over, one after the other.

"Orcas," Liza said. "Killer whales. Those fins are too tall to be minkes or humpbacks. They're feeding over there close to shore."

The black fins arched up again, spouts visible against the dark land. She handed James the binoculars and helped him focus them. He gasped as one of the whales breached, launching itself clear of the surface. The gleaming black and white pattern on its sides was a perfect geometry.

"They're hunting?"

"Feeding on herring, probably. And they go up some of the longer inlets in the winter to look for seals and sea lions."

"Sometimes I saw a whale by where I live."

He knew where he lived. Of course he did. Try again.

"James, you know where you live. Now listen. If there's some reason you don't want to go back, it's okay to say so. I won't make you go home until we know it's safe, all right? But I want to tell somebody that *you're* safe. Who can I tell? Your mom?"

"No," he said. He stared out the window, his elbows on the binnacle. "I don't got a mom. And my grandma knows I'm okay. She knows it," he said, desperation in his voice. "So you don't have to tell her."

"How could she know? You were out there in the water all by yourself, half-frozen when Sam and I found you."

The memory of that small shape huddled on the rock made Liza shiver. All at once she was angry at all this stalling. No way could his grandma know he was safe. Where was his grandma, anyway? She grabbed James by his sparrow-boned shoulders and whirled him around, bending over so their faces were inches apart.

"Now you listen. I won't make you go anywhere you don't want to go, but you tell me where you live, and what your grandmother's name is, and you tell me fast."

He stared straight into her eyes for a long moment, then flung himself at her, his arms tight around her waist, his sobs so violent he could scarcely stand up. "I can't," he choked out. "I promised. I promised."

Liza was instantly ashamed. It wasn't her right to overpower him, just because she was bigger and older. "Tell me for your own good" was such an empty argument. And how could she tell—it might not be for his own good. She sank to the floor and pulled him down into her lap.

"Never mind," she said. "If you promised, maybe we can find a way so you don't have to break your promise."

He nodded, then wiped his face with his sleeve. "I didn't want to, though," he said. "But he made me."

"Can you tell me who made you promise?"

"Goran. He said, 'remember this...remember this,...and he told me things I can't ever tell, because he knew those men would come, I guess. And then those men came on another boat and I saw Goran in the water and I tried to get him."

"You tried to get to him?"

"Well, he was floating in the water and I jumped in, but it was dark and I got too cold, and I don't remember..."

Tears were flowing again, and Liza held him tighter. Jumped in. He'd jumped in. She imagined the scene—Goran's body drifting away in the dark as James frantically tried to swim to him. This water was so cold it snatched your breath and numbed your thoughts. How could he have jumped in?

"You tried, James. You were very, very brave."

He nodded against her shoulder and sat up again.

"Did you recognize any of the men that came to the boat?"

He shook his head. "I don't know what was their names."

"*Please* tell me where you live. All I want to do is take you home."

She had a sudden vision of her mother, hunched at the kitchen table, going over and over the file of a small girl found wandering around the King Street train station in Seattle. The girl had refused to say who had been with her or where they had gone; Liza's mother dug away beneath the surfaces, searching for some elusive fact. Liza had stood in the door watching till her mother felt observed and looked up, smiled, leaned back in her chair to stretch, holding out her arms to Liza. The next day, or was it the next month or year, she was gone.

James was slowly shaking his head. "Those men would go there and get my grandma or maybe somebody else, and maybe throw them in the water like Goran."

"But the men already know where you live, don't they?"

"They don't, because we were out on our boat when they came."

"James, I won't tell anyone, I promise. I'll just take you home."

"But I guess they would know I'm here. On the *Salmon Eye*. So they could see us if you take me home."

Liza thought about that. A lot of people did know James was on the *Salmon Eye*. Was the lieutenant going to win this point?

Chapter 16

The village of Kashevarof had no more than seventy-five people plus several dozen cats and dogs. A muddy two-track was its main street, switching back and forth to the top of the hill. Houses lined the switchbacks, there was a general store, a storage shed next to the wooden dock where Liza would leave her freight, and an ancient cannery, long since defunct. The big attraction in Kashevarof was the Velvet Moose, a bar and grill run by its owner, Minerva Michaels.

By the time Liza had sidled the *Salmon Eye* up to the dock, a line of seven adults, three children, and assorted dogs had formed. The adults and children had books in hand—the dogs were waiting for Sam. Liza had had no intention of opening the library, but the line surged up onto the deck before she could say a word.

Lovie Peak was first. "I found that book I got from last time, and when I saw the boat in again, I just brought it down, and I want another book, and not one of those horrid murders, true crime they call them…" Lovie's fat cheeks were red and shaking with disgust, "…and then all these other people saw you were here again and they want books too. Who's that boy over there?"

Liza wondered how Lovie Peak could have enough breath to string together all those words without inhaling. She said, quietly, so James wouldn't overhear her lie, "He's my late husband's nephew."

James came over then, and she showed him how to change the date on the stamp and let him stamp the books and cards. The line kept growing: mothers with stacks of picture books and murder mysteries, Edward Polansky with three volumes on antique cars which were not at *all* what he'd been looking for.

"These ain't what I thought they was. See, I got to fix my truck. It's old. Kinda old. '43. These books, they don't say how to fix it, just how to pretty it. I ain't looking for no pretty truck."

"You want a repair manual, then, Edward. I'll look that up in town and see what I can get. '43? What make?"

"Oh, ain't only a Ford, see. Ford, they make a good truck. You don't want nothin' but a Ford, you gotta buy a truck."

Liza wrote his request in the back of the Kashevarof notebook, and James added the three volumes of antique cars to the returns.

When the last person had checked out, Liza chased Sam's black and white girl friend off the deck and closed the door. She put the returns into one of the fold-up milk crates she used for lugging books back to the library and shoved it alongside the two crates of new books she hadn't taken the time to shelve yet. Sloppy seamanship, she knew—they could fly all over the cabin in heavy seas.

As soon as she'd talked to Mink at the Velvet Moose, who knew everyone in the whole of Southeast Alaska, she'd unload the freight at the dock and they'd head back to Wrangell. Then she'd have to confront Paul Howard, tell him she wouldn't give James up till she found his family.

The Velvet Moose had been around since right after the century began, when Kashevarof's fish plant was operating in the narrow channel between the flats. The Moose was still the most imposing building in town with a towering false front and pillared porch, the interior open except for the giant spruce poles supporting the roof.

The bar, a curving oak counter nearly fifty feet long, ran the length of the building and came from the same sunken steamship whose salvage provided the huge bronze bell that hung above the bar. The tiered mahogany behind the bar had mirrored shelves for the bottles, a large oval portrait of Robert

Merton, owner-builder of the sunken steamship which bore his name, and a VHF radio so the bartender could hear trouble coming.

At 4:30 in the afternoon, when Liza, James and Sam walked in, Minerva Michaels, better known as Mink, was at the cash register, dressed in her bartender's uniform, jeans with red Alaska Fisherman suspenders, a man's white dress shirt, sleeves rolled to the elbow, topped by a purple bow tie. Her Brillo hair exploded from a black corduroy cap bearing the gold and red Kashevarof Volunteer Fire Department logo.

Not much taller than Tasha, Mink was built like an army tank, with all the same qualities of force and armor. The wilder the proceedings at the Velvet Moose, the quieter Mink's voice and the larger her dimensions. When she stepped from behind the bar and held the door open for someone who'd offended, few withstood the invitation.

Mink was writing figures on a piece of paper as she riffled through the till, counting up the take before the late afternoon crowd arrived. She glanced at them, finished counting the twenties and wrote on the paper.

"Shit. Look what drifted back to Meccaburg," she said. "What's that?" She pointed at Sam. "You, kid." She waved her hand at James. "Get that scrawny sumbitch outa here. He don't pay his way." She pointed at the door. "Get."

While James dragged a reluctant Sam toward the door, Liza looked around the room. The diehard coffee drinkers were seated at the center table, and the smell of overworked coffee mingled with the sour smell of beer. Elmer Hanson was draped across the far end of the bar, snoring, head on arms. At the center booth, four fishermen nursed a nearly empty pitcher.

In the last booth, a bearded man in faded army fatigues slouched against the wall, his legs stretched out along the bench. His gray hair straggled from a receding hair line to his shoulders. On the table beside him were a chess board, an overflowing ash tray, a small loose-leaf notebook, and three Pepsi cans. He was holding a portable VHF radio to his ear and tapped a folded newspaper against his leg as he listened.

While Mink finished counting, Liza walked over and gave the man a victory sign. He said something into the radio, held it away from his head, and lifted his newspaper in greeting. "Romeo," he said. "'Begin at the beginning, the King said gravely...'"

"Nothing, Tango. There's been a huge amount of Nothing in my life of late. What's coming down around here?"

"'I must become a borrower of the night for a dark hour or twain.'"

Somewhere in his lost past, Tango had absorbed most of Western literature written since the Golden Age of Greece. He had a memory to conjure with, and Liza wished she could see through to the mind that had retreated there.

Tango. The man Mink found on the beach and married so she'd have a pet. Or something like that. Her stories varied. Said she married him for his money. Said she married him to keep him from being sent back to Canada. He's Canadian? Well, he might be—at least, he doesn't want to go there.

All that was truly known of Tango was that he sprang full-blown from elephant grass after the Tet offensive and could not be separated from his radio. Whiskey Tango November, his adopted marine radio call sign, he alternated with Alpha Four from his platoon. "Sierra Zulu," Tango would shout when Liza and Larry walked in..."Romeo, gimme five!"

Mink believed, from circumstantial evidence, that he called in an air strike on a VC position, some mix-up occurred, and most of his platoon was blown to the other side of the river in very small pieces. Whether Tango gave the position incorrectly or the Skyhawks miscalculated mattered not to the course of history, except that Tango's life was permanently devoted to correcting the error. Regardless of what she said, Mink married him to give him the chance. When the radio voices got too loud, she parked him in the storeroom with a couple of joints and there was a pause in the bombing.

James returned from ejecting Sam and climbed up on a stool at the bar.

"Ain't s'posed to sit there," Mink told him. "Here—c'mon, you can sit back there where you can watch the TV. Kids allowed where the food is."

She grabbed a glass and filled it with ice and Coke. "C'mon. I got a sec—sit yourselves." Carrying the glass over to one of the booths, she stopped to pour Liza a cup of coffee from the percolator. She squeezed in on one side of the table, and James and Liza sat across from her.

"No getting rid'a bad pennies, hey? Who's this kid?"

"This is James. James Kitai. James, this is Minerva Michaels."

"Mink," she said. "Easier."

"You own all this whole place?" James said.

"Shoo-oot, you bet I do," Mink said, nodding solemnly. "Every little square inch of rotten floorboard. Right down to the clogged-up septic, young man."

"You got to use one of those rubber things on a stick," James said. "Like, you push it up and down and then all the water runs out when it almost went all over on the floor."

Mink's laugh growled up and the booth shook. "You got it, boy. You can fix it yourself next time. You got yourself a job."

"I gotta see if Sam's there," James said. "I'll be right back." Before Liza could grab him, he slid under the table and crawled out across her feet.

Mink turned her head, or rather, turned all of her from the seat up, and watched him go out the door. "Where'd you get it?" she asked. "He's kinda cute. Make a good plumber, anyway."

"Found him washed up on rocks over at Kindergarten Bay. I've started telling people he's Efren's nephew because somebody's looking for him. I don't know if they can actually recognize him, but they certainly know he's on the *Salmon Eye* because I radioed the Coast Guard after I found him. James won't tell us who he is or where he lives. Only person he's recognized so far is Crow, who won't talk."

"Crow? As in 'Old' or bird?"

"'Old,' I'm afraid. It's too long a story—Crow is, I mean. You know him, though. I'm sure you do. Bars are his only venue. Bars, detox, and the library."

"Gets his brainwashing three ways. Well, I never seen James before. He'll talk, though. You ain't mean enough. You gotta empty threat around a little—he'll crumple like last year's newspaper."

"He's pretty tough, Mink. A survivor—one of these kids that takes all the shit and turns out to be president."

Mink hoisted herself from the booth and picked up James's glass and Liza's coffee cup. "You couldn't stand up to a flea," she said. "You'd get eaten alive, man. What a feather bed." She steamed back to the bar and slammed the dishes into the sink.

James came back in and climbed up on a bar stool, standing on the top rungs to reach up and stroke the bell.

"Don't ring that," Mink warned. "You'll owe the house a round of drinks."

"This is a very humongous bell," James said. "Where did you get this bell?"

"Salvaged from the *S.S. Robert Merton* going down with all hands in the Narrows in '23. You want to hear a bell story?"

James nodded.

Mink leaned across the bar so her nose was almost touching his. "Okay, mister, I'll tell you a story if you tell me one. That a deal?"

James shrugged, nodded again, and sank down on top of the stool with his elbows on the bar, chin in hands like a life-long barfly.

"You ain't s'posed to be sitting up here to the bar," Mink said. "You see old Hap Farwell coming through that door sporting his badge, you scramble. Hap Farwell's the Village Public Safety Officer.

"Well now," she said, "I got stories would make your hair stand up like this corkscrew. I'll tell you what happened a while back, and then you're gonna tell me yours. Then I gotta go to work, get this place cleaned up and old Elmer there chased out before the next shift."

Elmer, hearing his name through a fog of sleep and alcohol, snorted violently, and raised his head.

"You there," Mink said. "You get."

"That's what you said to Sam," James said. "Everybody has to get."

Mink leaned herself on one elbow, swiping her towel in a circle. "While ago," she said, "one morning I come in to do some cleanin' up, and I'm scrubbin' out that percolator when I hear all this ruckus in the back room, glass breaking, lotta thumpin' bumpin', whole place shaking like an earthquake. Well, I grabbed out my old Colt pistol I keep in case we get an outsize emergency, and I walk over and crack the door a little and peek in, only it's dark in there. There's more crashing bottles and a lotta slurping noise. So I open the door wider and stick my head in and down there to one end is the biggest old brown bear you ever saw in your life, his nose an inch deep in a pool of whiskey."

Mink paused and pointed at James. "Bears ain't use'ta whiskey. You better believe that was one drunk bear. His bee-hind had no idea a'tall what his front legs was up to and when he lifted up his head, his bee-hind leaned way to one side and knocked down some more bottles crunching all over that cement floor." Mink stopped and sucked in enough air for Chapter Two.

James nodded. "You told it, 'You get,' didn't you?" he said. "Like you told Sam and that man over there."

"Well, I did," Mink said. "Exactly what I said, but that bear, he's too drunk to get. He leeans this way and leeans that way, and more bottles come crashing down, and I'm getting mad. Nobody gives away them bottles 'a whiskey, ya know. They cost sumbucks, them bottles. So when that bear can't get his eyes straight on that door he'd busted through, I shut my door up tight so he won't run my way, and I come over here and grab ahold 'a that bell clapper and I let him have it, kaDONG kaDONG kaDONG like this bar is gonna blow itself to doomsday.

"Well, there was such a racket in the storeroom I thought that bear musta took the whole wall right out. Wood splitting, glass smashing, crates going over…But he found that busted door finally, knocked it flatter'n Herb Dillon's birthday cake, and I heard him lurchin' and staggerin' off through the bush."

Mink reached up and swung the bell clapper back and forth without touching the bell sides. "That bear, he got such a fright along with his hangover, I do believe he'll never show his face down here again." Mink's deep laugh broke over them like surf.

James grinned and got up on his knees so he could lean across the bar. "You got some more stories?"

"Hey. It's your turn. I told you mine. Now you. You tell me one of your stories."

James shrugged. "One time me and my uncle went halibut fishing," he said. "And we got this very, very huge large halibut on the line. And we just only had the skiff because the troller had a broke-down engine till it got fixed."

He stopped, and Mink said, "What'd you say your uncle's name was?"

"Goran," James said. "Anyway I already told Liza his name. So this very humongous halibut was towing us all around and the boat tipping tipping like it was going over..." James's hands tilted and zoomed above the bar, "...and my uncle said he couldn't hold it and it would tip the boat over if he got it close to shoot it. You always got to shoot big halibuts or else when they get in the boat they break your leg or something."

James wrapped his arms around himself in the excitement of remembering. "So then, my uncle said maybe we better cut it loose, but we shouldn't do that because it was really a good fish, like we could eat it about for a whole month or year. And smoke it. So then..." He hugged himself tighter and laughed when Mink did the same thing.

"So then, we let it out a little more and more, and it was towing us everywhere around, and then it started getting tired and not pulling that much, and so my uncle started rowing hard, and I held on the line, and we pulled it to the beach, and then we got out of the skiff and we both of us pulled and we got it right up, right on the gravel."

He rolled his head around and around. "And it died dead, flop flop all over the beach. And that's all the stories I know to tell."

"Well, all I got to say is, that's the biggest fish story that's ever been told in this bar, and be-lieeeve you me, this old place has heard some mightly powerful fish stories. Lot of folks here would want to find that halibut hole. Where's that beach you hauled him to? That beach got a name?"

"No name," James said. "You got any more stories?"

"Naah, I gotta get to work," Mink said. "That was one swell fish story, though. Wait'll I try that one on my friends. They're sure gonna want to know where you caught it. Sure you can't remember the name?"

James climbed down from the stool. He gave his little shrug and said, "No name," once more. Then he went over and climbed up opposite Tango to look over the chess game in progress.

"...roger," Tango said, "that's Bravo Echo November, first name. Storm one. Alpha Four, out."

He set the radio down, jotted a couple of words in the notebook, and moved a white pawn. James nodded and moved a black bishop. Tango moved a white knight and James got up on his knees to see the board better.

From her perch, Liza could see the game proceeding slowly, interrupted occasionally by urgent radio messages, "Alpha one, Alpha one, this is Alpha Four, we have incoming..."

The door opened and a whole Wrangell contingent poured in, stamping water from their boots and hanging their rain gear on the coat hooks at the ends of the booths. She knew most of them. Rob Hendel of the wooden leg. Eric Sendhoven, the *Clara M.*'s skipper. Dan Jacobs, Butch Jim, Ross Elliot, Tasha's ex, Jake Fremantle from the *Aquila*, and a couple of timber cruisers, men Liza had seen flying helicopters for Tom. And Tom Morrison himself.

They jammed into one booth, dragging chairs around the end of it, and waved at Mink, who was already heading for them, a pitcher of beer in each hand. Liza didn't want to talk to Tom. She'd had enough of his complaints for a while. She slid off the stool.

A man was standing right behind her and she bumped into him, muttering "excuse me," as she extricated herself. The man wore a jeans jacket and a blue baseball cap turned backward. From his left sleeve dangled a metal hook.

Liza glanced at his face. His eyes, deep-set beneath hooded lids, were a startling yellow ringed in black. An eagle's eyes. Hypnotic. For a moment she felt like prey. The man backed away from her, turned and disappeared toward the restroom.

"Mink," Liza said, "who's that man who just came in? With the missing arm."

Mink, shoveling ice into one of the bins, said, "Likely Tenney Rushmore."

"James said he knew somebody with one arm. A fisherman."

"Owns the *Fighting Chance*, old double-ender. Hand trolls. Half-assed at fishing, but he's a pretty fair artist. Wood, mostly. Silver, too. Ain't no living in it, though—takes too long to make a thing right, him with only one arm working well. So he fishes on the side. Anyway, fishes so long as the *Fighting Chance* floats."

"Where's he from?"

"Damned if I know. Been around here, off and on, I'd say maybe three years. Got a floathouse over there on the north flat. He ain't around much, though, just in and out. But so's most of the fishermen."

"Find out where he's from, okay? Call me on the radio. If you learn anything, maybe I can use it to pry more out of James."

"You use a pry bar on that kid and you'll find out whatever it is you gotta know. Pisses me off watching you fuss around over him. He's a cute kid, but you gotta lean on him hard to find out where he comes from. I'll find out where Tenney's from and let'cha know." She moved down to the end of the bar and began to lever Elmer's head up, jamming a cup of coffee under his nose so he couldn't lie down again.

"Alpha Four, come in, Alpha Two," Tango was saying as Liza reached their table.

"Wrap it up, guys," Liza said. "James and I have to get our beauty sleep."

From the corner of her eye, she saw Tenney Rushmore emerge from the restroom and walk over to the booth with the four fishermen. They jammed together to make room for him. Liza decided to go over and make her own inquiry, but just then James conceded.

Tango stood and shook his hand. "'An adventurous child, thanks to the gods.' That's a quote from Horace. And another: 'Undeservedly you will atone for the sins of your fathers.'"

"Why do you talk on that radio?" James asked.

"As Horace says, so wisely, 'Change the name and it's about you, that story.' Come again. Your skill is challenging. I must go now, unfortunately."

He stretched out on the bench and picked up the radio. "Alpha Four—we're taking some mortar fire—Victor Charlie—

tree line." He sounded pleading. There'd have to be a bombing pause soon.

Liza, following James, saw him pause at the two crowded booths. For one split second he froze. Then he launched himself at the heavy door. Struggling to open it, he looked back at her. His eyes, his whole face, blazed with terror.

Chapter 17

Paul Howard was lying on his side, suspended over bottomless green water; a forest reflected in infinite layers. Trees rushed up at him. The metal roof of a green building hurtled toward him. Then the helicopter righted and began its slow descent, raising small tornadoes in the downdraft.

"You gonna be long, Paul?" the pilot asked.

"Don't know. I gotta find some guys, try to get a definite ID on this guy Patrick—the escaped felon—if they're around, it shouldn't take long."

"I'm running over to Burnett—I can stop back for you—have Ben gimme a call."

"Yeah, thanks—I hope this won't take long. I got enough mess over in town without some hassle over here."

Paul walked toward the green building. Across the bay he could hear the road equipment gouging another track across the mountains. Hadn't cut much over here on the bay side—probably change that quick enough, but right now the trees were thick as a bristle brush. Anybody wanted to hide themselves could do it forever in this forest. So why would the guy come in where everyone could see him? Dumb. Unless the object was to get them to search the wrong place. That wasn't so dumb.

Ben, the dispatcher, thought the guys Paul wanted were up at #7814 burning slash. Paul could take the jeep if he wanted or hang around till four—they'd all come in at four. Paul took the jeep.

The road was a washboard, a zigzag track punched along the side of the mountain, the rising curves precisely the arc required for the log carriers to get around. Boulders dangled precariously above his head, small rocks cascading down as he drove. Who would ever insure the life of a logger? God, it was dangerous just getting to a logging site.

He dragged the jeep around a deep mud hole. Concentrate on getting the information on Patrick. Don't think about the morning. Made a fool of himself.

One tire skidded in the mud and the jeep lurched. He gunned the engine and felt the rear wheels gain traction. He tried not to look over the ledge. A quick way down, only an occasional glint of water visible through the treetops, far below the road here.

Maybe he shouldn't have called Vivian so soon. But goddamn that Lizzie—she had no right to take the kid.

He gained the top of the ridge and saw smoke rising beyond trees down the opposite slope. Must be the burn. The road followed the top of the ridge, then plunged down the side and broke out into the clear-cut. He pulled up behind a battered blue pickup and climbed out.

A man in a yellow hard hat, bulldozer jockey, was pushing slash into a burning pile. Beyond him, a couple men with chainsaws were hacking through some scrawny downed trees and dragging them clear of the stumps. Paul made his way across the rough ground and shouted over the noise of the saws. The saws shut down and the men watched him as he walked over to them.

"Looking for Terry Madsen or Josh Calloway," he said.

"Both in one shot. Madsen here," the shorter man said, "and this is Cal. What'n we do for you?"

"Paul Howard, Wrangell Police. Heard you guys might have seen this guy Gordy Patrick. You get a look at him?"

"Kinda funny chance," Madsen said. "We went out fishing after work the other afternoon—what day was that?" he asked Calloway.

"Musta been Tuesday—shut down early because it was blowing so hard. Took the company runabout up the bay there to the mouth of Porcupine Creek. Getting real dark—we were heading back, and here comes this skiff with three guys in it. Seemed like they were trying to stay real close to the east edge."

"You get a good look at them?"

"Well, wasn't much light—raining so hard you could hardly see shore. Seemed like they were trying to go real quiet—we thought they might be doin' a little poaching, likely. We hung out—just drifted while we watched 'em."

"One fairly big guy," Madsen said, "musta been maybe six feet, a smaller fellow, kinda skinny looking, and a man with a beard. Got a look at that one through the binocs—they had flashlights—had one of those real bright kind, flashed it around and caught the bearded guy right in the face. For sure he was the guy in that bulletin they got on the office board. Scar right through his beard."

"Know where they went?"

"Went in over by that little float house in the hook there before the inner bay. Unloaded a bunch 'a boxes, looked like. Left one of the guys there. One with the beard."

"Did they see you?"

Calloway said, "No, I doubt they could see us—we were around the other side of that brushy point—only could see through the bushes what they were doing. Had the binocs, though."

"Anything about the other two except size?"

Madsen pushed his hard hat back and scratched his forehead. "Big guy was rowing—steel skiff, I think, Lund-type, something like that, had an outboard, but they weren't using it. Trying to keep quiet, seemed like. You remember anything else, Cal?"

"Big guy had his hood up, so you couldn't see much."

"Anything about the smaller one?"

"Nothing special about him I can remember. Black Helly-Hansen kinda jacket. Cap. Blue, maybe. Logo on it, but too far away to see it."

"Voices?"

Calloway looked doubtful. "We weren't close enough to hear 'em talk. They were keeping pretty quiet."

"Madsen?"

"Nah, nothing, I'm afraid."

"Well, I appreciate the time. If you think of anything else, give me a call. I'll see if I can get over there to the float house. The runabout usually down there at the office?"

"Yeah, unless somebody's checking log storage. Ask Ben."

Paul shook hands with each man and repeated his thanks before he headed back in the jeep.

Nothing, was what it amounted to. Tall guy, small guy and bearded one. Hunh. Like looking for that corpse carried out by the tide. He wrenched the shift and the jeep grumbled into low gear. Of course he knew Lizzie had actually found a dead man, but he wasn't giving her an inch. Let her fume. He wondered at his fury—fighting something, that's what he was doing. Fighting something he didn't want to look at.

He could see that James felt comfortable with her, leaned against her shoulder, watched her closely to see if everything was okay. Suddenly he remembered leaning against his grandmother, her arm around him, the safety of it. Loss gnarled like a fist to his ribs.

He kept the runabout out in the middle of the bay while he used the binoculars to look at the float house. Neat little place on a log raft—somebody's retreat, short dock connecting it to the beach. No smoke from the chimney, nothing tied up at the dock. Four crab traps stacked to one side of the raft.

He turned the runabout and went over to the small bight south of the float house, staring through the brush the way Madsen and Calloway had. Even in broad daylight it was pretty hard to make out very much. Heights, maybe, if they'd stood there on that dock together. Beard, only in very bright light, like the flash Madsen had described. Enough detail to identify the scar from the copier-made photograph in the APB? Hard to say. He wouldn't bet on it.

He turned the boat and edged around the point, clear of the bushes. Shoving the gear into neutral, he let the boat drift, trying to see any movement on shore. Boxes, they'd reported. Unloaded a bunch of boxes. Couldn't have been very large or heavy, if it was just a skiff, three men aboard, not even using the outboard.

He pulled in by the dock and shut the engine down. He checked again for movement, staying low behind the windshield while he waited to see if anyone came out. Patrick, if it was Gordy Patrick, didn't have a thing to lose now—wouldn't be taken without somebody going down.

Nothing stirred. He pulled his gun loose from its holster and climbed out. The dock warped across the surface of the water under his feet—three floating sections on pilings. He loped across them in a few strides, gaining his balance as he hit the beach, and jogged up the path to the shelter of the woodshed behind the float house. He stood there, breathing too heavily, and watched. There were curtains across all the windows—none of them moved. The door, he could see now, was padlocked on the outside. He moved cautiously along the path and kicked open the door of the outhouse. Nobody.

A small stream trickled down the side of the mountain and cut its way through the brush to the bay. He followed the stream, trampling salal and bunchberry, till it made a sharp turn and rose abruptly in a long, thin waterfall. The mountain rose in a series of rocky ledges above him. Behind him, where the brush line met the beach at the stream mouth, was a small clearing. Or rather, a small area had been cleared. Freshly turned soil. Not enough time for even the voracious undergrowth to cover it.

He scraped at the earth with his foot, then bent and dug at it with a stick. The furry smell of perpetual wet coated his throat. Something hard under there. He knelt and began to remove the loose earth with his hands. Plywood, still yellow-bright. He scraped farther and found edges. The boxes. Side by side, maybe eighteen inches on a side. He kept scraping, trying to see how many there were. Maybe there were some tools in the runabout he could use to dig them out.

Far up the mountainside, a raven gave a hollow warning and somewhere close to him, another answered. He heard a sudden flurry of calls, then a hushed whistle of wings as the whole flock rose and flew off. He jumped to his feet a second before a skull-crushing boulder ricocheted off the rock wall above him. It slammed into his left shoulder, hurling him to the ground. Pain exploded up his neck into his brain.

He felt for his revolver and fired blindly up the sheer mountainside.

Chapter 18

James backed himself under the bushes as far as he could get. It was a pretty dark forest and almost night and maybe bears could be coming out of their caves because it wasn't winter anymore. He could scarcely get his breath because he'd run so fast up the hill. Like when he jumped in the water off the *Sarah Moon*. Right next to him he heard something, so he tried to not breathe even though he couldn't really stop.

He reached his hand out and there was fur and before he could run, a tongue licked his face. "Sam?" he said, and tears started coming in his eyes. He could feel Sam's long ears and his tongue licking, licking, and he could hear Sam's tail wagging the bushes.

He buried his face in Sam's neck. Tears were coming in his eyes all the time because Sam was so warm and Sam was leaning on him. He tried to not cry but he couldn't, couldn't, stop.

It seemed like a long time and he was getting pretty wet from leaves and the ground was wet and he was shivering even with Sam. But he had to stay there hiding because of that man, the one that had come to the *Sarah Moon* looking for him when he saw Goran in the water. That man was there in that bar waiting to grab him and take him away like he took away his uncle. If he stayed hiding with Sam, the man wouldn't find him and he could go back to the *Salmon Eye* and Liza would be there.

Liza was trying to help, she was very, very nice of a person and anyway there was Sam and Sam was right here. He did not, did not, know what to do and he was now very extremely cold. He practiced the story words like Goran told him. 'That which is Nameless...' 'White Bird flies up...' 'the Listening Stone..." And then he heard Liza far away calling, "James, James."

He got farther in the bushes but Sam sat straight up and listened and Liza started calling, "Sam, Sam," and then Sam put his head up, his nose pointing at the tree branch above them, and he made this terrible howling noise like a wolf or something. James tried to shush him but he wouldn't. He just did it again, that creepy howling noise.

Then Liza was picking James up and holding him, hugging him with her jacket around him, covering him up with her jacket so he was a little bit warm and it was dark inside it. He could tell she was running because of the way he bumped against her. And her breathing was the same as when he ran up the hill. After a while she climbed on the boat and then he was in the sleeping bag, Sam on top of him.

A long time later he heard the engine starting up and then he didn't hear anything anymore.

Chapter 19

James had become very heavy, as though gravity was stronger at the bottom of the hill. Liza flung one leg over the rail of the *Salmon Eye*, then leaned him on the rail top while she caught her breath.

By the time she'd charged out of the Velvet Moose, James was gone, but she'd seen Sam's waving tail vanish around the curve of the muddy track called Main Street. She'd raced after him. Where the end of the track met the forest, she'd started calling. Sam, not James, had answered.

She found them huddled in the understory, dense evergreens a feeble umbrella over them. They smelled of ancient leaf mold and wet fur. Night had fallen in the brief time it had taken her to track them, and she tripped on every root, stepped in every hole and rotted trunk as she headed back downhill. James hadn't spoken. She could feel his shudders through her jacket. More than cold, this time.

Now, down here at the dock, the darkness seemed trenchant, a physical shape that pierced her from all sides. She felt rather than saw Sam leap onto the deck. He growled, a deep vibration against her leg. In such profound darkness there could be no shadows, yet she knew someone had moved on the foredeck.

Sam launched himself toward the bow. Whoever it was jumped for the rail, tripping over the coils of barbed wire that braced the crates of chickens. Instantly the chickens burst from their prisons and the air was filled with whooping chuckles. Distracted by the white feathers swirling around his legs, Sam skidded to a stop. The intruder was over the rail and gone before Sam recovered himself.

Get out of here, get out of here. Her hands shook so hard she couldn't find the key in her pocket. Finally something sharp and metal. She twisted the lock and carried James into the cabin, sliding him to the floor. She switched on her little penlight, dropped down the ladder and opened the gun rack. Larry had left all his guns aboard.

What to take? Something quick—something easy to grab. Larry's Browning 9mm automatic. No, he must have it with him. For bears. Well, never mind, go for distance—hope whoever was after them stayed far away. She took one of Larry's hunting rifles down from the rack. The bolt-action Ruger. She opened the drawer, found a box of Winchester .270's, loaded the rifle and stuck the box in the pocket of her jacket.

It had been a long time since she'd gone to the rifle range with Efren. She refused to hunt with Larry—"sissy," he called her, but she'd had enough of bullets and death after Efren was gunned down. Maybe she could still shoot, though. She'd been an outstanding marksman in those years he'd taken her to the shooting range every weekend. Practice, though. You had to practice. Don't kid yourself, Liza.

She leaped up the ladder and propped the rifle in the corner of the wheelhouse. Crouching over James, she pulled off his soaked clothes and rubbed him vigorously with a towel.

"We've done this before, haven't we?" she said to him. "Getting you dry and warmed up?"

From the shadowy edge of the tiny circle of light, he stared blankly at her, his huge eyes like black holes that gave back nothing. Perhaps his terror had gone too deep to be recalled. Her own terror was like a battery. Go now.

While she groped for the mooring lines, she could hear the chickens mumbling over beetles in the sagging planks of the dock. Hopeless to try to recover them. She didn't dare turn on lights—was the intruder out there in the darkness, lying in wait? Was it the person James had recognized?

Shrieks of laughter tumbled down on her head. Her pulse racing even faster, she stared upward into the darkness, trying to make out the source of the noise. Strange pale bundles were lined up on the crane. Seven Leghorn pullets perching. "And a par-triiidge in a pear tree," she muttered, rushing to the wheelhouse as the *Salmon Eye* swung loose from the dock.

The channel to the village of Kashevarof was narrow, the edges baring to long salt flats at low tide. Liza watched the radar and depth finder as though they were lodestars. She always tried to avoid the channel at Kashevarof below half tide. Now it was only half an hour before a minus .8 foot low. The depth finder flicked ten feet. The *Salmon Eye* drew almost nine. She shifted into neutral and crossed her fingers. Only luck would get them over the sand bar.

For once crossed fingers worked. The depth finder quickly showed twenty-three feet. Breathing again, Liza put the engine back in gear and shoved the throttle up. Visibility was nil. She should be able to see the light blinking on Round Island to the north, and beyond it the red beacon on MacNamara Point, but in fact she was driving through a long black wind tunnel.

Outside the channel, the southeasterly slammed into the boat. She turned to port to quarter the waves. Over the bow she could see them tower and crack their tops, dashing streamers against the windshield.

She looked at the radar screen to locate Tide Island. She'd head straight for it, then turn due south, again angling into the heavy seas rather than bucking them. Then what? Anchor up at Exchange Cove? Go through Ossipee Channel and run for it across Clarence Strait?

Clarence Strait was reporting forty-five knots and eight-foot seas. But she needed to get to Wrangell. She needed help. She hated to admit it, but she wanted Larry beside her. Right now. He'd know what to do out here, know whether they could get across tonight. She needed him.

She glanced at the radar screen again. A blip had separated from the shore. There was a boat behind her. She set the autopilot and waited for it to settle down. Then she opened the door of the wheelhouse and looked back. Nothing but rain sweeping sideways. How far away was that boat?

The screen was set on a one-mile radius. With almost zero visibility, she wouldn't be able to see its running lights that far away. But who else would be out on a miserable night like this?

She jogged the throttle up a little. The boat pitched as it surged into the steep mountains of water. After a few minutes, the boat on the screen seemed to have dropped back. The *Salmon Eye* was pulling away from it. She flexed her fingers. Her shoulders were rigid. She stretched and shook her arms over her head. It reminded her of her war dance in the police station. Mister Police Lieutenant Tlingit Warrior Paul Howard, where the hell are you?

Leaving the boat on auto another minute, she went back to check on James. Only the top of his head was visible in the sleeping bag. She thrust her hand in against his warm back, feeling his quick, slight respirations. He moved a little at her touch and sighed deeply.

Rock him in your arms, Liza. Erase his nightmares. You're a rotten mother.

"Mothers never have it easy, Elizabeth."

Right. What would she do now when she had to give him up? Her throat tasted the salt from a million tears.

She forced herself back to the wheelhouse and retrieved the steering from auto, inching the *Salmon Eye* through Ossipee Channel, another ugly shallow between islands. The tide had turned to flood. At the southern end of Snow Pass, standing waves curled in patterns like isobars on a weather map. The *Salmon Eye* yawed violently. Round black mirrors glinted on the surface, each one the vortex of a whirlpool like an underwater tornado. Liza threw her weight on the wheel, feeling the current suck at the keel.

The signal on Nesbitt Reef showed up on the radar screen. She turned east. Going east was impossible, though; the boat rolled on her beam in the waves beating up Clarence Strait. She turned south. She would have to tack like a sailboat, south, then northeast into Stikine Strait, and on to Wrangell.

At the edge of the radar screen was the blip she'd seen earlier. It came and went, right at the edge of the mile radius. Slow, slow trip both boats were making. She was throttled way down to keep from plowing headlong into the heavy seas. Who was that following? Or were they following? Her fingers played nervously with the throttle, nursing it a little, fiddling it forward while she tried to judge, by its rhythmic thud, the force of water against plank. The blip on the screen slid off the edge again.

The rush of adrenalin was dwindling, leaving her limp and exhausted. All sounds were rhythmic, drum of rain on window, drum of water on hull. Hypnotic. She jerked awake, knowing she'd dozed off the way one might doze on an empty ribbon of highway. She massaged the back of her neck. Dangerous when she couldn't force her attention any further. She grabbed the chart.

Steamer Bay. The GPS showed that she was three quarters of the way across Clarence Strait now, almost ready to turn northeast. She could see the marker on Mariposa Rock on the radar screen. Right beyond it was Steamer Bay. Safe anchorage, even if they'd roll heavily in the wind funneling down Porcupine Creek.

What about that boat following her? There'd be other boats in Steamer Bay on a night like this. She could even tie up at the logging camp if she had to. And maybe that boat, which wasn't showing on her screen right now, wouldn't pick her up if she turned in fast. She reached down and nursed the throttle forward a little more.

She wove between Mariposa Rock and the tip of Point Harrington. She was fully awake now, negotiating the rocky ledge at the Point. The inner shore on the west side of the bay was taking the full brunt of the wind channeled down the creek. There was a notch over there on the east shore where she could find twelve fathoms or less to anchor in. She could just make out a couple of anchor lights over there. Fishermen sitting out the blow.

She looked at the radar. That boat was showing again, closer than it had been, not over a half mile. Of course, she'd slowed way down to enter the bay, and the boat would probably turn up toward Stikine Strait anyway, the way she'd intended to go before she recognized exhaustion.

She inched the *Salmon Eye* toward the other side, keeping one eye on the radar screen, one on those anchor lights. People didn't appreciate it if you ran over their anchor lines or fouled them with your own. Plenty of room. The other boats were small, shrimpers, probably. Even over here, though, the water was lumpy, the small boats tugging their anchor lines straight.

She put the gears in neutral and the *Salmon Eye* rolled, taking the chop on her beam. As the boat leveled out, Liza shoved the door open and moved hand over hand along the foredeck, kicking loose the brake on the anchor winch. The chain rattled out to its splice with the nylon rode, then a fathom of nylon ran out. She watched in horror as the end of it vanished over the bow roller. The matched end, the *cut* end, remained on the windlass. The anchor, attached to nothing at all, lay at the bottom of the sea.

Somebody had cut the anchor line. Someone with a sharp knife and a death wish. For their deaths.

Move. Move. Look how fast we're drifting. Use the small anchor, the kedge. Head for the dock at the logging camp. Or just head out. The *Salmon Eye* pitched toward the small boats. She put it in gear and dragged the wheel over.

A boat was coming around the Point. A mass, denser than the black around it, moved slowly toward her. With no running lights.

She jammed the throttle to the top. Every plank groaned as the old schooner strained into the night.

Chapter 20

Paul Howard lay on his back in the runabout, listening to his own salvation. He thought he'd been lying there for hours—it was growing dark already, but time was a bird darting around him. He barely recalled getting to the boat, or the voice that answered his radio call. Sometime or other he'd heard a helicopter coming in over the bay. Now he heard an outboard, its mutter coming closer as somebody headed down the shore. The pain in his neck and shoulder seemed to thrust straight into his brain.

The outboard was close now—must be turning toward the dock. Paul pushed himself up with his right arm, waited while the ceiling spun around him and settled down again, then got to his knees. Through the back of the canvas dodger he could see an open skiff pulling in on the other side of the narrow dock. The motion from its wake made him grab at the dashboard, and a black hole appeared before his eyes.

Someone was bending over him.

"Jesus, Paul, you're really smashed up," the chief said. "Why the hell didn't you get backup before you came over? That guy's brutal!"

"Wasn't thinking," Paul said, his voice sounding tinny and distant to his own ears. "Didn't think he'd be hanging around here—too many people. Dumb."

Woods supported him on his good side, and he launched himself to his feet. "Found some crates they buried. Don't know what's in 'em—somebody shoved a goddamn huge boulder down the hill—if I hadn't stood up, I'd be flatter'n roadkill."

"We've got troopers up trying to find the guy—he's too smart to light a fire, though. And it's way too dark to pick him out unless he lights something."

"Probably long gone. They likely had a pickup all fixed. I maybe walked right into it."

"Well, it's not really our turf, anyway."

"Maybe not, but this is turning personal. And I got an idea what's in those boxes. I got a flash—let's take a look."

"Jerry's over there poking around. You're in no shape for digging. Let him."

"Yeah." Paul tried to step out onto the dock and winced as his shoulder brushed the door.

"Come on, I'll take you back. Jerry can bring the skiff."

A pencil of light appeared on the beach, and Jerry said, "Pulled the tops off those crates. Full of Indian stuff. Boxes, masks, baskets. Looks like somebody cleaned out a museum or something."

"Thought that's what it'd be," Paul said. "Lemme look."

"How 'bout tomorrow? You got something broke in there, or dislocated, or something."

"Just lemme look. I can tell if it's some of the missing stuff we been getting reports on." He moved cautiously along the dock, supporting his left elbow to keep his arm still. Jerry held the flashlight beam at his feet and Paul moved forward as though the path were mined.

Jerry had cleared the tops of three wooden packing cases and used the tip of the shovel to pry loose the lids. He held the light on the nearest box. In slow motion, Paul lowered himself to his knees. He reached out with his right hand and lifted a small bentwood box. Touch took him home.

The rounded corners where the steamed cedar had folded, the dovetail stitched with spruce root at the single joint, a grinning bear with abalone teeth, its deeply tooled outlines as familiar to his fingers as his own face. A box almost like this one had sat on his grandmother's shelf. The box had been carved by her great-grandfather.

"Old," he said. "Very old." He reached in again. Beneath a layer of wood chips was a rattle, and a leather pouch fringed with puffin beaks. "Shaman," he said. "Look at how this has all been preserved. Somebody was keeping it safe." He dug through the chips with his fingers. "And look at this. A Raven mask. And a headdress. Mountain goat horns."

"This the stuff you were looking for?"

"Hunh unh. Mostly pieces of poles, those are. And not in the best shape. This stuff's been kept somewhere like a museum. Or in someone's house. It's been covered and kept perfect. Not easy to keep wood. Gets dried out. Cracks. Or gets wet and rots."

Paul set his right foot flat on the ground and levered himself up with his hand on his knee. The darkness whirled and the chief braced him with his arm. "Can we take this stuff out tonight?"

"First thing in the morning, Paul."

"It won't be here. You can bet your life they aren't going to lose this haul. It's all master craftsmanship. Wherever it came from, they've staked a hell of a lot on getting it transferred."

"Good. We'll watch and see who comes back for it."

"You lose this, you lose a lot of the heritage of the Tlingit nation. Jerry's only uncovered three cases, but I bet there's a hell of a lot more here."

"Why would they use such an obvious place? There's always loggers around."

"We gotta start asking. Loggers, timber cruisers, they cover a lot of territory. Could be some link." Paul bent over and tried to lower the lid on the packing case. The next thing he knew, Woods was helping him into the runabout. He sagged onto the seat and put his head in his hands.

Where the hell had those things been? He'd seen a Chilkat blanket folded around something in the center of the crate, touched the wool. Mountain goat wool soft as cashmere.

A fierce longing seized him. He wanted to go back. Those objects meant only a criminal plot to the chief—a theft. But to Paul they were as dear as his own childhood, objects lovingly created, designed for a purpose, treasured for their usefulness. A whole culture of wood, of spruce root and cedar bark, replaced by Tupperware and stainless steel utensils. Even his grandmother had come to plastic and pottery, but each spruce root basket and wooden bowl on her shelves had a designer and a story, and he knew every story was true.

"This is Gonakadet, the sea serpent," she'd say of a carved wooden bowl. "Listen how Gonakadet tricked Killer Whale."

The pilot and Jerry boosted him aboard the helicopter and in a minute, Woods came out of the building and wedged himself in back. In moments they were over the landing pad north of Shoemaker Bay.

As the helicopter settled down he tried to see the harbor, see if the *Salmon Eye* might be back in its slip, but the yellow lights turned the docks into a forest of rigging and poles and he couldn't tell one boat from the other. He knew he'd find a rectangle of black water where the boat should be. His whole head felt like a rectangle of black water. He wished he could just slide into it and float for about a year.

"My car's here," he said, when Woods tried to get him to go in his car. "I can manage it—drive one-handed."

"Listen, Paul, you gotta see the doc. You're battered like a quarterback on a bad call."

"Naah, little sleep, coupl'a aspirin's all. You get on back. If I don't show up in the morning, mark me in sick. I got a few days coming."

"You're the goddamnedest stubbornest fool I ever got crosswind of."

Paul waved his hand, then regretted it. "If it isn't better tomorrow I'll check with the clinic. You go on. I'll putz in slow and easy. Got some undercover bourbon I'm looking forward to."

The chief looked hard at him, then shrugged in defeat. "You call if you need anything. I'll bring the report forms over tomorrow."

"Who's gonna cover the goods over there?"

"State uniforms—they lost that guy—now let'em take him back."

"You better get 'em over there quick—they may already be moving that stuff."

"I called while you were getting in the 'copter. They oughta be there already."

"Yeah, well, they better not lose it." Paul turned and walked carefully toward the Blazer. He felt in his pocket for his keys and was grateful they were in the righthand side. His left shoulder and arm seemed both hot and numb, which struck him as odd—if something is numb how can you feel it flaming?

He unlocked the door and tried to climb onto the seat without moving anything on his left side. Even raising his leg pulled his shoulder. "Knee bone connected to the...thigh bone..."

The day had developed a color all its own. Purple mixed with brown, he thought. Totally ugly. He drove the few hundred yards to the Shoemaker parking lot and pulled in facing the north finger.

The *Salmon Eye*'s slip was empty. He couldn't see the black rectangle of water, but the high bow wasn't visible. And no chickens. Goddamn what a fool he'd made of himself the whole goddamned day. A toad-colored day. The pain in his shoulder was the least of it.

Chapter 21

Over the roar of the engine Liza could hear waves thundering onto the rocks at Steamer Point. She stayed offshore as far as she dared without losing distance on the other boat. A flood tide with wind like this could set any boat on the rocks. If she could get safely around the Point, Stikine Strait would be partially protected from the southeasterly by the high ridge of Etolin Island.

Now she was far enough out to see the Steamer Point blinker. Had the boat behind her closed the distance slightly? She couldn't be sure.

Behind her, through the sweep of rain, she caught the blinker on Nesbitt Reef. She looked back the other way for the light on Key Reef. She couldn't see it. The other boat must be passing between the light and the *Salmon Eye*. She stared at the screen. Could that boat actually be heading northwest? Was it all her imagination that it was following her?

She was very close to the Steamer Point light now. Already the waves were easing a little as she turned into the east-running section of Stikine Strait. No, the other boat was turning too. All she could do, then, was hope the huge old engine had a few more horses than whatever powered that one.

On the screen, the boat was closing in. She'd better radio for help. By the time anything got out here, though, even a helicopter with state troopers, the other boat would overtake—men swarming over the rails, grabbing James, throwing her overboard...Radio. Tell someone you're in trouble, Liza.

A tiny red dot appeared on the starboard side of the windshield frame. Her mind stumbled a beat—no—it couldn't be. She dropped to the floor and the window flowered into a million petals.

The wheel spun from the force of the current on the rudder. She raised her hands and grabbed the lowest spokes, trying to drag it to center. Blind. She was steering blind. Surf at the Point boomed, reverberating against the wooden planks under her head. Too close. Then she heard a voice. Very faint.

"What was that noise? Sam, get off me. Liza?"

"James, stay where you are. Don't stand up. Stay flat. There's some trouble." Her voice stuck in her throat. Could he hear her?

She tried to turn so she could see down the companionway. "James," she shouted as loud as she could. "Stay down. Don't move."

"Okay," he said. "But Sam wants to go there. Where you are."

"Well, let him go. But you stay flat. Don't move till I tell you."

The red dot appeared above the starboard door. Laser scope. She pressed herself so flat to the floor she thought she'd melt into it. Flowers bloomed in the glass of both doors. Her breath was forced out in explosive bursts.

The floor planks arched rhythmically under her body. Lying there, the boat alive beneath her, she wondered again what had flashed through Efren's mind when the joy rider had come blazing out the front door of the crack house. And afterward, when he lay dying on that unforgiving concrete walk. Maybe nothing—maybe there wasn't time. Yes. Yes, he'd thought of her—his last thought.

Her attackers had something very high-powered. A sniper type of weapon. And they must have closed on her fast. Irrelevant fragments galloped across her brain. I came to Alaska to escape. The word "escape" brought hysterical tears to her eyes. Carbonated laughter rose like sobs.

She rolled on her side. Sam was there, his head drooping above her. "Drop," she whispered, and he flattened himself against the floor, his nose jammed under her chin. Her breath still coming in sharp gasps, she got up on her hands and knees and tried to set the autopilot. The wheel swung hard to port—

she reached up and fingered the dial till the wheel centered again.

She snaked her way back to the door of the companionway where she could see both the radar screen and the GPS from the floor, Sam moving beside her as though they were joined at the hip. And there was the Ruger.

She pulled it toward her. Hit something blind? Never do it. She imagined the red dot on the outside of the door opposite her heart—they knew she was in the wheelhouse. And whatever they were using with that scope would penetrate the wood door like a knife in butter. An invisible, distant target from a rolling boat? Forget it.

You're a dumb shit, Liza.

God damn it—what would Efren say?

"Go for it," that's what he'd say. "What've you got to lose?" But he'd done something crazy too and lost his life.

She slithered over to the smashed window and knelt. Jamming out the bottom of the fractured glass, she tried to get an angle— they'd been to port, directly abeam, to hit both doors.

She inhaled deeply, held her breath and pulled the trigger. She dragged the bolt back and fired again.

Suddenly a brilliant light washed across the wheelhouse. They must be training a spotlight. But from where she knelt, the radar screen showed the other boat dropping back. A larger blip had appeared behind it, moving steadily into Stikine Strait.

She raised herself to eye level in the shattered window and looked back. A skyscraper of bright lights was bearing down on the stern of the *Salmon Eye*. The Alaska State ferry. The ferry would pass through Stikine Strait, then turn east toward town. An escort. By god, she had a naval escort.

The ferry came on, traveling perhaps five knots faster than the *Salmon Eye*. Floodlights blazed, lighting up the gold North Star and Big Dipper on her blue stack. Her bridge made a brilliant half circle above the high bow. On the radar screen, the smaller blip was being overtaken by the larger one.

Now the other boat was turning across the ferry's bow, trying to stay on the same side of the channel as the *Salmon Eye*. Too late. The ferry horn sounded, deep, and double-toned. A brilliant spotlight again lit up the exploded glass in the wheelhouse.

Liza stood up and stared out, but not in time. The ferry, playing the light across the other boat, had already moved between them. Liza punched off the auto-steering and turned to starboard. The ferry was hard astern now and she had to move over. She'd never pushed the *Salmon Eye* this hard. The boat was making twelve knots—must be the current pushing her.

By pulling the *Salmon Eye* to starboard, she'd signaled her intention to let the ferry overtake to port. The ferry was abeam now. The *Matanuska*. The avenging angel *Matanuska*. She plowed past and arced away from the *Salmon Eye*, heading toward town. The smaller blip on the radar screen had dropped back farther.

At her present speed, Liza thought she could just about make Wrangell before the other boat caught up with her again. And every moment would bring more light. She could actually see the black ridge of Elephant's Nose outlined against the sea. Somewhere back of that ironclad sky, the sun was rising.

Chapter 22

"Shit, can you believe it?"

"Get him in here. Has he got a pulse? Goddamn it, look out—he's bleeding like a fucking pig."

"He's still alive. Hey. Hey. Can you hear me?"

"Get...me...Gotta...get..."

"See? He's even talking."

"Just winged him, maybe. Lucky shot."

"How the hell'd she do it? Ya know? I keep askin' myself how the hell."

"I told him 'no heavy metal.' We'd'a boarded her if he hadn't taken that hit. Shit. For all we know, he hit the kid."

"She'd be screamin' all over the radio if he'd hit the kid."

"Don't know how she did it. Anyhow, we'll take him in and dump him off at the hospital tonight."

"No. Reck...nize...be awright...gotta..."

"Ahh, shut up. You're dead weight now. Or dead meat. Your choice."

"...they'll get me...they..."

"Get him cleaned up, see what the damage is. Far as I'm concerned he's done anyway. No way we're carrying him any farther. With that scar, they'll pick him out a mile off."

"Yeah, but he's got all those other sales contacts down south."

"So twist his arm a little. I want those names. We're gonna go with the highest bidder once we find it."

"He ain't lookin' too good, hunh?"

"He's dirtying up the floor. Take him down and clean him up. If he comes around, tell him, 'you want to get well, name your contacts.' Move it, man, before he croaks right here."

Chapter 23

At five forty-seven a.m., the *Salmon Eye* backed into her slip at Shoemaker Bay. Liza climbed over the rail and cleated the mooring lines. The familiar smells of sour tidelands, diesel fuel and fish drenched the back of her tongue like a salty communion. Her knees buckled and she clung to the boat like someone drowning.

There was a light touch on her hair and she raised her head. James's face was inches from her own, his eyes so close they seemed like the dark pools she was drowning in. She blinked back tears of exhaustion, or were they love for this resilient child?

Back in the cabin, she sank to the floor and pulled James into her lap. She could feel a live current running through his spine and she rubbed his back and shoulders with one hand, easing him against the curve of her body as he slowly relaxed. Finally he pressed his face into her shoulder and began to sob.

Sam came over to lick James's ear. James tried to cover it, giggling through his tears at Sam's rough tongue. "I saw the windows," he said, inhaling in huge gasps. "They got shot."

"They did," Liza said. "Somebody chased us. But we beat them. We're home now, safe and sound." She realized as she spoke that James wasn't home—that she still had no idea where his home might be, and safe it certainly wasn't. James nodded, though, apparently accepting the idea of "safe and sound."

She pushed him away from her shoulder and turned him in her lap so she could see his face. "James," she said, "I want you to tell me who you saw before you ran away from the Velvet Moose. You recognized somebody. Who was it?"

"A man. I saw him and I remembered he was on the boat that came. He got on the *Sarah Moon* and then my uncle got put in the water. They turned on these bright lights and I saw him and I wanted to get him…But I couldn't…I couldn't see him any more and it was cold…" He started to sob again, rubbing his face on her sweater.

"I know this is hard for you, James. It's terrible to think about. But I have to know who that man was. Tell me what he looked like."

"Well, he had on a cap. Black, I guess. And his hair isn't black, it's sort of…you know…a little…"

"Brown? Blonde?"

"Well, a little like brownish, I guess. And kind of long."

"Shoulder length? Over his ears?"

"Sticking out from his cap."

She sighed. "Does he have a beard?"

"Well, no, that one doesn't got a beard."

"There was *another* one?"

"Yeah, on the boat that came there was two men. And one got a beard and one didn't."

"Okay, let's go back to the bar a minute. Did you recognize somebody else in the Velvet Moose?"

"No, because I was so scared that other guy would get me I didn't exactly look at anyone else."

She tried to picture the crowded booth, but she'd been so startled by James dashing out the door, she hadn't paid attention. "Where was the man sitting? The one you really looked at. Were you looking straight at him, or from the side?"

"I guess he was middle. Like there were a lot of people all around him. But he was looking at me. I know for sure he was looking at me. He saw me and so I ran. I was scared."

"Any idea what he was wearing?"

"Maybe a shirt or something, but I think bibs—I think he had those straps like he didn't take off his wet stuff before he came in there."

Somebody wearing oilskin overalls. The fisherman's uniform. Thousands like that, except that most of them would have taken off their wet gear before heading for the bar. That, and no beard. She ran through the possibilities. Dan Jacobs, Rob Hendel, at least one of the men who flew helicopters, all had beards. Tom Morrison had no beard. Nor did Jake or Ross Elliot or Eric Sendhoven.

She tried to see who was wearing bib overalls, but the scene was fading, the edges losing focus. If she couldn't see it, imagine how it looked to James, whose terror had been consuming. She hugged him, then lifted him to his feet and unfolded her stiff legs, revolving the foot that had gone to sleep under Sam's weight.

"We'll go see Andy," she said. "His mom will fix us breakfast. Throw me the electric and phone lines. They're coiled up on the base of the crane."

One of the herons that patrolled the harbor was standing on top of the electric panel. It lifted its wings and glared at her with one eye, defending its territory. When she insisted on plugging in the lines, it squawked a protest and sculled over to the bowsprit of the *Nereia* in the next slip.

"Is that blood spattered on your face, or paint?" Tasha said. "You're looking a tad frazzled. Motherhood getting to you?"

Liza tried to laugh but it came out as a wail. "Tash...somebody's after him. Somebody chased us all the way back from Kashevarof...shot at us...you should see the windows in the wheelhouse. They'll kill to get him. Will you keep him while I go and report to the cops?"

"As long as you want. Days—months—whatever you say."

"I don't want to give him up, Tash. He's wormed his way inside. He's the toughest kid I've ever seen. Toughest individual, child or adult."

"You eaten yet, or you both running on empty?"

"Empty. Feed James, and I'll be right back."

"You want to wash up first?"

"Am I a mess?"

"Your face—must of got some of that glass."

"I can't take the time—maybe they can track that other boat if I get in there right now."

"Be off—we'll be here whenever you get back. It's Saturday, so half the kids in town'll be messing around here. He'll be one of the crowd."

"Saturday? How did it get to be Saturday?"

"World turns, dearie. Get going, then go and sleep. You look like you haven't closed your eyes this month."

Liza went out to the back porch where James was sitting with Simi. "I'm going to run into town a minute. You can stay and have breakfast and play with Andy. I'll be right back."

He stared at her, then nodded. She noticed that Simi was leaning heavily against his shoulder. He stroked her ear a little. Dog and boy swam across Liza's vision.

The Wrangell Public Safety building was one of the more imposing buildings in town—a modern two-story building housing the fire department as well. Liza turned left into the parking lot and cranked the truck into one of the visitor parking spots. She slammed the door and headed for the entrance. Facing the building was a white Blazer. Descending from it, as stiff as a Frankenstein monster, was Lieutenant Paul Howard. Without moving his head, he turned his whole body to look at her.

The left side of his face was a virulent purple, red tributaries running through it. His left eye was swollen like dough before baking. His left sleeve hung empty; his left hand dangled beneath the waistband of his worn leather jacket. There was something comical about this split personality, but again, Liza felt tears rising. It seemed an eternity that they faced each other before she said, "What happened?"

"What happened to you?"

She raised her hand to her face. It felt gritty; for the first time, she noticed how it burned. Her hand came away with a tiny needle of glass.

"Where's James?" The lieutenant's voice was hoarse with tension.

"He's with Tasha. He's fine."

She reached up and felt her hair. Loose strands were raked over her ears, some drifting over her eyes—she must look like a war refugee. "We have to talk," she said.

"You eaten?"

Tasha had asked the same thing. She must look emaciated as well as disheveled. "Not for a while, but I've got to tell you what happened."

"I gotta check my desk. Then we'll go eat. Come on."

In the office he hit the button on the message machine and she heard Chief Woods's voice. *"Tried to get you at home—suppose you're in the office, though. Got a report from a log truck driver that Patrick was picked up by speedboat not long after you got smashed. We'll take the crates out this afternoon. You take some time off."*

Liza asked for the restroom and he pointed down the hall. Switching the light on, she was confronted with a monstrous sight in the mirror. Her face was measled and glittered with glass dust. Her hair had blown into a firm mass from which long wisps had escaped. A streak of black below her right eye— was it oil or stove soot?—rambled over her cheek to the corner of her jaw. She started to laugh, then bit her lip as tears ran over. Good lord, she must be at the end of her rope to cry like this.

She soaked a paper towel and began blotting her face to get the glass off. Little specks of blood welled up from nearly every pore. She threw the towel away and started over with another, working carefully around her eyes. Her upper eyelids were dotted, too. Reflex must have closed her eyes at the sound of glass exploding. How could nerve ends operate at the speed of sound? Lucky thing. She took a comb from her pocket and began to work at the nest of hair.

"Start at the ends and work back, Elizabeth. How you get yourself in such a mess I do not know." Her mother, teasing. Liza leaned forward. In the mirror, she could see the shadowy shape of the wolf, the black wolf, draped across her shoulders.

Chapter 24

Paul followed Lizzie into the café, noticing the weary hunch of her shoulders. From the counter, all eyes turned to look at them and Maggie, at the cash register, whistled. Paul lifted his usable hand to their audience. Lizzie hesitated, looking back at him, and he was startled all over again—something so odd about her face—it looked like it had been sandblasted. Her eyes seemed recessed in her skull as though the bones of her face had absorbed them.

"Smoke?" she asked.

He shook his head and instantly regretted it. She turned in the other direction and walked to the corner table. He moved to pull the chair out for her but she waved him off and he sank gratefully into the chair across from her. Goddamn. This was going to be a siege. That bullet in his shoulder in '77 had never hurt this much. But he was younger then. Old now. An old man.

Maggie came over with menus and coffee. Paul held his cup right side up for her and gulped half the coffee before setting it down.

"You sure you got the right place?" Maggie said, looking from one to the other. "Hospital's right up the street. I hope you two have made up."

Lizzie laughed, but Paul could only roll one eye up. "You oughta see the ones we left behind," he growled.

"Don't think I care to. You guys know what you want?"

"Scrambled eggs, toast, hash browns," Lizzie said.

"The works," Paul said. "Two easy over, ham, hash browns, toast, large o.j. And splash some more of that brown stuff in here before you go." He hunched. He straightened up and turned sideways. He leaned his right elbow on the table. A knife stabbed his left shoulder. He lowered his elbow and bent forward slightly. He could feel Lizzie's eyes on him. Don't say anything, he willed. For god's sake, no pity.

"I'll start," she said. "It's such a long story we'll probably be here till lunch. But here goes. I went over to Kashevarof. I thought maybe Mink would recognize James. The Velvet Moose is such a landmark, everyone turns up there sooner or later. I know I was technically violating our agreement not to leave town."

By supporting his head in his right hand he could see her out of the corner of his eye. She raised her eyes and he looked away immediately. Then he realized her last comment had actually been a question. Her stillness, that listening air—she was waiting for him to say something.

"Yeah," he said. "Vivian's pretty bent out of shape. Says she won't take the kid now."

"I didn't know then that...I shouldn't have...But the chickens..." In an instant, her sorrow dissolved into laughter. She tried to cover her mouth but laughter leaked around her fingers. "The chickens..."

"Goddammit. Those chickens...carried on like there was a fox in the coop." He grinned with the side of his mouth that functioned. "What'd you do with 'em?"

"Well, that's part of the story. Sorry. I have to tell it in order. Let's see...Kashevarof..." She stopped again. "You know, the condition of your face is incredibly distracting. I hope I'm going to get an explanation."

"Yeah, yeah. But you first."

"Well, we talked to Mink, and James played chess with Tango, and then a bunch of men from Wrangell came in and sat at one of the booths." She began listing names.

"Butch Jim, Rob Hendel, Ross Elliot, Tom Morrison...a man named Tenney Rushmore, a one-armed fisherman Mink knows..."

"I'll get that list of names later if it's important."

"It is important because after James finished playing and we were leaving, he stopped and looked at the men in those booths. Only a second. I mean, barely even a split second. And then he started running. He was all the way up the hill by the time I got out to the road. And his face, when he was shoving the door open—you should have seen it—stark terror."

"So you think he recognized some of those men?"

"One of them for sure. I questioned him after we got in this morning. It was one of the men he saw on the boat that came before his uncle was thrown in. One of them had a beard and one didn't. Only two items narrow it down at all—the man does not have a beard, and he was wearing bib rainpants. Oh, and he doesn't have black hair—brownish, James said. Which probably means not Butch Jim or another Native American. So where does that leave us?"

Maggie returned with food. "Want me to cut up your ham and spread your toast?" she asked Paul. "You do it with one hand?" She snickered. "Eggs at two o'clock, hash browns at seven."

"I'm not blind," he snarled.

"Couldn't prove it by me," Maggie said. "One-eyed jacks. I'll be over with more coffee in a sec."

"Cute," he said to her back. "So James is running up the hill." He picked up his fork and flipped the eggs onto the potatoes.

"He was deep in the forest when I found him. Sam followed him and gave away his hiding place."

"Sam doing okay?"

"He's slowed down—that's why I could still see him when I got out to the road. Otherwise, his leg seems to be healing up. But James was nearly hypothermic again. There was old snow under those trees, and he was huddled down right against an old rotted tree trunk. I wrapped him in my jacket and carried him back to the boat.

"When we got there, somebody was on the foredeck. He ran but it was too dark to see who it was. He tipped the chicken crates over and the chickens escaped and flew all over the dock and roosted on the crane." She smiled. "See? It could have been a lot worse the other day."

He nodded and pain shot through his neck. Dammit, why couldn't he remember not to shake his head? Lizzie saw him wince and looked away. At least she wasn't all sloppy with sympathy.

"The boat was locked up," she continued, "and I was pretty sure nobody'd gotten in. It wasn't till later that I found out what he'd done. Ugly weather, but I headed out—I wasn't going to hang around and let them take James at gunpoint, or whatever they were planning.

"I crossed the Strait and tried to anchor in Steamer Bay. But somebody followed us, stayed right at the edge of the radar on the one-mile setting till I got close to Steamer, then started closing with us. The anchor went straight to the bottom—the line cut. That's what the guy was doing on the boat. When he heard me, he tried to hide."

"This boat following you—you get a look at it?"

"Not once. You know how dark it is out there—thick sky, no city lights reflecting—just totally black. And they weren't carrying running lights. Freaky. I set a speed record getting out of there."

"You able to outrun them?"

"Well, I outmaneuvred them at the start—I think they expected me to spend more time trying to anchor than I did. But they were starting to close with us after we got into Stikine Strait. And then they shot at us—something tremendously high-powered like a sniper weapon. Had a laser scope. I saw the red dot on the woodwork and dropped."

"How'd you know what it was?

"My husband, remember? The cop? I used to go with him to the shooting range."

"You shoot?"

"I used to. Pretty good, too. But I haven't kept in practice. Up here all you can do with a gun is kill something. And somebody killed my husband with a gun. But I actually took one of the hunting rifles that Larry leaves in the rack and shot back."

He stared at her in amazement. Lord, this woman had a steel gut. "In the dark? You have a night scope?"

"Nope. Just fired at random. One of the dumber things I've done in my life. But all it did was waste a couple .270s."

"And make yourself a perfect target for their scope."

"Yeah, I thought of that. Figured they had the dot right over my heart while I fired."

A picture flashed across Paul's mind of her crouched in the wheelhouse, trying to take aim at a moving target in the dark. He was stunned at how horrified he felt. "Obviously you made it back," he said, trying to concentrate on his plate.

"The ferry came along. The *Matanuska*." She laughed. "Cut them off, so they had to cross behind her. By which time I'd pulled away. And it was starting to get light—not exactly dawn, but enough to make out the islands. I think they're scared of being identified—they dropped back till they were off the screen."

"You got any ideas about that boat?"

"It's big—as big as the *Salmon Eye*, I think—has a slightly more powerful engine. Or engines. They pulled up on us whenever they wanted to, but not at high speed."

"Another packer?"

"Could be. Or a tug, I suppose. Something in the sixty-to-eighty-foot range, I'd say."

"Easier to track thugs than tugs."

She smiled at his little joke, then grew serious again. "At least James is okay."

"Have you gotten anything else out of him?"

"For what it's worth, I know that he 'doesn't got a mother.' He said his grandma knows he's all right. Can you believe it? This is the kid I found on a rock the sea covered minutes later. The kid that someone will kill for. But his grandmother knows he's all right? He's scared that if he tells me where he lives, the men will go there and throw his grandma away like they threw his uncle away. He's stubborn as they come."

"Like I told you, he's got this loyalty. It's a family thing. His family's the whole village—a tribal house." Paul laid his fork down. He took a deep breath and lightning tore through his rib cage. "My grandma was all I had, too," he said. "My mother drank herself to death before I could walk."

He stared across the street at the truck where Sam yearned from the window. "Sorry. Forget it. That has nothing to do with James." He picked up his fork and waved it over his plate as though he could brush the words aside. But she was looking at him intently.

"So you know what it's like," she said.

"To not have a mother?"

"To have a mother die." She pushed her plate to the side. "My mother disappeared when I was twelve." She laid her hands on the table, palms up, as though holding something out to him. "She's dead. I know that." She took a shaky breath. "But her...body never showed up."

She glanced at him, her eyes flat and unreadable. "It's the black wolf on my shoulder," she said. "I carry it everywhere."

She was holding herself stiff as a mast. She had opened a tiny window to him but he could see she was afraid he'd trespass. The faded plaid of her flannel shirt stretched into curves as she tensed her shoulders. He stared at the worn plaid in silence, afraid to meet her eyes.

When she spoke, her voice was barely audible. "Now you tell. What happened to you?"

"Dumb. Rookie kind of mistake. Went after an armed-and-dangerous and he was. I was actually just going to get information, but then I stupidly followed up on it without backup. Somebody shoved a boulder down the hill—caught my shoulder instead of my skull. So it coulda been worse."

She knotted her hands more tightly and nodded. Not meeting her eyes was becoming painful. After another long silence she said, "You were right about James, lieutenant..."

"Paul."

"Paul. I can't keep him."

He did look at her then. Her eyes were full of tears. He could no more say, "I told you so" than he could allow himself to touch her clenched hands.

"Even James sees that being on the *Salmon Eye* is dangerous because they know where he is."

"What do you think you'll do with him?"

"Is it my choice? Then I'll leave him with Tasha. She'll scarcely notice an extra and...she's one hundred percent Indian."

He flinched. "Sorry about that. I was out of bounds."

"I was pretty obnoxious myself."

"Well, Tasha told me not to turn everything into Wounded Knee. And she's right. There's no reason at all."

"There is a reason. You were right. I'm half Indian with an all-white mind. I know nothing of Native American ways. Nothing. Only those stories everyone knows. My dad didn't want my mother to "turn me Native." I just don't want anyone else to have James."

The tears had reached her voice. "But I know I have to let him go." Her hands were bolted together like a steel latch.

His own hands grew huge and clumsy as he gripped the edges of the chair seat to keep from touching her. "At least he'll be safe," he said.

Chapter 25

Again Liza watched Lieutenant Paul Howard in the rearview mirror as she turned out of the Police Department parking lot. What a dark spirit he was, brooding, like Hi-ya-shon-a-gu on the Raven totem, charged with holding up the whole world.

They had laid their deepest selves on the table at the local café. No, it wasn't that, exactly. They'd begun stories they alone had the right to tell. But their stories were safe. In some way there had been comfort in their exchange. Paul Howard's darkness held profound compassion—he was spiny like a sea urchin to protect the delicate, vulnerable part that lay inside.

"You must watch this man, Elizabeth."

What do you mean, watch, Mother?

Silence. All at once she caught a flash of her mother's dark eyes rolling upward. She fell to giggling.

She turned into the parking lot at the hardware store. In the summer, the lot was filled with lines of tourists off the cruise ships, waiting to use the pay phones to contact civilization. "Once you've seen one mountain, you've seen 'em all." "How could anyone live in a place like this?" they'd say to grandchildren and neighbors and the next person in line.

"Because people were born here, raised here, can't extract spruce forests and salt flats from their morning coffee," Liza longed to retort and indeed, had done so on one embarrassing occasion.

"It's like a park," said a blue-haired lady whose stentorian voice could have reached Toledo without the phone. "They should just make it a park so These People can't cut down all the trees."

Liza had turned on her. "Of *course* we won't cut down all the trees. They're why we live here. We *love* them. And we love the mountains and the ocean. And we don't need somebody from Ortonville, Ohio, telling us how to take care of it. We take care of our home because we *love* it."

The lady had made her lips into an ooo and raised delicate fingers to cover them. Liza had stomped into the hardware, her face blazing. Of course they *would* cut down all the trees if the payoff was big enough. What on earth had gotten into her? The don't-tell-me-what-to-do attitude must be dissolved in Wrangell's water supply.

The hardware store, also boat supplier and purveyor of popcorn, had a fifty-pound anchor that would do for the moment. She had decided to set up a second working anchor—sixty or better, but for now she could get by with the fifty plus her kedge, which she'd bring up on deck.

"You hear we got cut back on cruise ships again?" Alice asked, while she ran off Liza's credit card. "Fish are disappearing, mill's gonna go—what else is there?"

"The place has lived on its gristle and bone for eight thousand years. It's one tough community. Do we really need all those tourists in their shiny jogging suits?"

"Oh right. Maybe they'll strike oil out there by Five Mile."

Liza looked at Alice's tired face and thought about the years she'd stood at a cash register, hoisting cases of motor oil and nails. Every one of these Southeast towns lived on roller coaster luck. Most of them had enough diversity to survive the downhill ride. Wrangell, though. Wrangell had lots of history but not much of anything else. Never enough of some things. Except toughness. Independence. Wrangell had plenty of that. Liza was proud to live here in this working-man's town that wasn't all gussied up for tourists.

"I'm sorry, Alice," Liza said. "Not a lot of options at the moment, are there?"

"None that pay the rent," Alice muttered, going to get the hand truck for the anchor.

In the parking lot, Liza passed Eric Sendhoven climbing into his pickup. He nodded curtly. She was already out in the road before she remembered that he was skipper of the tug *Clara M.* Could it possibly have been the *Clara* following the *Salmon Eye* last night? But what could Sendhoven have to do with James? The man was deep-down angry, though—the fates were always against him—maybe he'd just flipped out after some new injury. She had a certain sympathy for people who were pushed over the edge. She'd been to the brink. Next time—ahh, god...next time...

As she got to the corner, a man, his back to her, was entering the Old Russian Bar and Grill. He was dressed in uniform— rubber boots, jeans, denim jacket, baseball cap pulled forward against the rain, dark, shoulder-length hair, beneath it. Nothing to single him out, except that from his left sleeve dangled a hook, not a hand. Tenney Rushmore.

Liza's eyes were slow to adjust to the flickering dimness inside the Old Russian Bar. Over the bar was a moose head like an over-inflated football beneath a giant rack of antlers. The antlers were outlined in miniature Christmas tree bulbs on alternating flash.

Smoke hung like strands of wool from the dim ceiling lights, and endless repetitions of the Rainier sign were traded between the rear window and the mirror behind the bar. Through the opening at the far end, Liza could see the pool table, a man leaning over it, another standing beside him, holding his cue like a lance.

Billy Pete, the bartender, gave her a sideways glower when he saw her by the door. His glance made her want to hurry. She looked carefully at the two men seated on the bar stools. They had two hands apiece.

Opposite the bar, two booths were empty and three had one occupant each. The day drinkers. The Old Russian Bar and Grill was home to them, and one thing Liza could say for Billy, he let them stay as long as business permitted, shoving coffee at them from time to time. When he moved them on, they'd go to the shelter, if their legs could carry them. If not, somebody from Tasha's group, or Paul Howard's, would get them there. Crow was often one of them.

There were five people in the last booth. Facing Liza was Tenney Rushmore. For an instant, their eyes met, and again she felt that hypnotic yellow gaze; a man, she felt certain, who would do anything he set himself to do.

Eric Sendhoven passed her and slid onto the seat beside Tenney. She took a step toward them when hands grabbed her arms. Tom's voice said, "Don't leave home without me." He spun her around. "Liza. Good lord, what happened to your face?"

Shoving her onto a seat facing the front door, Tom slid in across the table from her. For a moment, fatigue drained her resistance and she leaned against the back of the bench, her whole body ticking like a watch.

Tom reached across and took her arms again, levering her hands onto the table and taking them firmly in his. "Okay, now what happened?"

"Tom, I can't stay, I've got to talk to somebody. And I've got to get back—I left James at Tasha's." Suddenly she shivered, wishing she could eat those words. Nonsense. How stupid. There was no way Tom had anything to do with laser scopes and murder. But lately he always seemed angry. Even now he was gripping her too tightly, his eyes boring into her face.

"Turn him over to the authorities. You don't have to be the good Samaritan for everyone, Liza."

"He's such a nice kid, and I think he's starting to trust me a little. Or at least he trusts Sam."

"Tell me what happened to you."

"My face?" She shook her head. "That's much too long a story to tell now." She started to rise.

Tom tightened his hands on hers. "Liza...good god, I was worse than obnoxious the other morning, wasn't I? But you know how I feel...I mean..."

She could feel his eyes demanding hers and looked away.

"I...listen. You know how I feel about you. You've seen it, haven't you? Larry's my best friend, though, so I'll make no claim." He leaned far across the table toward her. "But I worry. It makes me goddamned rude and ugly and I want you to know I'm sorry."

Somebody upped the ante on the jukebox—the whine of steel and thudding percussion drowned out voices that resurfaced immediately at vastly increased decibels.

"Thanks for your concern," she hollered over the noise. "But I'm okay. See? I told you I could handle the weather. It was nothing."

"But something terrible happened—look at your face. And how come you're back? I thought you were going a lot farther. That's what worried me."

"And I thought you were going out for at least a week."

"TraCo canceled. I'm getting sick of those guys: 'do this, do that,' 'we gotta have the survey by this afternoon,' 'oh no, forget it, we settled out of court.' Shit, what a stupid job."

"What about those Japanese that Larry brought over?"

"Japanese? Ahhh, timber's dead. Time to get out of it."

"And time for me to get out of here." She forced her hands out of his and stood up, turning to look at the last booth. There were only three men there now, none she'd ever seen before. Eric Sendhoven was gone. So was Tenney Rushmore.

She hadn't seen anyone leave through the front door—maybe they were at the pool table. She dashed toward the back, but they were gone. Shoving past the pool players, she flung the backdoor open and looked up and down the alley.

Puddles next to the dumpsters sparkled red and blue from the beer signs. Steam rose from the heating vents and hung in the wet air. A rusty pickup with one wheel on a log was crammed against the frame siding of the next building. There was no one in sight.

She went back through the pool room and the bar. Tom's coat was still on the table, but Tom was gone. She was half running by the time she got to the narrow entryway. Tom was there, leaning on the wall, the phone receiver crammed against his shoulder while he lit a cigarette. He looked startled when he saw her, muttered, "Take care, now," and jammed the receiver back on the hook.

"I'm going out again tomorrow," she called over her shoulder as she opened the door, wondering who he'd hung up on so abruptly.

"How come you came back in? You never said."

"Tell you later. In gory detail. Then you'll really worry."

"You do it on purpose," he shouted, as the door shut.

James was playing Monopoly, Simi stretched out on the floor next to him. Andy and Margie were arguing over the rent due on Park Place.

"Sure," Tasha said, when Liza asked if James could stay. "Long as you want. You clear it with Paul Howard, though. I don't want Custer's Last Stand in my living room."

"It's all fixed with him. He's just relieved that I'm willing to let him go. Tash..." Liza felt her eyes begin to fill. She was too tired to keep the tears back, too tired to think of anything but sinking into oblivion. Tasha put her arms around her.

"Just go and sleep. Come back for dinner. James is going to miss you—you'll have to come by very often."

Liza nodded and wiped her eyes with her sleeve. "I'll come. If I'm awake. Or alive. I'm totally brain dead right now."

She went back and bent over James. "I'm going to let you stay with Andy a couple days," she told him. "I think you'll be safer away from the boat till we catch the bad guys."

He jumped to his feet and looked up at her anxiously. "You better not go there either," he said. "On the boat. They might come back and they got those guns they shot the windows with."

"Guns?" Andy said. "Somebody shot you?"

"Well, they didn't get me," James said. "But they got the windows. And maybe they were trying to get me." He stood a little straighter. "For sure they were, but Liza beat them."

"We both did, James. But the Lieutenant will catch them, and then I can take you home."

"Could you stay here, too?"

"I need to fix things on the boat. And I'll have Sam to warn me if there's trouble."

James's face fell. "I was thinking maybe Sam could..." He took a deep breath. "I guess you would need him, though."

"And you have Simi. I can see Simi's already a best friend."

"Your turn." Andy said, suddenly the nonhero. "James—it's your turn—hurry up."

Liza gave James a hug and he flopped down next to Simi. "Come back right away, though," he said, as she followed Tasha back to the kitchen.

"Thanks," Liza said. "And I'll even take you up on dinner." She tried once more to say how she felt, but "thanks" seemed to be the limit of her vocabulary.

On her way back to Shoemaker she passed Ross Elliot in his pickup. He waved vigorously and stopped in his lane, rolling his window down. Liza pulled up opposite him and said, "What's up?"

"Didn't get a chance to talk to you over at the Moose. My god, what happened to your face? You okay?"

"For an old salt. How come you're back? I heard you were headed the other direction."

"Schedule change. Thought I'd see the kids while I'm in. Looks like I'll be out several weeks on the next trip."

"I just added Efren's nephew to the family," she said. He was headed straight to Tasha's house so he'd see James anyway, and Ross Elliot would never have followed her and shot at her in the middle of the night. But why all these schedule changes?

With the hand truck, she inched the new anchor down the ramp and along the dock. She had enough chain—she'd have to use a shackle assembly on the nylon—she was far too weary to splice it. She could feel Jake watching her through the dark glass of the *Aquila*'s door. Jake's paranoia could keep a shrink in business for a lifetime.

She turned into her own slip and there was Larry straddling the rail, his blue Pacific Air Charters cap pulled down at a jaunty angle, his gray eyes narrowed against the reflection. He swung down onto the dock, his grin disappearing as he saw her face.

"My god," he said. "What the hell happened?"

"Glass. Did you look at the windows?"

"I just got here a second ago. And I can't stay—these Japs," he said in disgust. He was staring up at the wheelhouse now, the exploded windows stark against the varnished brightwork.

"Liza, my god! What was it?" He pulled her tight against him so her voice was muffled by his jacket.

"Somebody shot at me again. The window glass left tiny shards in my face."

"Shit, Liza—I don't want you to go out again. Ever." He hugged her so tight her head swam and she had to pull away. "Where's the little boy?" he said. "Is he all right?"

"He's all right. He's at Tasha's. I didn't dare keep him any longer after all the attacks on us."

"Okay. Listen. I have to take these guys to Ketchikan to catch their Seattle flight. As soon as I get back, we'll make him tell us where he lives. Then we'll fly him there. Nobody would follow a plane—he'll know that."

He tipped her face up, winced at the marks, and kissed her thoroughly. "Sorry to leave you when things are so bad—I'll be back tonight, though. You better leave the boy at Tasha's— we got some catching up to do." He kissed her again.

She pulled back to look at him. His gray eyes seemed to turn back the gray sky. His face was very serious. She felt herself ease against him, press into the hard muscle of his chest, his hand massaging the ache in her neck. Let him take away the numbing burdens of past and present.

Say yes, Liza. Tell him yes. Tell him now.

She rubbed her face against his shoulder. No, wait till he's here tonight, holds you in his arms, makes love to you.

"Tonight," she said, hugging him tighter.

She watched him jog along the dock, vanishing behind the *Susan Marie* and reappearing on the ramp. She watched him till he backed his new red Cherokee out of the parking place by the dumpster.

"Gotta impress my clients when I meet them at the airport," he said when he bought it. "Richer's better."

"Solitude's best," she'd responded. But no, it wasn't anymore. She needed this man.

She still had one more job. She used the Skilsaw and cut sections of plywood to nail over the windows in the wheelhouse. One window was mostly gone where she'd hammered it out with the butt of the rifle. The other had an elaborate dahlialike rosette around the bullet hole. They might not give way, but she was taking no chances.

At one o'clock in the afternoon she climbed into the bunk and pulled sleep down like a window shade.

Chapter 26

"He's one hundred percent liability. We're not keeping him another day."

"So we leave him here? He can walk okay. And he's got enough stuff, food and stuff, to last till he gets better."

"And why would we want him to do that?"

"Get well? Because he's got those other contacts."

"Right. The ones on the list in the chart table."

"How'd you get that?"

"Pretty easy to persuade someone to buy insurance when he's scared he's gonna die."

"We're not taking him south?"

"He won't be in any condition to go south."

"We going that soon?"

"As soon as we get the information from the kid, find the Stone, and take care of a few loose ends. Like our friend here."

"He's not going?"

"He's not going."

Chapter 27

There was a hot wind on her face. Sand filled her boots—she couldn't lift her feet, but she had to hurry—she had to find someone, someone invisible in an endless desert. Sand shifted under her feet and the hot wind sang in her ear. She opened her eyes.

Sam was sitting on the floor next to the bunk, his nose inches from her ear, his breath steaming her cheek. As soon as she turned her head he stood up, his tail flailing so hard his head wagged back and forth.

"Unnnnh," she said, tugging on his ear. "You want to go out. What time is it?"

She switched the bunk light on and looked at the ship's clock on the bulkhead. "Four ten. I hope that's afternoon, not morning." Three hours could just as easily have been seventeen the way she felt, struggling back to the surface.

She stared at the ceiling till Sam reminded her, shoving his nose under her shoulder and prying her upward. She'd jog to clear out the fog in her brain, assuming it was actually daylight above deck, then shower, and go to Tasha's. She swung her feet to the floor and Sam danced back and forth between the bunk and the door. "In a hurry, eh? Okay, okay, I'll be right with you."

She pulled on her sweats and running shoes and opened the door. A thin ray of light tumbled over the rungs of the ladder. Still day. Still, she hoped, the same day.

They jogged south along the highway, past Wrangell Institute. The elegant buildings still gleamed white beneath their collapsing roofs. A chain-link fence surrounded the entire Institute, three padlocked gates along the highway. Alder and fireweed were reclaiming what was once a carefully kept lawn.

Three buildings faced the road, a girls' dormitory and a boys' dormitory, the larger classroom building in the center connected by mission-style arched passages. The simple serenity of the architecture made its demise all the sadder. The whole place was filled with asbestos.

The campus was beautiful but haunted. Shadows and voices and leftover spirits wandered, and when the buildings vanished, Liza knew the collective memory would inhabit the shore.

Students had come there from all over Alaska in the days before oil money provided schools in each village. Liza tried to imagine having to send a small child hundreds of miles away to boarding school, to a distant island and foreign culture. Imagine sending a child like James away to strangers. But wasn't she a stranger to him? And where was home to James?

A man was walking toward her; when he was closer, she recognized Crow. He saw her and stopped. Turning away, he glanced back at her over his shoulder, his chin retracted so that his long hair fell forward to cover his face. A man hiding in the open like a fox crossing the tundra.

"Crow—wait a minute," Liza called.

She caught up with him and said, "Crow, those books with the pictures—you know, the ones you mentioned at our meeting—do they have something to do with James?"

"Didn't see 'em lately. You aren't ever there," he said, accusingly. "You don't go there anymore, eh?"

"I do, Crow, but only to get books to take out to the villages and logging camps. I don't work the desk anymore. But Mary will be glad to help you find books—old pictures and things. She's very interested in history, too."

"Nahhh, she only thinks, hey, old guy, old drunk Indian. Is all she thinks. Sure can see it, what she thinks. You better go back there. People like for you to be there, you're always pretty good with books, know what people like to read, things like that, eh?" He stroked Sam's head, muttering to him.

"Listen," Liza said. "I have to find James's family—find out who he belongs to. Can you imagine how worried they are? Their *child* is missing. I know you know who he is. Help us, won't you?"

"Kitai ain't one gives up easy. He looks all right. You keep him. He ain't somebody gives up."

"But his *grandmother*, Crow."

"She thinks she knows where he is, and even if he's not there, he's good. So she's good. She's all right."

"I promise you, you won't be in any kind of trouble. Please. All we want to do is return him."

"He's all right, now. He wouldn't be if you took him back. Wouldn't be any kind of trouble for you or me, see. Would only be some others' trouble. You leave him be, Liza." Crow stepped around her and walked on along the highway.

By the time Liza jogged back toward the harbor, the security lights had come on at the park across the road from the Institute. The exercise had improved her mood—she'd pushed herself a bit and her mind had floated into a meditative state that salved the worst of her worries.

As she approached the old school, Sam veered suddenly and slipped through the loosely fastened gate in the chain-link fence. Nose to the ground, he trotted up the overgrown two-track. She could see his bony shoulders rising and falling like pistons, his back leg still gimpy, hobbled by the bandage, his russet coat making a bright gleam against the fireweed, turned silver and limp after the winter.

Liza went over to the gate and called, "Sam. Come here, Sam." She whistled. He'd vanished—she thought he'd headed behind the classroom building; the black, windowless eyes stared from the pale structure like holes in a skull. She whistled again, then shouted, "Sam. Come."

It wasn't like him to run off and not come when she called. His collar should jingle from his tags; if he were running toward her, she'd hear his feet thumping on the broken weeds. She strained her ears.

Waves slapped the gravel beach across the road. The wind was rising and a sudden gust rattled a board against the fence. A raven in the woods behind the school set up its one-note evening bell and farther up the mountain another raven passed it along. No cars went by.

Out on the road there was still daylight, but darkness was creeping out of the forest and beginning to envelop the grass and alder behind the school. The sweat she'd worked up on her run had turned to cold rivulets. She shivered. Irritated at Sam's absence, she pushed the gates apart as far as they would go and ducked under the loop of chain.

She felt in the pocket of her sweat pants and took out the penlight she always carried. Darkness in Alaska was only a matter of degree. She'd been ambushed by the night often enough to be prepared.

Thrashing through the spindly alders, she paused every few feet to listen. At the back of the main building, she turned left and walked along the clearing behind it. The door to the basement was ajar. Had Sam gone in there? And if so, why hadn't he come out?

She hesitated, then walked down to the door and shouted. From far off, somewhere deep inside that ancient structure with its collapsing roof, came a jingle. Sam's collar. At least he was moving around. Why didn't he come?

She flashed the penlight through the door. Its narrow beam stabbed into the dark basement room and made a tiny circle on something yellow. New wood? Liza swung the light back and forth and outlined a wooden crate.

She stepped forward and pushed the door farther open. The light skipped across the room and picked out other crates, some with their lids open, others nailed shut. Over the edge of one of the open crates drifted a length of black hair. Human hair. Fine and long and carefully combed.

Hours seemed to pass before Liza could breathe. The mildew in the basement was sickly sweet in her throat and the damp air felt like another skin. Blood drummed in her ears. Finally she took a step forward and held the flashlight high over her head. She looked down into the crate at staring eyes ringed in red and black. At puffin beak earrings and a nose pierced by a long copper nail. At a wide grin of bear fangs. At a wooden mask.

Her sigh of relief could have shaken the supporting posts off their foundations. She flashed the light over the floor. She had walked into a museum. The crates held a collection of Native art which, even in the tiny circle of light, was clearly genuine.

Still to be packed were a spruce root basket so finely woven it looked like silk damask and a stack of Chilkat blankets. A carved bowl bore the head of a frog and tapered into a halibut with inlaid eyes. A bentwood box sat next to the bowl, an object crying out to be touched. She picked it up. With her finger she traced the grinning faces of Beaver and Wolf.

Suddenly the circle of light included Sam. Her senses must still be in shock—she hadn't even heard him. He was crouched in front of her, his head lowered, his hind legs drawn up beneath him. She bent and put her hand on his head. Instantly he leaped up and started through the door to the inner part of the building.

"Sam, come," she ordered. "Come on. We're not supposed to be in here."

He stopped, then turned and faced her, tail wagging slightly, front paws dancing with impatience. He turned away, came toward her again, pranced back to the door, making a widening circle away from her. She understood as though he'd spoken. Follow me, follow me. He had to show her something.

All at once she was terribly afraid. She didn't want to see what Sam had found. The flashlight beam trembled. She took one step toward him and he rushed forward into the darkness beyond the inner door.

Gripping the flashlight like the proverbial straw to a drowning man, she stepped through the doorway. Sam was waiting for her at the foot of a flight of stairs. She moved toward him and he bounded up them, his feet thudding over her head. She paused on the first step and shone the light over them. Sam's tracks showed on every other step, glinting wet and darkly outlined by the light. He was waiting, head lowered, ears drooping over the top step.

"Come back," she whispered hopelessly, already climbing.

The door at the top of the stairs was wide open. Dim gray light still drifted through the broken windows. Sam trotted along a hallway and abruptly disappeared through a doorway on the right. She looked through it without entering. A cloying, sour-sweet odor of something spoiled, moldy food rotting, was added to the general smell of decay.

Somebody had been camped in the classroom. A thin mattress was doubled over in the corner. In the center of the floor was a green Coleman camp stove, a battered saucepan set on one burner. Several cans of baked beans and a box of cornflakes lay next to the stove. And something wet had spilled. A river of something dark and wet ran toward the center of the room, Sam's footprints streaking it here and there.

Sam had crouched again and was inching along the floor as though stalking something. Something she couldn't see because the half-open door hid it. Something she didn't want to see. She took a deep breath and walked around behind it.

A man lay there, face down, his head turned away from her. The side of his head was shattered. The dark spill on the floor was blood. Blood had run from the huge wound and flowed downhill on the sloping floor toward the center of the room. She was standing in it.

She gagged and threw herself backward, hitting the corner of the door behind her. Whirling, she shouted, "no, no," hearing only her own whisper against the dark.

"Think, Elizabeth, don't run. This man defiles the place— children laughed here, played, wept—you can't run away."

She swallowed repeatedly, then leaned across him, trying to see what was left of his face without touching him. He had a heavy gray beard with a wide gap in it made by a scar like a smooth white snake. The eye she could see was slightly open and pale. His stringy gray hair had straggled down the back of his neck into the blood. A gray man—gray shirt, gray pants, gray boots.

Get out of here. What difference does it make what he looks like?

Because the last body disappeared? Because you want Paul Howard to believe you this time? That's suddenly very important, isn't it?

A gust of wind blasted through the empty window. Somewhere below her, a door slammed. Adrenalin surged through her veins. "Sam," she whispered. "Come on." But Sam was already heading for the hall.

Chapter 28

Paul kept thinking about those crates. Drove him crazy, thinking about all that lovely Native work, the bowls and baskets, those Chilkat blankets. Uggghhh. He needed to go back to Steamer Bay. He had to make sure those things were packed up perfectly and taken out before whoever it was came back to get them. He called the helicopter service. Yeah, somebody was going over there with a couple loggers—yeah, there'd be room.

By the time Paul got back to Steamer Bay, they had finished loading the crates. He saw Chief Woods revolve his finger in front of his ear.

"Yeah," Paul said, "crazy, but I had to check it out. That stuff belongs to all of us, in a way. So I gotta see it's okay."

"The stuff's okay, Howard. Holy shit—I know it's valuable. We're handling it like the crown jewels. Lock and key till we find the owners."

"The owners'll be the last people that used those things. The grandchildren of the makers. Great-grandchildren. Everything there was made to be used. And every one of 'em has a story."

"Well, you can just ride back with them and make sure nothing happens."

Paul shook his head, then clutched at his neck. "I'll stay and poke around here a little longer," he said. "Helicopter's stopping at the yard later. I'll catch it back."

Woods stared at him a second, then with obvious deliberation turned his back and walked away. Paul made no attempt to unfasten the lines holding the barge at the dock. They had three healthy uniforms with them—no need for a disabled old goat to do the work.

Two deep trenches marked the location of the crates. He stared down at the holes—maybe four feet deep and a little wider to allow the diggers to remove earth from the sides. This had taken time. How had the thieves managed to bring that stuff in, dig these holes, and get out without being seen?

Well, actually, they had been seen at least once. The two loggers had seen somebody, maybe Patrick, get dropped off. But most of the crates must already have been in place. They must have worked in the dark, hoping none of the fishing boats would come in this far and notice them.

He noticed something bright at the edge of one of the piles of earth and picked it up, blowing the dirt from it. A nose ring. Where had he seen a nose ring recently? Oh, yeah. On his desk. Lizzie had taken it out of James's pocket. He turned it over in his hand, rubbing it between his fingers.

Was there some connection? Did James know something about the contents of these crates? Something the thieves didn't want spread around? Then why hadn't James told Lizzie? He seemed to trust her. And why would someone keep trying to get him? Wouldn't they figure he'd already told everything he knew?

He wandered over to the dock again. There hadn't really been any need to come back over here—he'd known that—knew they'd take care of everything. Steve Woods was a thoughtful, careful kind of guy and justifiably annoyed that Paul wasn't accepting orders to take care of himself. But after his breakfast with Lizzie, after he'd made a fool of himself all over again, he'd wanted to get out of town.

He turned back, walking along the beach, noticing for the first time the lineup of black boulders. He stopped and stared along the line, then nodded. Of course. It hadn't been only crates of artifacts, baskets and blankets. They were stealing petroglyphs as well, hiding them right out here in the open because a casual observer would think they were part of the landscape.

Paul walked back along the line of black rocks, counting. Seventeen. A big group of the petroglyphs remaining in

Southeast. And once upon a time, thousands. The smallest one was turned over and Raven stared out at the forest behind the beach. Why had they left that one on its side? Dead giveaway if anyone happened to pass by. Which he should have done. Which he had not. A dereliction. Why the hell hadn't he noticed these right away?

The last one in the row was chest height and as broad as Paul was tall. It weighed tons. They must have used a crane to move them. How else could it be done? Shallow though, this beach. Must have some kind of landing craft with a crane.

All at once he thought of Eric Sendhoven. When he'd asked at the mill, he'd learned that the *Clara M.* was moving a camp to Steamer Bay from the other side of Etolin Island. Heavy equipment coming into the bay. And the *Clara* had come into Wrangell right after Lizzie had seen a tug passing when she was shot at. Sendhoven was a loner—not a guy he'd like to run up against in a dark alley. Maybe...

The rotors of a helicopter snapped over the ridge and Paul watched the bird drop to the pad over by the green building. The signal on his radio shrieked and he switched it on. Norma.

Call came in, Paul. That Romero woman. Found a man's body at the Institute. She asked for you but I've got the Chief and Luke on it. Just thought you'd want to know.

Good god. That Lizzie..."born to trouble as the sparks fly upward." He lowered himself into the skiff and yanked the cord on the outboard with his left hand. The pain that raced all the way to his shoulder wasn't nearly enough to consume his anger at everything, especially at himself. He steered left-handed, relishing how much it hurt.

Chapter 29

Woods ignored him when Paul entered the upstairs room at the Institute. Paul walked over to the body. Badger, the photographer, already had lights set up and was taking angles on the body. Jerry was squatting over a Coleman stove in the center of the room, scribbling in his notebook. When Badger moved back to get more of the room, Woods crouched over the body. He pulled the dead man's shirt open, exposing a filthy, bloody bandage around the rib cage.

"It's Patrick," Paul said.

"No kidding. Nice friends he had. See?" He lifted the bandage. "Shot him twice. Somebody out hunting just happened to wing him, I *don't* think. Can't see why they didn't finish it, though. This one's old—least a day or two. Some reason they waited? The other one killed him—high-power pistol—close enough to flame out, see there?"

He rolled the body to the side and Paul saw where the bullet had shattered bone and scorched the skin. "Very recent," Woods said. "Blood's only just drying now. Went right through. It's over there in the woodwork. I need an angle, etc., etc. Can't figure why they'd shoot him once and not finish him off."

Paul stared at the chest wound, mulling over a possibility. Maybe Lizzie had hit her target, after all. Pitch dark, rolling boat, no night scope, and she'd hit him? Not likely. Why would Gordy Patrick have been out there chasing the *Salmon Eye* and now here, dead as a beached cod? And downstairs, all that Native art being packed up, crates exactly like the ones they'd found over at Steamer Bay. Was Patrick offed because he knew too much?

"You call the doc?" Paul asked.

"Says send him up to Juneau—he doesn't want to be the M.E. Got enough trouble between the kid with a hatchet in his leg and caesarean twins."

"Where's the Romero woman?" Paul asked.

"I left her at the office—Luke's taking a statement—I'll be going in soon to check it out."

"Stay till Badger's done. I'll check things out with her and then head home. Per instructions."

"Okay, check in and then get yourself some rest. Rate you're going, I'll be looking for a replacement tomorrow."

"I oughta have my head replaced anyway. I shoulda followed up on Patrick yesterday. Shit, the whole thing in the palm of my hand and I let it go."

"The guy's no loss—the state woulda spent big bucks taking care of him for life. Now get outa here."

She was sitting cross-legged in a chair opposite Luke's desk at the back of the main office, her feet, in white crew socks, partly tucked under her knees. A pair of running shoes lay on the desk, soles up. She glanced at him as he walked toward the desk and nodded without speaking. Luke stood, his mouth pulling into a whew of relief.

"I've taped the statement up to her finding the crates of stuff in the basement," he said. "You can maybe do the rest of it? Took some notes, here." He pointed at a yellow pad covered with illegible black marks. Luke was not known for literacy, though he was a highly organized and observant young cop.

"Yeah, sure. Let's move into my office," Paul said.

She padded silently ahead of him, sat down and tucked her feet up again, folding her arms tightly across her chest.

"Cold?" he asked.

"A little. I was jogging so I'm not dressed for sitting around, and my feet are cold."

He looked at her again. Gray sweatpants and a worn navy sweatshirt with a small Wrangell logo. Probably no shirt under it. And plenty of other reasons to be chilled through.

"I'll get you something," he said, crossing the outer office to grab one of the jackets that hung in the closet. He scanned the lineup of rubber boots and chose the smallest.

She thrust her feet into the boots and pulled the jacket up around her neck. "Thanks. I was pretty shivery. Mostly reaction, I guess. Shock."

He set the tape recorder on the front of the desk and rewound the tape a moment before pushing Play.

"...behind the door. There was a lot of camping gear in the center of..."

Her voice stopped as Luke, seeing Paul, had pushed the button.

"Without replaying the whole thing, can you give me the gist of what you were doing in the Institute? Dangerous place to run around."

She explained how Sam had vanished. "I heard the tags on his collar jingling inside the building. I went in and then I saw those crates."

"What do you know about those crates? You ever seen any like those before? Ever delivered crates like that some place?"

"No. I mean, I do deliver some things in wooden crates, or on pallets. Engine parts are crated sometimes—appliances. But usually bigger than that. Those looked like they'd been specially built—all the same size."

"Have you ever seen a container—any kind of container—filled with Native art?"

"No, I haven't. Not till this afternoon."

She was looking at him so directly he was forced to look down at the yellow pad. "Dog climd stars," caught his eye. "L. go to."

He wanted to tell her how a nation's legacy was being systematically stolen, wanted her to hear how one race was still destroying another, one hand giving Natives land they already owned, the other robbing them of a different heritage. He could hear her angry response:

So? Does that make them victims?

Yeah. They're getting screwed.

*But they know something true. Like Crow. So they have pride—
something to fight for.*

Shit. Why did she stir up all these undercurrents?

Into his long silence she thrust, "Why did Luke give me the
Miranda warning? Am I under arrest?"

"Nah—we read the rights to witnesses in case they become
suspects. So anyway...let's take the rest of it."

It took another fifteen minutes to get the whole story. He could
believe it all. All but the coincidence. Two bodies in four days?
Why had this woman been on the spot so soon after two murders?

She'd gotten into his head, was the trouble. There was
something stoic about her, some barrier she'd erected against
pain and fear. But it was clouding his judgment. He had to
stay impartial with a witness.

He shifted uneasily in his chair. "I want to go back to last
night," he said. "When you guys were out there trading gunfire."

"What about it?"

"Do you know if you hit somebody?"

"Given the odds, I'm sure I didn't. I only fired at all because
I was so mad."

"The rifle still on the boat?"

"Yeah, sure. Propped in the corner of the wheelhouse right
where I left it. Why all the concern?"

"I think you did hit somebody. But didn't kill him. At least,
we're assuming your shot didn't kill him."

"What are you saying?" She flung the jacket aside and sat
forward, her stare suddenly hard as a blade.

"The man you found at the Institute—he'd been hit with a
rifle bullet. Probably didn't have much velocity left when it hit
him—shot from long range. Like maybe from a boat at 300
yards? Maybe farther, even. We'll have to check the ballistics—
see if your rifle fired that bullet. Somebody'd made a crude
bandage. But that wasn't the bullet that killed the guy," he
said. "Somebody shot him through the head. Right there in
that room. And so far, we only got your prints and the dog's."

She shuddered, and Paul felt a longtime grief grow
consumptive. "I gotta tell you, Lizzie, even though we have
your story and no reason so far not to believe it, we gotta
consider you a suspect."

Chapter 30

James felt bad that Simi couldn't come with them. "Why not?" he asked Andy.

"Because she tells our hiding places," Andy said. "She follows us and barks and it tells where we are."

"She's pretty fat for a dog," James said, stroking her neck, wishing he could stay with her.

"She's getting puppies," Andy said. "It makes her get fat. Sam's her puppy, only big now."

"Sam's pretty good," James said. "I'm going to get a dog. Like Sam. A boy dog."

"Maybe you could get one of Simi's puppies next time," Andy said. "Come on. Willy and Marge are already hiding."

James gave Simi a last hug and followed Andy out the door and up the path behind the house. There was quite a lot of blackberry and it got caught in his jacket and Andy got pretty far ahead, but then James caught up when they got to the muskeg. His boots sank in and the mud felt like it was trying to suck him down and his boots made squatchy noises when he lifted his feet. Andy waited for him till he got across the muskeg.

It wasn't much light in the woods, totally dark in there actually, and he tried to keep right behind Andy on the deer trail. Then Willy started firing at them from some bushes, "pow, pow," and Andy fired back, "ka toooo, ka tooo," and Willy went crashing away off in the trees.

"It's army," Andy said. "We have to hide and creep up on the enemy like in a war."

Behind James, Margie suddenly fired a machine gun, "Uhuhuhuh...uhuhuhuhuhuhuh..." and Andy turned and disappeared in the bushes. A long way off, Willy shouted, "pow, pow," and a little bit closer, Andy hollered, "ka toooo, ka tooooooo."

James tried to follow the sounds, but he couldn't find where Andy had gone off the deer trail. It seemed like there was devil's club all over next to the trail, so he kept going, trying to hear where the others had gone. Roots were all over too, and he tripped and fell. The moss was covering up the roots and it was soft but it was wet, too, and his clothes were getting a little soaked.

He heard Margie's machine gun and it seemed far away. Then it got real quiet around where he was. All he could hear was a raven gulping and a whistling noise like some crows were flying over. And really too dark to see any more underneath all the trees. And he needed to pee. Bad.

He turned away off the trail a little bit and he heard this sound behind him like somebody breathing. He looked over his shoulder but he couldn't see anybody.

"Andy?" he said, not so loud because he didn't want to get Andy mad at him for giving away his hiding place. He couldn't hear the breathing anymore though.

He felt under his jacket for his pants zipper. Breathing again. Right behind him. Something came on his mouth and nose. A hand. He hit backwards with his head at whoever was there. This wasn't a fun game, it was scary.

He tried to shout, "Stop it," through the hand over his mouth and nose, but whoever it was was much much bigger than him, bigger even than Willy, and strong, holding him so tight he couldn't even breathe. He kicked backward and bit the hand as hard as he could, but everything got black in his eyes and his ears sounded like waves beating and pee poured hot down his legs.

Chapter 31

"A suspect. We gotta consider you a suspect." Was it only four days ago that she had set out from Kindergarten Bay to deliver chickens? No missing children, dead bodies, gunshots in the night? No policeman with eyes like a map of his mind?

From the curve in the highway Liza could spot Tasha's place because all the lights were on. Her electric bill must exceed the food bill most months. She pulled in, stopping behind the disabled bike. Through the windows she could see the blue flicker of the TV. Leaving Sam in the yard, she clomped up the back steps in the boots she'd borrowed at the police station, opened the back door, bracing herself for Simi's onslaught, and shouted. No dog, no answer. She walked through to the sunporch, where the TV reigned. No one there.

"Halloooo," she shouted again, "anyone home?"

Silence.

There seemed to be no dinner preparations in the kitchen. Liza opened the back door again. Sam had disappeared. Tasha's little yellow Rabbit was sitting abeam the pickup. Somebody had dumped a bike on the ground behind the Rabbit. No wonder repairs were required so often. She walked around behind the cars and shouted again.

Between Tasha's yard and the forest, salal and devil's club and salmonberry formed a nearly impenetrable fence. Beyond it, the mountain began. Forest surrounded muskeg, deep layers of peat holding water like a bowl. Stunted shore pine and spruce clung to the edges of pools, searching for soil. A treacherous place, the ground sinking at every step. Liza knew the kids kept a deer trail trampled down so they could play guerilla armies in the woods. It was dark though—much too late for them to be up the mountain.

Liza started back toward the house. A voice shouted and someone answered. She looked up and saw lights flickering through the trees, partway up the mountainside. She put her hands around her mouth to project her voice, and shouted, "Halloooooooo."

"Hallooooooooo" came back like an echo, and in a minute she saw a light on the narrow trail, a flashlight probed the underbrush, and Tasha's small, dark shape burst from the trail end.

"Liza," she said, trying to catch her breath, "listen—I'm sorry—he's gone—I mean, we can't seem to find him." She stopped to pant. "James. The kids were all up there playing army—Margie and Willy and Andy and James—and when they tried to get everybody back, they couldn't find him."

"But it's dark," Liza said, irrelevantly. "Maybe he's still hiding." Her whole body was ice-cold.

Tasha pushed the hood of her parka back and rubbed her eyes wearily. "We've combed the area where they were playing. Ken and Erin are up there now. And Simi's just going nuts. I mean, you just have to look at Simi tracking, and you know she'd find him if he was still there."

"Where else could he be, though?" Nine-tenths of her mind was committed to denial, the other tenth too terrified to respond.

Tasha grabbed Liza's arms. Liza could see her frightened eyes, worry carving valleys in her forehead. "There's something really screwed up with his story. He knows something. Something somebody doesn't want anyone else to know. I bet they've grabbed him."

Panic burned up the back of Liza's neck. "Goddammit, give me that flashlight—I'm going to look." She grabbed the flashlight and started toward the trail.

"We better get the police," Tasha called after her "We've looked, Liza. If Simi can't find him, he's not there."

"How long have you been looking for him?"

"Maybe fifteen minutes—half an hour—I don't know, I don't even know what time it is."

Suddenly, far up the mountain, Sam bayed. The primitive howl clawed at the back of Liza's neck. Simi joined with her deep, quick bark.

"Maybe they've found him," she yelled at Tasha, and plunged up the trial.

Across the muskeg, her feet sank into the bog. Then she was in the dense understory, sphagnum moss shrouding everything. She tried to stay on the trampled trail, but brambles tore at her jeans, and every twig spilled cold water down her face and neck.

She could hear the kids calling back and forth, and Tasha panting behind her. The ancient floor was crisscrossed with roots and moss and half-rotted leaves that slipped underfoot, but fear was a powerful stimulant—they reached Willy and Andy and Erin in minutes.

"I heard Sam," Liza said. "Any trace?"

"He acts so funny," Willy said. "He goes round and round in circles and then he goes back to the same place and howls that way he does."

"The hound in him. No sign?"

"Erin and Andy and I stayed with the dogs, and Ken and Margie went up—they thought he maybe got all the way to the top and didn't know which way to go down."

Sam bayed again, and they headed for him, beating their way across the face of the mountain. The darkness beyond the slim pencils of light was as impenetrable as the underbrush.

The dogs heard them coming and plunged noisily through the brush. Sam burst out, throwing himself at Liza's legs and whimpering. Simi lumbered through in his wake, her tongue hanging out a foot from the effort of dragging her girth over such rough territory.

"Find, Sam," Liza ordered, snapping her hand forward, finger pointing. "Find."

Sam launched himself into the darkness, holding his back leg stiff, which gave him an odd, sideways gait. They followed the sound of his passage. In another fifty yards or so, they broke out of the black canopy into a small clearing, another patch of swampy muskeg. A person could drown in his own footprints in muskeg, Liza thought.

Sam circled the clearing, nose to the ground. After three circumnavigations, he sat down, threw his head back, and bayed.

"See that?" Willy said. "That's what I meant. Sam loses his trail, right there, right at that exact same spot every time."

Willy went over the ground around him. "Hey, look at this." He stood up and held something out.

Liza flashed the light on keys suspended from his hand. "James found those keys when we were walking up the ramp. I let him keep them in his pocket. He was wearing that parka of Andy's, and he put them in the side pocket with the Velcro flap."

Her eyes stung when she remembered how carefully he had put them away, his fingers checking from time to time through the pocket to be sure the keys were there.

"Either he wanted us to find them," she said, "or somebody lifted him so they slid out under the flap of the pocket. Sam says he's not up here. Call Ken and Margie back—Sam knows he didn't go that way. I'm going to call the police. And get Crow. Crow knows all about James. We've got to find Crow."

Chapter 32

"Shit. I told you not to hurt him."

"I didn't hurt him, for god's sake—he's okay. He's all right."

"Scared the piss out of him. All you had to do was tell him who you were, tell him she sent you to get him—he was supposed to go back to the boat with you. I told you. Con him. He's just a little kid—he'd never have caught on. But no. You gotta go in like some bush cow-boy on a smash 'n' grab. Now he's scared shitless. He'll never talk."

"All those other kids were around—I couldn't tell when one of 'em would come running out at me. He'll calm down—I told him we're taking him home."

"Did he buy that?"

"He isn't talking. Just stares at me. He'll come around, though, when he starts thinking about his grandma. Bet he's crazy to get home."

"He's smarter than you think. If he's so crazy to get home, why isn't he already there? Ever wonder that? Because he hasn't told anyone where he lives, is why."

"Yeah? Most kids'd wanta go home so bad they'd be screamin' in their sleep. Ya know?"

"Right. So he hasn't told anyone where to take him. Very, very smart, that boy. Knows if he goes home we'll know where to find him. And now he won't talk because you scared the hell out of him."

"I'll try to calm him down. Maybe if he eats something?"

"Forget it. You're the bad guy now. You take over the wheel. Head for Conclusion Island. I'll go down and try to pass the peace pipe."

Chapter 33

Liza drove fast, trying not to think. Sheer terror had torched all reason. Beyond the harbor, along the south side of the bay, she could see the security lights at the mill and a tug tied up under the crane.

In the rearview mirror, she noticed a car with only its parking lights on, coming up behind her very fast. Intending to turn off at the Shoemaker parking lot, she slowed down and pulled over to the right. As the car passed, she recognized Eric Sendhoven in the passenger's seat. He turned his head away, but she knew it was Sendhoven. She couldn't see the driver, though, and didn't recognize the car—an old blue Japanese make, rusty dents making it a clone of most of the vehicles on the island. The tug at the mill must be the *Clara M.* Maybe it was the *Clara* that followed her that night—someone aboard had fired those shots.

If James was in that car, they were taking him to the *Clara.* She'd check the *Salmon Eye*, then head for the tug. But she'd better get an army if she was going to take on Sendhoven and his crew.

The Lieutenant would go crazy when he heard that James was missing, but as soon as she checked the boat, she'd tell him what she thought: Sendhoven had kidnapped James and taken him aboard his tug.

She swung into the parking area above the harbor and jounced through the potholes, pulling up beside the Dumpster. The ramp seemed exceptionally dark. She looked up and found the main overhead light had burned out after a week of humming and flickering. Sam galloped ahead, turning into the slip, and vanishing behind the *Nereia*. In a moment she could see his head above the *Salmon Eye's* stern rail—he'd recovered his jumping form in spite of that leg wound.

As Liza turned along the dock, a black shape hurtled past her head so close she ducked and flung her arms up. A hoarse screech identified the heron, disturbed in his evening patrol.

Trying to quiet her galloping pulse, Liza climbed over the boat rail. Sam was pressing his nose to the door and clawed at it, unable to wait for her to open it. His eagerness would have made her certain James was inside, except that Sam's tail was low and stiff. His fur stood in a knife edge down the back of his neck.

As soon as she removed the padlock, he forced the door back with his shoulder and lunged forward. Inside, he circled the cabin, nose to the floor, then bounded up the steps to the wheelhouse and vacuumed every inch with loud whuffs. No James. Together they searched every inch—head, engine room, crew quarters, lockers. Nobody.

Help. You have to get help. God damn it, Larry, where are you? I need you. You said you'd be back by now.

She'd have to go back to Tasha's. No, she could call the police dispatcher—they'd reach Paul Howard by radio. She grabbed the phone and dialed. Nothing. Not even a dial tone. She jumped back on the dock. The phone line was still plugged into the jack on the dock, but two feet of it dangled into the water, the other end hanging loose over the bow roller on the boat.

Suddenly she realized that the *Aquila* was gone. She stared at the shiny black hole in the water where the *Aquila* should be, and remembered someone watching her, safe behind a reflection. Someone? Would anyone but Jake have watched from the *Aquila*? Stop it, Liza. The whole damned question is irrelevant.

With Sam at her heels, she raced along the dock to the public phone. The receiver had been cut off and wedged under the phone. The residents of Shoemaker Bay were rendered speechless.

Suddenly she was afraid to leave the absolute safety of a dead phone. She leaned against the rickety cage surrounding it. The lights in the harbor were dimmed by mist that clung like pollen to every surface. Just over the crest of the mountain, the moon ran like a damp watercolor. A halyard clanked against an aluminum mast—water whispered and chuckled under the dock.

Her shivering rattled the graffiti-covered phone cage as she tried to scan the fingers of the dock for unexpected movement. In the hazy moonlight, every object seemed translucent but cast an impenetrable shadow.

"All right, Sam," she said, glad to hear any voice, even her own. "We're off to Tasha's. Home team's down two-zero."

Sam led the way, looking back to make sure Liza was smart enough to follow. Suddenly he stopped and lowered his head, his tail rigid.

She could just make out a shape, motionless, halfway down the ramp. Sam's throat whirred and Liza froze in place. The shape moved further down the ramp, and Sam lowered himself to the dock, ready to spring.

"Careful, Sam," she whispered. "Stay."

The dark shape stopped again. Liza made out the figure of a man, cap pulled low on his head. Sam half rose, growling vigorously now, and she spoke to him sharply. There was something tentative in the posture of the man—Liza felt he was not a threat, and almost immediately Sam agreed. He darted forward, tail waving in greeting, and nosed into the man's leg, causing the man to grip the railing with both hands to steady himself.

"Eh, Sam," he said, "you, is it?"

"Crow?" Liza said. "Is that you? What are you doing here?"

"Come down to find you," he said. "Been up along the road, there. Looking for something." He shoved the cap back and wiped his forehead with his sleeve. "Guess you're not going to town, eh?"

Blackmail time. No information, no ride. "James is missing, Crow. Somebody's taken him. You *have* to help us now." She reached out to shake his arm.

"They got him?" he said. "Yeah, they'd do it. I thought maybe they'd get him. They want what he knows, see. And he could finger 'em, too. Little kid, maybe don't know names, eh? But he knows who they are. He'd see 'em and he'd know, see. So they got him."

"Who, Crow? Who got him?" Worse, though: "What'll they do to him?"

"Take him back, likely. After he tells 'em what he knows. He goes back and he can't tell on 'em, see. Won't matter then."

"But *who*, Crow? Who's got him?" She had to clench her hands to keep from clawing the answers out of him. "Where have they taken him?"

Crow rotated his head, rubbing at his eyes with one hand. He sighed heavily. Liza knew she didn't have the leverage to get the rest out of him. She'd have to let the Lieutenant try.

Crow straightened suddenly. "Gone," he said. "They got the little kid."

The information must have penetrated to a critical level of his brain. "They've got him, Crow," Liza repeated. "And I'm going to get him back. If you won't tell me anything, I'll get Lieutenant Howard, but by god, I'm finding that child."

"No cops," Crow said. "They find out the cops is after 'em, they gotta get rid of him. They won't hurt him if there ain't no cops on 'em. We can take your boat and go after 'em. Just you 'n' me." He started along the dock, his gait unsteady.

Sam's tail whipped Liza's legs. He whined and pranced back and forth between her and Crow. Sam said Crow was on his side. If she couldn't trust her own intuition, could she trust Sam's?

"Your mind is too tortured to reason, Elizabeth. You need help."

Liza followed Crow to the *Salmon Eye* and climbed aboard.

Chapter 34

Paul's mind had finally hit the "Shred" button. He couldn't cling to a single thought—words and images spun together in a whirling light show. He shucked his boots on his own back porch, groped for the kitchen light switch, and shut his eyes against the fluorescent glare.

The sink held the remains of his last meal, whenever that was—a dirty frying pan, a plate and coffee mug. There was a faint odor of decayed food—he hadn't taken the garbage out all week.

He opened the cupboard under the sink and the garbage pail tilted into a gray fog. He gripped the edge of the sink with one hand and straightened up. His head throbbed, his whole left side was frozen into granite, and he was a hundred years old today. Happy birthday, Paul Howard.

The hell with the garbage. Hot shower, bourbon, and bed. He ground his way up the stairs like the mills of the gods, pausing to glance into Joey's room, the Hudson Bay blanket neatly tucked at the edges, animal posters papered to the walls.

His grandmother's hand stroked his neck and Joey's dark head pressed the pillow down at the edge of the blanket.

Your mind is broken down, Paul Howard. Sweat this.

He plunged into the bathroom and turned the shower knob all the way over to hot, letting the steam rise till his face was lost in the mirror.

His hand was pawing for the phone on the bedside table long before he woke up. "Unh," he said. "Yeeuunnh?"

Reportthe…missing…woodsback…searchteam.

Darnell, the night dispatcher. "Come again?" Paul muttered, struggling painfully to a semi-upright position. He looked at the red blinking numbers on the radio clock. Nine fifty-seven. He'd only been asleep a half hour—he felt as if he'd died.

Romero woman called in to report a missing boy—some kid staying at Tasha George's. Search team's in the woods back of the house. Chief wants to know if you know anything more about the kid's background.

"Nothing. Not one thing. I'll get over there."

Chief said "don't come," just give him anything you know.

Paul had already dropped his pajama pants and was trying to get his shorts on with one hand, clutching the phone in the other. "What time did she report it?"

Norma's got a note here. '8:38 P.M. L. Romero—report James Kitai missing from George house. Will check boat at Shoemaker Bay. Will contact.

9:20 P.M. T. George—James Kitai missing; L. Romero hasn't returned from Shoemaker.

9:22: Radio contact Sgt. Farrell.

Norma signed out at 9:30.

Paul dragged his trousers on and fumbled with his belt. "Why the hell wasn't I called when Luke got the report?"

Guess nobody wanted to disturb you after your accident.

"Who's on it?"

Luke, Jerry and the chief are over there at the George's place.

"Everybody except me. Shit. Has Romero called in again?"

No. It was Tasha.

"So has anybody checked at Shoemaker to see if Romero found him?"

I don't know. You want me to call and find out?

"Hell no. Of course she didn't find him, or they wouldn't be looking. I'm not awake. Hold the fort. I'm on my way."

He stood there staring at the receiver in his hand as though it held a secret, tears of sleep and frustration clouding his vision. He replaced it finally and picked up his shirt, working the left sleeve up his sore arm before thrusting his right arm in the other. God, he was stiff. He sat on the bed and pulled his socks on, then padded downstairs, got his jacket and cap and jammed his feet into cold, damp rubber boots he'd left at the back door.

James missing. His mind stumbled around on what he knew as he drove through town and headed south on Zimovia Highway. First report at 8:38 P.M. A little after 10:00 now. If James had been at Shoemaker, Lizzie would have called to let them know. No chance he was there, then. Funny she hadn't called back, though. You'd think she'd call the second she got to the boat and discovered he wasn't there.

He slowed down at the drive to Tasha's house. He could see the two police vehicles parked side by side at the top, Tasha's Rabbit and the old trucks beyond them. The ditches at the sides of the driveway were lined with assorted vehicles. On the other side of the highway, several old cars and pickups were pulled off at the edge. The town had turned out.

He waited for an oncoming car while he looked for the green truck with its crown of moss. Not there. Where was she, then? Missing, too? Had she taken James and run? This goddamned night was expanding as fast as the universe.

He decided to go on to Shoemaker, make sure the boat was there. She'd probably left the truck and come back to Tasha's with somebody else. Another pickup pulled into the ditch at the side of the highway, and two young men in insulated overalls climbed out. He slowed down and opened the window.

"Heard there's a kid lost," the nearest one said.

"I just got the report myself," Paul said. "There's a search party out there. I'll check the harbor—he came in on one of the boats—mighta gone back there."

The men nodded and headed for the drive. Trouble was like a magnet. Pulled all the scattered, warring parties together. One small missing child could hold the entire town in a moment's fragile union.

The Chevy was there. He swung in next to it, slammed his door and looked inside the truck's cab. There were some crumpled newspapers on the seat and Sam's muddy footprints on both the papers and the worn seat cover. Lizzie's driving gloves were lying next to the papers. And the keys were in the ignition.

The doors were unlocked, so she hadn't inadvertently locked the keys in the car. She'd been in a rush or she'd expected to come right back.

Without further thought, he opened the door, took the keys out and locked the doors. He had some vague notion of protecting the truck. He had some vague notion of preventing Lizzie from returning to it and giving him the slip. Vague notions were part of the chaos that had substituted for his brain.

The ramp light was out. At the deeply shadowed foot of the ramp he turned right and headed for the outer finger past the work float. A tug had the outside slip beyond the *Salmon Eye*, an old wooden workhorse, superbly maintained with pristine red and black paint. The classic-design sailboat *Nereia*, with her sweeping sheered rails, sat on the side closer to him; the *Salmon Eye* always towered over her. Turning the corner onto the last finger, Paul could see the tug silhouetted against the breakwater. The *Nereia*'s raked masts stood out against the tug's black hull. There was nothing in between.

He stared into the water where the *Salmon Eye* should be. Why had she gone? She must have taken James. Or was she chasing after someone who'd taken James? Then she would've called for help. She'd run with the kid. But she knew it was dangerous for James to be with her—she'd told Paul so this morning.

In a flash he knew he knew nothing. He thought she'd given herself away at breakfast this morning. But this empty slip told him more than all her words. She'd planned to run. In some way, she was involved with a gang. But murder? He felt as if he were tearing in two.

Behind him, a boat was turning in, backing to swing her bow into the slip directly across from the missing *Salmon Eye*. Automatically he walked over and reached up to take the lines from the skipper, a heavyset, grizzled man who returned to the wheelhouse as Paul cleated the stern. *Aquila*, the name on the bow. A large fiberglass gillnetter with a drum on the stern and a couple of crab traps stacked next to it.

"You pass the *Salmon Eye* anywhere?" Paul said, when the skipper stepped back on deck.

The man looked sideways at him as he swung down and readjusted the lines. "You looking for her? She ain't here. Dunno why she's running at night. Better not be picking crab. Somebody's been haulin' my traps."

Paul thought about it for a minute, then realized his question hadn't been answered. "Did you pass her anywhere?"

The man came over to him, standing so close his huge belly was practically touching Paul's jacket. "Who's askin'?"

"Paul Howard, Wrangell Police Department."

"She do somethin'?"

"She left a boy with someone and he's missing. Just wondered if she might have picked him up and not reported it. Thought you might have passed her boat."

Jake glared at him in a fierce, piggish squint. Finally he nodded. "Yup. I did."

"You saw the *Salmon Eye?* Where?"

"Not far—'bout atop Woronkofski—Elephant Nose."

Paul raced through the options—Search and Rescue, Coast Guard, a helicopter, commandeer this boat…Of course, it wasn't his jurisdiction at all—nothing off island was, actually—they had to get clearance from the state troopers. The chief would have a cow if he went off island without clearing it with him. But he had to get to her first…find out what the hell was going on.

"Listen," he said. "I need to catch her before…You be willing? I'll reimburse you for fuel and time. Could you catch her?"

"We…lllll, dunno. She was haulin.' But I ain't loaded. Get about twelve knots with no load. She didn't do nothin' bad, though. She'd never do nothin' bad 'cept maybe haul a coupla traps." Jake shrugged, looking sheepish. "Naw, actually, she wouldn't do that even. I been watchin' her. She ain't taken no crab."

He turned to climb back aboard, then looked over his shoulder. "Why don'cha just radio?"

"There could be some trouble, Mr.…?"

"Jake's the name."

"Jake. Didja see the wheelhouse windows when she came in this morning?"

"Naah, never noticed."

"Shot out. Could be dangerous—you better know what you might be getting into."

"Yeah? Well come on, fella, let's go."

Chapter 35

The mist had cleared away, and the water was a rolling mirror, the moon still tangled in spruce on top of the mountain. Liza figured she'd stay along the edge, crowding the rocky shore, hard to catch on radar. But there would be little hiding on such a clear night; whatever boat had carried James away would be silhouetted against an ebony surface. As would the *Salmon Eye*.

What made Crow think James was on a boat? Why did Crow imagine for even one minute that they could find it? And what on earth would they do if they did? She had to turn around. Madness, to undertake a chase. You're not thinking clearly— how could you be so stupid?

Crow came in from stowing fenders and pointed. "Nor'west," he said. "Go topside Zarembo. They likely went that way, maybe Red Bay, see, or maybe they'll keep going. They'll take the kid home, but they gotta keep outa the way, see."

"Listen," Liza said. "No way can we find them by ourselves. It's just you and me against a bunch of crooks, right?"

"Be all right," he said. "We can find 'em. I know where they're like to go, see."

"Great—so what if we do find them? We going to take over their boat like a couple of pirates? Swarm over the sides with pistols waving?"

"We can get him back, Liza. See, we want him, and he wants us. So we can do it, eh?"

"We *can't*, Crow. We've got to have help. We'll endanger James's life, chasing after him by ourselves."

"Naah, not us. We can get him. I know how, see. More danger to him if the cops try."

Larry, she thought, where are you? She needed backup. Muscle. Wouldn't that strange electricity between them relay that she was in trouble? The idea lit a spark of hope.

Despite her intention to turn back, they were already passing Elephant's Nose. The black hill slept against the lighter sky and a few stars trimmed its back. On such a night, one should be filled with the serenity of mountain, sea and sky. Liza was filled with terror.

Crow sat on the stool by the chart table. Liza studied his half-profile. In the dim light, shadow chased light across his face, and his eyes gazed upon some inner space. His right eye was hidden, and an image of the one-armed artist of the fierce eagle eye crossed her mind. "Do you happen to know a one-armed artist named Tenney Rushmore?" she asked Crow.

He turned his head away and looked out the window in the door. After a long interval, he said, "Know him."

She waited.

"Yuuh, I know him. Long time ago, I knew his mother, little bit. More'n a little, even. My cousin, his mother is."

"Your *cousin?* You're *related?*"

"Ain't seen Tenney in a couple years—he ain't one to come to town much. His mom, Martha, she was John Jack's niece, went off to Angoon with one a' them Angoon men, came back after he drowned in a storm, fishing boat down with all hands—she came back with her kid, Tenney. He musta been maybe two, three, then. John Jack, he sees Tenney's got the eye, so he trains him for the carving, but then Tenney, he goes off to that Vietnam war and gets his arm blown to bits.

"When he comes home, he says to John he's gonna go on doing the wood and the silver, too, like he did before, and John, he says, no way you can do it, Tenney, but Tenney, he goes off to some rehab place, like a detox, I guess, that sort of place anyhow, and they fix up his arm so he can use this pulley, like, and hold on a clamp sort of thing, and first off, there he is, cuttin' away, tap tap tap with the chisel, cuttin' out with the little scribes.

"He made one a' them poles, once. Should'a seen how he held that log—big old cedar he towed up from the south coast—used a chisel, adze, like he got two arms—had a bent-around holder—clamp, like, and drove them cutters around, tap tap tap on th'ends of 'em, like he got maybe three arms, even. He's a good carver, is Tenney." Crow paused and heaved a sigh, as though he regretted Tenney's talents.

"That pole he made. A ridicule pole it was. Shame on a debt can't ever be repaid. Shame on somebody he knew a long time. Shouldn't have made that pole. It'll come back on him some way."

Liza wondered if it was the ridicule pole James had talked of. The Marten shame pole that had embarrassed the whole community.

"A Marten pole? James mentioned that."

"We got two," Crow said. "Beaver and Marten." He didn't say which one Tenney Rushmore had carved.

Liza headed the *Salmon Eye* a bit more northwest to pass between Zarembo and Vank Island, realizing as she did so that she had no idea where they were heading.

"Tell me where we're going. Are they out on the water in Sumner Strait, or do you think they've gone in somewhere?"

"Red Bay. They got one storage there, even though their boat's deep for that bay. They set the poles 'round high slack, get back out quick when she turns. Might go in there, now, or might not. Depends."

"On what, Crow?"

"Depends if they think we're on 'em. If they think we're on 'em, they like to get on a ways, maybe head up north on the Strait, Douglas Bay, Totem Bay, someplace—maybe just run out there to Kuiu before we get to 'em. Who knows?"

"But that's just it—who does know? Do we go to Red Bay first?"

"Yuuh, right, go in there, see what's what. Only a couple places they'd be in there—it's shallow, you know. We can swing behind Danger Island, and look around, see if they're there."

Liza picked up the coordinates for Red Bay off the chart and checked the distance on the GPS. It was 24.3 miles to the entrance to Red Bay. They were doing 8.5 knots but in the satin waters of the Strait could make 10. They'd be there by midnight.

She checked the chart again and shoved the throttle ahead. The engine's pulse rose and steadied, water hissed past the bow and curled over, tinseled phosphorescence marking their passage. Sam pawed his cushion out from behind the binnacle, circled and collapsed in a pile of ears and tail.

"Now," Liza said to Crow. "Now tell the story."

Crow raised his head, staring out at the moon's path. "Kitai family," he said, "comes from a place out at Kuiu. Old house, maybe five, six families to the start of it, Kitai was one of 'em. I'm a Kitai. My grandfather, Chief Henry, was father to Sarah, who was Goran and Anna's mother. Anna was James's mother, see."

"Our house didn't mix up with others except for marriage," Crow said, "hid themselves away, kept to the old ways for a long while, fishing, berry picking, weaving blankets, baskets. Kept hid, so we didn't get warships like Angoon, no missionaries telling us to burn our own totem poles like Kake. When the Institute came in Wrangell, all the young men got sent there for schooling. But they had to go back to Kuiu Island and teach the young children so the old ways would stay mixed with town ways. That was our law. But some of the men didn't..."

"*Whiskey Tango November. Whiskey Tango November. 'Wherefore art thou, Romeo?'*"

Tango. Calling the *Salmon Eye* on Channel Sixteen from the VHF radio on the shelves behind the bar of the Velvet Moose.

Liza grabbed the transmitter. "Whiskey Yankee Romeo. Go to other channel. Over." He'd go to to their usual talk channel without giving it over the air. She switched the dial.

"*Tango November. Base One relay asking, 'where are you? Do you need recon?'*"

Base One. Tasha. She must have called Mink, who'd turned the radio over to the master operator. If Tasha hadn't called the police at the same time, telling them the *Salmon Eye* was gone, then Liza was alone, heading straight into the arms of a gang that was using her kid as a hostage.

She was startled when Crow spoke; clearly he'd understood Tango's question about recon. "Tell him, don't call the cops," he said. "They'll run if he calls the cops—take the kid and run, maybe get rid of him."

"Tango," Liza said. "Romeo. No cover, no recon. Relay Base One, no cover. No Victor Charlie in vicinity. Over."

"Roger, no Slicks, no Hogs. Alpha Four standing by. Tango November out."

She looked at Crow, who was shaking his head violently. "Don't need nobody," he said.

Someone needed to know their approximate location and destination, though. Liza glanced at the chart. They were swinging slightly south, now, past Northerly and Southerly Islands.

"Whiskey Yankee Romeo. Civil War's a long time passing," she said. "Heading for a Commie regime. Victor Charlie country. Over."

There was a long silence. She knew Tango had pulled out the half-dissolved chart from the drawer under the cash register. Then she heard him laugh. *"Hey, Romeo, hang five on Echo Delta. Bluuue Bayou, and here's to you, sweet, Yank."*

He'd gotten it—running past Northerly and Southerly, (sweet Yank) headed for Red (Romeo plus Echo Delta) Bay, (Blue Bayou.) All he had to do now was phone Tasha and tell her, "don't call the police," and there she'd be, all by herself in a landscape the size of the Milky Way, searching for something like a quark.

She knew Tango was already dialing Tasha's phone number. *"Ahh, Romeo,"* he came back, *"'Seal up the mouth of outrage for a while, till we can clear these ambiguities.'"*

"Whiskey Yankee Romeo, clear," she said.

Tango had not sprung from elephant grass spouting Horace and Shakespeare; some memory had not been erased by that explosion that bloomed into bright confetti across the river.

"He's a smart one, that Tango," Crow said. "Got it figured, didn't he? Nobody else would know what he said, hey?"

"He's good, all right. He's had twenty-five years of daily practice—he oughta be. But he interrupted your story. You were telling me that not all the men wanted to go back? After going away to school? Something like that?"

"All of 'em went back a while, seems like, but some of 'em, they weren't satisfied. Some of 'em, they wanted more of the things they saw in town, like they wanted a TV and a fancier boat, stuff like that. Or some of 'em, they wanted booze. Village voted dry, see. Can't buy it, can't bring it in, can't use it atall. Some of 'em, they got drinking while they were away in town, and they didn't want to stay there in a dry village."

The radio crackled again. *"Mammoth Mama to Yankee Romeo—you on here, Romeo?"*

"Romeo here." Mink this time. She must have wrested the transmitter from Tango for a minute.

"Call from Base One. Myrtle J. says Crow is mixed up with some kinda gang. Shamed Marten house. Base One: Myrtle says, 'Look out for Crow.'"

Tango was on again. *"As Horace says, 'The little crow moves our ridicule, stripped of its stolen colors.'"*

Crow hunched down on the stool and turned his back. Liza stared at him. "Look out for Crow?" Sure, Myrtle Joseph, I'll do that. Should be easy—he's sitting two feet away from me this very minute.

All at once, she saw it. Somebody had kidnapped James, and Crow had kidnapped her. James was probably still in town, held somewhere to keep him from talking, and Crow was taking her on a wild goose chase. Shit, what an idiot you are, Liza.

She scanned his motionless back, for the first time looking for a telltale bulge under his jacket. Did he have a gun?

Her hand was gripping the transmitter the way a drowning man would clutch the seaweed engulfing him. She finally got the button pressed and muttered, "Romeo here. Whiskey aboard is Old Crow." Her voice shook so badly she wasn't sure they could get it. She repeated the words, hoping they understood.

"Roger, Romeo," Mink said. *"Relaying that to Base One."*

"Alpha Four." Tango's voice was low and sharp. *"You got a dust-off comin' up, Yank. Sending birds. Watch out for sniper fire. We got you covered, centerfield, heigh ho away we go."*

From the corner of her eye, Liza saw Crow make a swift movement. He had the transmitter before she could call again. He clutched it in his fist, his face inches from her own. Sam leaped to his feet. A sound deep in his rib cage vibrated against Liza's thighs.

"Tell him no," Crow ground from clenched jaws. "No birds, no dust off. Tell him Crow's gonna pay back. Don't send the cops. They'll kill the kid if the cops go in."

They stared at each other, Crow's skin ghastly in the green light from the radar. At last she held her hand out for the transmitter, their eyes still locked. She could see doubt in Crow's eyes, and fear, too. The sound she could feel became audible in Sam's throat. If Crow had a weapon, so did Liza Romero.

Slowly Crow's fist opened and he held the transmitter out. Liza took it from him. The tremor in his hand was precisely the same frequency as the shiver running up her arm.

"Yankee Romeo here," she said, never taking her eyes off Crow's face. "Negative dust-off at this time. Stand by. This is Yankee Romeo. Out."

Chapter 36

It was like the engine was roaring right next to his ear. It must be very big of an engine—through the wall by the bunk it sounded like one of those humongous bulldozers that made the logging roads.

There was a lightbulb in the ceiling, too bright to look at. Bunks all around him, not hardly any blankets except his. He pushed the blankets farther in the corner and sat on the bare mattress, hunched under the bunk above him. He didn't need those blankets anyway. That engine on the other side of the wall was so big it made the whole entire boat hot.

His pants were getting dried a little bit, but kind of stiff. His grandma would say never mind, what's an extra wash, don't you mind now. Tears kept coming in his eyes when he thought about his grandma. And Goran. No, don't think about Goran.

He wished he knew where those men were going with him. Maybe faraway and he wouldn't get to see his grandma again, or maybe Sam or Liza or anybody. Emerson, even. Emerson was about his only friend that he played with, and maybe he wouldn't get to see him again.

Tears kept on coming and he rubbed his face on his knee and tried not to think about if they were taking him home or else faraway. "Remember this," Goran had told him, so he would try and remember the entire story.

"That which is Nameless can never be found. Where White Bird flies up and Raven waits for Salmon, the Great Chief carved an ear in the rock so Spirit of Stone could hear. Stone listens to

Wind's music and Raven's voice. In spring, when the wild currant blooms and in autumn, when the Bear grows fat, day is as long as night. Then the Chief climbs the hill to tell his story to Listening Stone."

Across from James, under the bright lightbulb, the door to the bunkroom opened. A man came in, a man James had never seen before. The man was smiling a funny no-smile.

"James," the man said. "I'm sorry you got scared. We're taking you home. You want to go home to your grandmother, don't you?"

The man sat down on the edge of the bunk and ducked his head under the top bunk to look at James, who was pushing his back against the corner as hard as he could.

"You want to go home. Of course you do," the man said. "I'll bet your grandma's just about wondering now where you could be. Thinking to herself, 'My, I certainly will be glad to have that boy home again.' Aren't you glad we're taking you to her?"

James stared at the man's face. He had lightish hair that stuck out from under his cap, not very long, and light-colored eyebrows. And his eyes were funny-color, pale, no-color eyes like water or fish scales. And the man kept smiling, but his mouth didn't show his teeth like if you were really smiling because of being happy.

"You hungry?" the man asked. "You must be pretty hungry by now—it's late. Way after dinnertime. What would you like for dinner?"

James kept on staring at the man's face. His nose was small and not at all round—sharp, more, like a little beak, like a wren's beak or a robin.

"James, we need to have a little chat. I know you're worried about your uncle. We're going to get you two together again, you and your uncle, but we need to find out a couple things first. He gave you some directions, didn't he? Where something's hidden. So we'll take you back to him, but first we have to know where that something is."

The man's chin was sort of bony, like all the way back to under his ears. He didn't have a beard.

And anyway, Goran was drowned. He knew that for sure. Goran didn't ever get out of that water.

The man reached up and pushed his cap back a little so he could look at James. He leaned himself on one elbow so his face got even closer to where James was sitting. "I'm going to bring you something to eat, and then you can tell us where those things are, and before you know it, you'll be sleeping in your own bed at your grandma's house."

The man ooched himself out from under the top bunk and stood up. Then he leaned over and looked in at James. "Hamburger," he said. "With french fries. And ice cream." He was still smiling the funny no-smile when he closed the door.

Chapter 37

Liza hung up the transmitter. "You tell me what you know, and fast. If it doesn't add up, I'm calling Tango and he'll get the police."

Crow sank back on the stool again, and Liza saw his legs trembling. He lifted his hands, spread the fingers out on the chart table, raising each finger separately as though he were playing music on an invisible instrument. "Chief Henry Kitai. My grandfather. He been ninety-seven before he died."

"So are you the chief now?" Liza asked, wondering where this was leading.

"No, it ain't me. Goran's Chief, not me. See, it passes Chief to nephew on the mother's side. That way keeps the mother's clan in a straight line. Eagle marries Raven, see, and the kids, they have to be same as the mother. The mother's brothers raise the kid, they being the same as the mother's clan. So after Anna, James's mother, died, Chief Henry's daughter who is James's grandma, and her son Goran, Anna's brother, they got to raise James."

"And after Goran, the chief will be..."

Crow was nodding. "Be James."

James. Chief James Kitai, eight next time. Chief Goran Kitai, dead. Liza wondered if Crow knew Goran was dead. She wasn't ready to tell him. How far could she trust this man? Suddenly a new fear lit up like a neon sign. "Is there some plot to get rid of the Kitai Chiefs? Will they..." She couldn't finish the sentence.

"See, every Chief gets told a story. The story tells where something is. Maybe valuable, maybe just legend. I think they're after the story."

"The story is some kind of directions?"

"I think that's it. Lot of talk about what the story tells, but only a Chief can hear it. Lot of talk—sometimes it's told that there's a special stone carved by First People, and it marks something old as Earth. Something maybe hidden under it? I don't know—there's a lotta talk that don't seem like much sense. Nobody knows but everybody's sure smart about it."

"Only the Chief actually knows?"

Crow nodded, and Liza looked at him, puzzled. "Why would they kidnap James? How would he know the story?"

"All Kitai Chiefs, they learn from the earliest time that story. Every one of 'em knows it—first story they learn. So these men, likely they figured out James would know it."

"*Who* has figured it out? Who's got James?"

"Likely some of those timber fellas. Some people, if they can't buy something, they steal it, see. They try to buy the hand art, poles and all, but the council says no, not enough money anywhere to buy those things. What happened, though...some of the boys got hooked up on town ways. We was only twelve then, thirteen or fourteen—school was to eighth grade at the Institute, and then we got sent over to Sitka.

"Few of us used to get away after lights out, go in the bars, sell some of the small stuff from home, jewelry, charms, that sort 'a thing, buy a coupl'a bottles. Wasn't any good, Liza. Wrecked up, some of us.

"So these timber fellas, they find some 'a those men that come back unhappy from town school, and they make a deal with 'em, pay 'em money and liquor, and the men snuck things out to 'em."

Crow sighed. "Goran, he tells those timber fellas he knows where there's poles all over the forest, Kuiu, Dall, Prince of Wales, but they have to pay him so good he can get settled in town when it's done. It's money, see. But then, Goran maybe starts feeling bad. Those poles and stuff, they belong to the whole village. So he was likely going to tell what he done."

Crow inhaled deeply as though the next part of the story required all the oxygen of his lungs. His hands on the chart table were curled into fists. "I wrecked up, too, Liza, drinking. That Marten pole Tenney made—shame on me," he said. "It's shame on the whole community when one goes bad. Shamed my family with drinking. Tenney, he made that shame pole, but I can't never pay off the debt."

Crow turned and looked at Liza. The light from the radar screen turned his face into a relief map, his eyes like caves. Liza had a sense that he was trying to size up the effect of his story. Something was wrong with it. All at once, she knew what it was.

Would a village put up a pole shaming one of its own for nothing more than drinking? Alaska would bristle with ridicule poles if alcohol was sufficient cause. Swallowed another one, didn't you, Liza? "Fool me twice…"

"Crow? Sorry, but I don't buy it. You weren't shamed for drinking. Who are we kidding, here? What did you do?"

There was a long silence. In the green light, Crow's eyes suddenly glittered. Keeping Sam between them, Liza grabbed the transmitter again. Before she could call though, Crow spoke.

"Wasn't Goran—it was me. What I did, I sold those timber fellas the keys to the Marten Tribal House and a map of all the places our people had kept from the early time. Burial grounds with sacred objects. Petroglyphs. Old poles, some gone, some rotted, but a lot good. A lot that could be made new with oil and paint.

"I copied maps from the old picture books, put Xs where the sacred burial sites were, all over Kuiu, all around on Kupreanof, some down to Sea Otter Sound, even. Then I put all the maps together in one map. And I sold 'em that map."

"Who did you sell the map to? You must know some names, Crow. Who has James?"

"No names—didn't never tell me who they were—sent a guy I ain't never seen before to get it and pay off. Had a big old scar down the side of his face—ain't never seen him before."

Instantly Liza pictured the body on the floor of the old school. "A scar? Like a snake running through his beard?"

"Yeah, that's him. You know him? Know his name?"

"I've seen him, that's all. In Wrangell." She tried to erase the picture of the man with the scar through his beard. Somehow it was all connected, but she still didn't have the key. "How did they find out in the village that you had sold their secrets?"

"My grandfather. Chief Henry. A lot of things went missing before he died. From the tribal house. And he wanted to be buried at the tip of the island—went there to choose the site, and the poles were gone. I don't know how he knew it was me, but he did. He came and told me 'keep out of the village, you shamed House of Marten forever.' I don't know how he knew. He was one of the great Chiefs, and great Chiefs know men's secrets."

Crow stopped and stared out the window, his fingers knotted together in his lap. Then he turned and looked straight at her. "I wrecked up, but I ain't going to let James get wrecked up, too. We'll get him, for certain."

Hearing the rumbling intensity of his promise, Liza felt a surge of hope, ill supported by the evidence of her eyes. Their forces consisted of a drunken thief, a gullible woman, and a dog.

A high white moon floated above and below, painting a center line across Sumner Strait. Prince of Wales Island was a black monument to the south. To the north, the red light blinked on that truly named ledge, The Eye Opener, while far to the west, the ridge of Kuiu Island rose above a slim white bedroll of fog. The satin surface of the water looked like a sheet of ice.

"Right there," Crow said, pointing at the impenetrable shore, "there's Red Bay, past the rocks on Pine Point."

A glittering line of surf broke where the slow swells met the Point. Liza switched the light on above the chart table and checked the depths. Rising tide, near slack—a good time to enter, but no place to get trapped. Imagine turning in behind the Point, slipping along behind one of the entrance islands, and suddenly coming bow-on to the other boat.

"Crow, I don't think we should go in," she said. "What if they're there?"

"Slide in close to Bell Island," he said. "Slide in, throw over the hook and I'll take that raft and have a look around. The raft goes quiet, and there ain't much current right at slack."

Liza didn't answer, not wanting to commit to such a plan till she got a feel for it. She was watching the radar like the Holy Grail—heading into shore off that moon-bright water was like coming in out of the sun.

She gave the reef plenty of distance before she crept close to Bell Island, working the *Salmon Eye* into the shallows as far as she dared. "No farther," she said, watching the depth finder blink fifteen feet. "And you better be quick. There's no water at all in here by midtide. Can you get the anchor?"

Before Crow could answer, a frog as large as a skiff rose ahead of the bow. Moonlight on water could cause hallucinations, Liza knew, but that frog was *there*, eyes bulging beneath drooping lids, mouth splitting its head in an eerie smile. She yanked the throttle back and jammed the gears into reverse.

"Them's the poles," Crow said. "See 'em? Lying there in the water? Look like logs, eh? Rafted up there just like logs."

Gradually Liza's eyes made out the dark lengths of the floating totem poles; a snarling sea wolf, a killer whale, and a beaver with its cross-hatched tail; the narrow end of one pole bore Raven, the trickster. Above them all loomed the smiling frog. The slow swell and dancing moonlight gave the creatures life.

"Real nice, ain't they?" Crow said quietly. "Seems like they're alive, eh? Real pretty, them poles."

His voice carried them home to the dense spruce forest, wind mourning through the branches. Liza's neck prickled; she had to blink back tears.

Crow went out on deck and released the anchor. Sam sat on the deck, supervising Crow's preparations. While Crow pulled the raft in, Liza clung to Sam's collar. No way was everyone going to leave her. She grabbed a life jacket and tossed it in the stern as Crow let himself over the side and shipped the oars, waiting for her to release the painter. One moment he was there, the next moment, swallowed by the dark, only the faint shush of the oars reporting his passage, then silence.

Gradually the night sounds resumed—frogs beginning spring courtship, a gull's sleepy irritation, the slip, slip of water over gravel, and the occasional distant boom of surf over rock. Sam lowered himself to the deck at Liza's feet, head raised, ears alert to any sound. She was grateful for his warmth against her legs—the clear night air was close to freezing—cloudy nights were warmer, the cloud blanket holding in the earth's heat.

After fifteen minutes or so, Sam sat up again, then stood, tail held stiff, ears back and wide to catch some inaudible sound. She strained to hear, too, finally catching the rhythmic hush of oars in water. She braced herself against the rail, ready, if those oars weren't Crow returning, to leap for the anchor, dash to the wheel and start the engine. The darkness was solid, and only Sam's tail beginning its wave told Liza who was there.

"Nobody here." Crow's words came from nowhere, and then he was gripping the bottom of the rail, handing her the painter, jamming the oars back in their rubber straps.

"Then where have they gone?"

"Eh, maybe out to Kuiu. Hard to say, eh? Maybe we gotta wait till it's light—might pass 'em along shore if we go now."

"You think we should stay around here till daylight?"

"Could. Probably be the thing, eh? We ain't gonna find 'em in the dark. We can go early, get a start on 'em. Likely they'll head out there to Kuiu. They gotta track down what James knows about, see."

"On Kuiu? That's where it is?"

"Well, that's what ever'body says. Something hid on Kuiu."

She sat there on the stool, staring out at the poles.

The incredible frog made its slow roll and dip; its smile seemed full of some joke yet to be played. The creatures rose in the light and vanished into the deep shadow like animals creeping in and out of caves and tunnels. Go. You have to keep going. James is in terrible danger.

In the main cabin, Crow was already snoring. Liza backed the boat into deep water. Stay until daylight, that's what Crow had said, and she was too exhausted to go any farther. She went out and dropped the anchor again. This bight northwest of Red Bay was plenty deep to anchor.

Back in the wheelhouse, she put her head on her arms. She tried to conjure Larry's voice, his strong hands massaging the back of her neck, but Paul Howard's face seemed engraved on her mind, his brooding eyes turned sideways at her, sardonic and angry.

"Shoulda left it all to me," his voice grumbled, and the words became entangled in her dreams.

Chapter 38

After the engine got shut down it seemed like it was pretty quiet, nobody coming in, just sometimes the boat creaking. Maybe even he slept a little bit, but he didn't want to sleep because those men were here on the boat and he didn't know what they were going to do. The food they brought him smelled okay and he was hungry, super hungry actually, but maybe it could be poison or something, and anyway, he wasn't taking stuff from those men, no way. But it smelled good. But he wasn't going to eat it anyway.

He hated that light bulb that was too bright and it was always right in his eyes if he didn't stay all the way back in the bunk. Maybe he could reach the chain for it if he got in the top bunk.

He stood on the lower bunk and dragged himself up with his arms and got his knee up and then pulled himself all the way. He turned around and reached out and he could just get it with the tips of his fingers. When he pulled the chain it was so dark that in one second he felt like he was going to fall down and down like in the water when he jumped over, but he got back on his heels all right on the bunk and hung down off the edge till he could feel the bottom one. He was glad it was dark. It made him feel a little bit safer because they couldn't right away see where he was.

Then he heard a lot of feet banging over his head like somebody running on the deck, a lot of somebodies running, and he heard a snap, snap that was like a helicopter very close to the boat. The feet stopped and there was a motor noise like an outboard, but he could hardly tell it because the helicopter was so loud it sounded like it was coming right through the deck. But no feet anymore. Nobody shouting.

He felt his way to the door and turned the handle. He thought probably it was locked but it wasn't. The helicopter was so loud he wanted to cover up his ears. He could see steps going up—there was light up at the top of them. He started up the steps, scared somebody would come and see him, but he kept going and when he got to the top, there was just a small place with a door on each side like a little hallway, and a ladder going up higher. He looked out the window on one door—dark—nobody he could see on the deck—the roar of the helicopter was so bad he didn't want to open the door. He climbed the ladder in front of him. The wheelhouse was there. Nobody in it.

He looked back and there were floodlights turned on and there was a helicopter with a log or something hanging under it and men were standing on a log boom with long poles trying to get the log straight over the boom. The noise made his whole face squinch up and he put his hands over his ears while he watched the log coming down lower and lower.

This was a tugboat he was on and those men were doing helicopter logging like him and Liza watched. He looked around the wheelhouse. The radar was on, and that thing Liza had showed him with the numbers. The GPS, that was what she called it, like a computer. Next to it the radio.

The men had the log grabbed with those pole hooks now and they were pulling it straight down. When it got down onto the boom, they unfastened the chains holding it and the helicopter started going up.

He looked back at the screens above the wheel. The GPS had numbers just like Liza showed him. She had told him how he could call and tell those numbers to somebody if there was trouble—if the *Salmon Eye* got in any trouble. And there was the radio, too. The radio was right there next to it.

He looked back. The helicopter was gone, and the men were getting into a skiff that was fastened at the side of the log boom. He climbed onto the swivel chair behind the wheel and took the transmitter off the hook.

Chapter 39

She was dreaming in whispers. Whispers soft as breath, coming from everywhere. She woke terrified. Sam leaped to his feet, and began circling the wheelhouse in a frenzy, tail lashing her legs, thudding the stanchion and binnacle. He whined and Liza grabbed his head, rubbing his ears to quiet him so she could hear the whispers that were real.

"Liza…Liza can you hear? It's five six, dot dot, three one, dot, one two; one three three, dot dot, four one, dot, zero zero, is where the boat is."

James. Calling on the radio.

She grabbed the transmitter, whispering back—he must have gotten into the wheelhouse alone and called, but would his captors be able to hear her answer? "This is Liza. I hear you, James—we're on our way to get you. We'll be there soon. Hang on."

After an eternity, he whispered again, this time his voice thick with tears. *"I guess you can't hear—this is what it says the boat's at."* He repeated latitude and longitude.

She realized he didn't know he had to release the transmit button to listen. He didn't know he'd reached her. She pictured his despair and her arms ached in their emptiness.

After endless moments of paralysis, she grabbed the chart. The coordinates plotted almost exactly at Trouble Island, a tiny dot just around Point Barrie on the northwest arc of Sumner Strait. Trouble Island. How appropriate. No time to waste anchored here. Hang on, James, the troops are on their way.

She started the engine and switched on the instruments. In a minute, a sleepy Crow poked his head through the door.

"We're going," Liza told him. "James called. They're at Trouble Island. Must be anchored, if he could get to the radio alone. Otherwise, somebody would be in the wheelhouse."

"Yuuh, Trouble Island. Right across, see. Maybe take him in by skiff when it gets light. Don't want the big boat going in there. They never go in the bay, always pick up someplace else. Don't want any one to see 'em."

"Right across? Where's the village, then? The chart doesn't show anything straight across."

"Village isn't on the chart. Isn't mapped. See here...No Name. Village is in a little way from No Name Bay. They call it No Name so it doesn't exist, see. Names make things be."

No Name. "That's what James told Mink when she asked him where he'd caught the halibut. We thought he was just refusing to tell us where it was."

"See, it doesn't exist, eh, because you can't name it. James, he's smart, he knew what you'd think, eh?"

Smart, yes. In trouble, yes. "Come on, Crow, let's go."

She threw the door back and he went out to pull the anchor. She listened as it came up, putting the engine in gear as soon as she heard it clank against the bow roller. As the boat swung, the poles danced up and down in a phosphorescent wash.

"We'll be back," Liza said aloud.

She turned west-northwest from Red Bay. The moon was still visible to the southwest, almost touching the black ridge of Prince of Wales now. The white roll of fog had moved eastward and rainbow ghosts floated up from it. Crow waved his hand at it.

"Can't see anythin' in there," he said. "They'll be hiding, waiting out that there fog, see. They can't get the kid in to No Name because there isn't any radar in the skiff. They're anchored, see, over there by Trouble Island. Gotta wait this out, likely."

"Take the wheel a minute, would you?" Liza said. "I want to plot a compass course for Trouble Island."

She entered on the GPS the coordinates James had given her and came up with a compass bearing. Then she unrolled the chart and laid out the parallel ruler to double-check the information.

Crow eased the wheel a little to the bearing she gave him, his eyes checking over the gauges, flicking up to the radar screen, as though he'd been a captain all his life.

"Haven't done this in a while," he said, half to himself. "Used to go out with the *Eldred Rock*, inland barge it was, made a bundle doing it, even though I'd already took up with liquor. Sober up quick, then, couple hours and we were off and running Chatham, or Lynn Canal. No problem, those days."

"Glad you weren't running an oil tanker."

"Isn't good, liquor. Polish the edges, that's all it's good for, smooth off what's all the time rough, scarred up. All it does. Isn't good. You sure you got that course set?" Crow asked. "We're going in."

Liza glanced out the window and saw the water disappearing. The bow loomed against a gauze background that folded around them and sealed off the world.

She'd set a course that would take them straight across to No Name Bay, but when Point Barrie appeared on the radar screen due north, she'd turn and make her way toward Trouble Island.

"Hold till we pass Point Barrie," she told Crow.

"You could sleep a while, you gotta be kinda tired," he said.

"I'm too scared to be tired. I wish James would call again. Maybe they've moved."

"See, there's some boat coming on the screen, right now," Crow said, waving his hand. "Little blip there, see?"

Liza had to look hard to pick it up. The sweep showed another moving object just southwest of Totem Bay on the north edge of the Strait. She wouldn't have noticed it if Crow hadn't had such sharp eyes.

All at once the radio stuttered and Liza fiddled the squelch button to decrease the static, hoping to hear that little whisper once more.

"...*moth Mama...Romeo...come in...*"

Mink again. Two thirty A.M.—she must be ready to leave the bar and decided to check up on them again. They were getting out of range with the ridge in between.

"Romeo," Liza said, switching channels.

"*...Mama...on the way...*"

She couldn't get it. "You're breaking up," she said. "Try again. Over"

"*...send...ten...cops...heard...tote...Get...two hours...*"

Hopeless. Was Mink getting any more at her end? She had to try something. They weren't going as far as Conclusion Island, they were heading for Trouble Island.

"We will not get to the *end* on present course because of *difficulties*. Do you read? Over."

Pause while Mink studied the chart. "*Rog...difficul... destin...Romeo...wait...wait...send...ten...cop...wait. Over.*"

Ten cops? "Crow, do you think someone's sending ten cops?" she asked.

"Better not be," he said. "She says wait, but if it's cops we better get there a long ways ahead of 'em."

"Too late to wait for anybody, now," she said. "We're on our own."

It was no use trying to get any more from Mink. "Whiskey Yankee Romeo, clear," she said.

"*...standing by...*" came back, and Liza clung to the thready sound a moment before she put the transmitter back on its hook.

Soon the screen showed two dots rounding Point Baker, staying close together. Probably a tug and barge, the skipper no doubt calculating his time to Wrangell Narrows in order to enter at slack tide. The tide flooded in from both ends of Wrangell Narrows, meeting in the center in a swirl of standing riffles; a boat faced S curves, drying flats and ledges. Liza wished she were headed that way, twisting through the red and green blinkered midway. She should be making some simple delivery along the shallow Narrows, not on a life-and-death mission to save a child.

The shroud of fog was so dense it was difficult to see the *Salmon Eye*'s own bow. Once in a while, a little hole developed overhead as though they were trapped at the bottom of a well. The sky seemed brilliant and lost, the stars dropping as though launched by a flamethrower. Then the hole would seize up again and they were traveling in slow motion through featureless space.

Crow raised his head to look at the radar and Liza looked, too. "'Nother boat comin'," Crow said, waving at the screen again.

Just at the edge of the screen, another boat showed clearly, following the *Salmon Eye* along the Strait, though still miles away.

"Maybe a boat coming out of Wrangell Narrows," Liza said.

"Better not be ten cops, is all."

"They'd have something a lot faster than that. Could be the Coast Guard, though," she said, with a glimmer of hope. Crow was so insistent on no police. She hoped there wasn't an ulterior motive to his resistance.

"They ain't dawdlin', whoever," Crow said, and indeed the other boat seemed to be catching up.

"That one," Crow said, pointing at the enlarging outline, "that one might be somebody. That one sure could be ten cops. They're movin', right? They're gonna catch us b'fore we get up 'round the Point if we stay off this far. No place to hide out here, either. We turn up close and maybe we can beat 'em behind Trouble Island, eh?"

"And then what?"

In the darkened wheelhouse, they turned to stare at each other.

Chapter 40

The *Aquila* moved swiftly once it had passed the breakwater. Jake hunched over the wheel, his weight making the captain's chair look more like a tripod. He hadn't said a word to Paul since backing out of the slip. Paul was grateful for the silence. Seated on the bench next to the door, he leaned his elbows on his knees, put his chin in his hand, and tried to bring order from chaos.

Lizzie had taken James and run. Why? "Jake," he said, standing up and walking over next to him. "You pick her out on radar?"

Jake stared at the screen, then reached up and fiddled the range. "Probably her," he said, pointing at a tiny blip, barely a dot on the expanded range. "Just past St. John, there. Could be her. 'Nother one north there, mighta come out'a Wrangell Narrows."

Jake adjusted the range downward, trying to get a larger image of the *Salmon Eye*, if indeed it was the *Salmon Eye*. "Likely her—seems like that's about where she would be, 'bout that far ahead of where I saw her."

"Can you catch her?"

"She's haulin.' I dunno. Maybe, maybe not."

Paul watched the black spot that the radar seemed to redraw on each sweep. It had moved to the very edge of the screen now, toward the black mass that was Prince of Wales Island. Staring at it, it occurred to him that this was the dumbest thing he'd done in all his police years. He had no business being this far from Wrangell Island. He had to call the state troopers, call the chief. He reached for the radio transmitter.

Lizzie's voice suddenly filled the wheelhouse. "*...Yankee Romeo. Go to other channel. Over.*"

The other channel. One she'd use without naming. Try to locate it before they stopped talking. He pushed the channel scanner.

"*...mie regime. Victor Charlie country. Over.*"

Her face, across the table at the café, flashed in front of him, amusement in those hooded eyes. Then tears. Sheesh.

"Base One says, 'Look out for Crow.'?"

"That's Mink over at the Velvet Moose," Paul said. "Who's Base One, I wonder? What's she mean, 'Look out for Crow'?"

"Romeo here. Whiskey aboard is Old Crow." Her voice was very low, almost a whisper.

"Shit," Paul said. "Must mean Crow's with her."

"She could be in big trouble," Jake said.

"She *is* big trouble—she's run off with that kid," Paul growled.

"Nahh," Jake said, turning to glare at him. "She wouldn't hurt a flea. A loner, maybe, but she keeps an eye out 'round the dock, gives a hand when somebody's got down on his luck or somethin.' You ain't talking trouble with the *Salmon Eye*'s skipper, Mister."

"Listen, she'll have the right to tell her side of it—we better hear her out first. And could be she's in trouble, Crow aboard and all."

Me too, he thought. Trouble with a capital T. Off my turf. Wrangell Island's the boundary. What the hell am I doing?

Jake shoved the throttle up and the pulse of the engine rose to an urgent drumming, water curling past the bow in a glittering wave.

Paul stood at the door and watched the moon following them. Exhaustion rose like steam in his brain. He sat down on the bench, staring at the radar, a cat's eye, green, circling... circling, water hissing past the bow, forming words, distant conversation, words he couldn't quite make out, radio words, white noise from the radio. Then dimly he did make them out: *"'...the little crow moves our ridicule, stripped of its stolen colors.'"*

Tango—doesn't know if he's an English professor or a grunt. He should call her too—get her on the radio, say hey, Lizzie, wait for me—you don't have to run, don't have to run anymore, Lizzie, your mother...she wouldn't have left...your mother...

Jake was shaking him. He stared up at the radar screen. Everything looked the same. "Where've we gotten to?" he asked Jake.

"Right beyond there's St. John Harbor," Jake said, pointing at the small islands off Zarembo. "Looks like she mighta gone into Red Bay—hooked into the shoreline someplace around there, anyhow. Can't see her on the screen."

Paul tried to straighten his back, which felt permanently pleated from his slumped position on the bench. God, why couldn't he think straight? Okay, call the chief. Confess. He took the transmitter off the hook again.

"Wrangell Police Department—Howard calling. Over."

"Dispatcher—Wrangell. Over."

"Yeah, Darnell. Can you get the Chief on the wire?"

"Yeah, okay—how's he get you?"

"F/V *Aquila*—WYP 4577."

"Roger—I'll try him. Stand by."

Jake was swinging the boat to the south now, aiming just north of Vishnefski Rock. There was no sign of the *Salmon Eye* on the radar.

"You sure she went in there by Red Bay?" Paul asked. "Seems like a strange place to go—too shallow for that big old packer, and the entrance is real hairy with those rips 'n all."

"Last I saw she was heading over there and then I lost her. Must be right up against something there so she doesn't stand out anymore."

"Aquila, Aquila, WYP 4577. Steve Woods, Wrangell Police Department."

"Yeah, chief. Howard here. Say listen, I think the Romero woman has the kid aboard—she's running, is all I know. I picked up this gillnetter coming in at Shoemaker—skipper's name's Jake...?"

"Fremantle."

"...Jake Fremantle. Says he passed the *Salmon Eye* going around Elephant's Nose. We're following her right now—looks like she's in the Red Bay vicinity—anyway stopped showing up on the radar around there somewhere."

"You're outa bounds, Howard. What the hell are you doing?"

"Well, I thought we should check and see if she has the kid. We're heading over there."

"Don't try anything, Howard. If you locate her, just watch her till we get somebody out there."

"Yeah, roger, Chief. *Aquila,* WYP 4577, out."

He switched back to Channel 16, the all-call station. "Want me to take her for awhile?" he asked Jake.

"Nope. I'm wide awake. Can't stop thinking what the hell this is all about. This is gotta be some mistake. Ain't even a possibil..."

Paul raised his hand and bent forward. A faint whisper hissed on the radio. He shoved past Jake and pressed his ear to the receiver, straining to hear.

"...dot, four one, dot, zero zero, is where the boat is."

There was a momentary silence. Then Lizzie's voice, whispering, too, but louder, the words slow and clearly articulated:

"This is Liza. I hear you, James—we're on our way to get you. We'll be there soon. Hang on."

Silence. Jake turned his head and glared at Paul, who still had his ear pressed to the receiver.

"See? The kid ain't with her. She's hunting for him. She ain't no kidnapper. I knew..."

Paul flung his hand up to shut off Jake's grumble.

"...it says the boat's at five six, dot dot, three one, dot, one two; one three three, dot dot, four one, dot, zero zero."

There was silence on the radio then and silence in the wheelhouse of the *Aquila.* Jake tilted his head back and stared over at Paul, who still hunched next to the receiver.

When Paul was sure there would be no further exchange, he straightened and looked out at the moon-bright surface. "Hunh," he said, expressing the burden of his thoughts.

"She's comin' out." Jake gestured at the radar screen, and Paul saw a tiny black blip clearing the top line of Prince of

Wales Island. "See? She's going to rescue the kid. You wanta still go over there, or maybe we should head for the position the kid gave."

"Did you get it?"

"Pretty close—56° 31'—133°41'. Pretty close anyhow."

"Let's see where that is."

Jake fiddled the charts on the GPS. "Some place close to Point Barrie, looks like."

Paul stared at the radar screen. If that was the *Salmon Eye*, she was moving very fast, making a long diagonal across Sumner Strait. The *Aquila* was a long way back now, and dropping farther all the time.

"You pretty certain that's the *Salmon Eye*?"

"So who else would be haulin' across there after getting that message? She's going for the kid."

"Okay. Head for Point Barrie. Doesn't look like we can catch her, though."

"She's puttin' some distance on. She's in a hurry. 'Nother boat out there, too, see? Cut down outa Totem Bay. Crazy place to be at night—rocks growin' up like a wheat field. Why the hell'd anybody be in Totem Bay at night?"

Paul tried to massage his neck to loosen the stiffness. Goddammit, he couldn't go into some crazy situation disabled. And he sure couldn't put Jake out there like some decoy. Whoever had the kid wouldn't give him up now without somebody going down.

"Fog out there," Jake said.

Paul looked where Jake was pointing. Far to the west, a fog bank, white in the moonlight, had hidden Kuiu Island and the southwest corner of Kupreanof. Point Barrie. "Can we go any faster?" he asked.

Chapter 41

"Where's the kid? He's not in the bunkroom."

"He's not? Looked like he was sleeping last time I went in. Maybe he's in the head."

"I checked. Looked all over down there. Didn't see him anywhere."

"Shit. He's hiding. He's gotta be somewhere on the boat. Find him. He's really scared even though I told him we were taking him home. Keep telling him we're not going to hurt him."

"I looked everywhere down there—he's not below."

"Look again. If he isn't there, he must be out on deck. He'd never try to swim again. He must have found it damn cold last time."

"We're pretty close to that island. Maybe he thought he could swim that far."

"No way. He's right here on the boat. Bring him in here when you get him. It's going to be light in a couple hours and we gotta be ready. Get going."

Chapter 42

The *Salmon Eye* passed the bulge in the coast north of Point Barrie, and Crow turned to the northerly bearing Liza had given him. Ahead, Trouble Island was a tiny black blob in the green sweep; she adjusted the radar range. Trouble Island appeared to be only a few hundred yards long. A thin pencil of land ran out from the coastline southeast of it. Between the peninsula and the island, almost indistinguishable from the land itself, was a shape too regular and symmetrical to be an island. Behind it were radar markers at each end of something being towed. James had read the right numbers. Liza knew he was on that tugboat.

She stepped out on deck and pulled the door shut behind her to keep Sam from following. She didn't trust Sam not to bark—his ears were so keen that he'd hear the slightest sound of voices, even at that distance. She could feel his weight pressing against the door as the latch clicked.

The fog coated her face in a chill net. Somewhere far away, a bell buoy tolled a slow dirge. A thin line of white spray spilled from the bow of the *Salmon Eye* and vanished into the dense cloud that sat everywhere across the water. Nothing beyond the rail was visible—they were alone in some trackless space.

She went in and took the wheel from Crow. She wanted to be able to back out of this at any second, and she was in no hurry to meet up with any of the boats showing up on the screen. They were well south of the boat she believed James was on, south of the passage between Trouble Island to the west and the peninsula jutting out from the shore of Kupreanof.

She pulled the throttle back and the *Salmon Eye* gradually slowed till it was barely holding against the current.

Crow was standing next to Liza watching the radar. "He's on that boat for sure," he said. "You pull up along here and put down the hook, and I'll take a look on the quiet."

"I don't like the idea of being anchored. It might take too long to get out if anything went wrong."

"Shallow here, don't need much line out," Crow said. "So we can pull it up quick. Come up, now—we're close enough. Don't want to make a ruckus they can hear." He watched the screen. "This'll do, here. I'll let go the anchor and go over there and check on things."

"I'm going too."

Crow opened the door. This time Sam was ready. He had his shoulders through the door before Crow could push it shut, clawing his way past. He pranced to the bow and put his front paws on the railing, leaning out as far as he could, his tongue hanging down and his nose quivering to catch every passing scent. His tail swept the deck, but he didn't bark.

Liza wanted to go out and stand beside him, whisper to him to keep him quiet, but Crow had released the brake and was looking back, waiting for her.

She looked at the depth—thirty-eight feet—and waved at Crow to start the windlass. The chain rattled and she could see it angle away before it disappeared—the boat was drifting back quickly as the tide ebbed.

When Crow slammed the brake down, Liza put the engine in reverse. The *Salmon Eye* swung slightly and she killed the engine immediately. They could drag with so little scope and a strong ebb, but she intended to be back very soon. The instant they returned, they'd be out of there.

Liza looked again at the radar screen. The small boat was bouncing along the edge around the Point. The boat that had been following them was no more than eight miles east of Point Barrie and still coming on strongly. Were those boats coming to help her, or help their quarry? Or were they innocent of the whole thing? Assume everyone's an enemy. Count on Liza, count on Crow.

She went out on deck. Crow was at the stern, pulling in the raft, Sam pressing over his shoulder, tail beating the wet air to a froth. She peered at her watch. 4:13 A.M. This night, this endless night, would have no dawn in such a fog.

Crow cleated the painter for the raft, and Liza felt Sam tense. In a single motion she lunged for his collar and he lunged for the raft. Crow whispered, "Let 'im go, he'll find James first."

"No," she whispered back, "we can't take him—he might bark and give the whole show away."

"He won't," Crow said. "He's gotta get the kid, see. He's smart, this dog."

By then there was no choice. Sam was already in the raft. Dragging him back on deck was going to make an almighty scene. Count on Liza, Crow, and *Sam*.

Crow climbed over and pulled the oars out, jamming them into their rubber oarlocks. He looked up at Liza and nodded. She handed Crow three life jackets, which he stowed under the seat. Then she climbed over, unfastening the painter before she sat.

The little raft tilted, riding low in the water—not a vessel designed for major search and rescue ventures, but Crow stabilized it with the oars. "Sit, Sam," he commanded in a loud whisper, and Sam obediently lowered his hind quarters to the floor, facing forward as the bow watch.

Liza concentrated on sound. Beyond the slow tolling of the bell buoy, she could hear the drum of waves breaking on rock, the sigh as they receded. Their own progress was a steady spill of water from the oars.

In a minute, there was a pulse barely audible through the thick skin of fog. An engine running inshore of them. Close enough to hear.

Liza remembered the *Coast Pilot*'s description of Trouble Island, "at the edge of the foul area..." "...small craft with local knowledge can pass through this area, but should not attempt it when the kelp beds are not showing." Not only were the kelp beds not showing, they couldn't even see the water.

Then a chink in the wall opened abruptly, and Crow pointed. Through the draggling mist, Liza saw a boat. Her port running light was only a few yards off the raft's stern, its red haze illuminating the name below it. *Fighting Chance*.

"Do you know that boat?" she whispered, watching as the hole closed and gobbled up all trace of it.

"Belongs to Tenney Rushmore. He fishes some, along with his carving."

Tenney Rushmore. The one-armed man with yellow eyes.

"He knows the back ways," Crow said.

Tenney Rushmore was clearly heading for the other boat. "He's one of them, Crow. This is a trap."

"He's turned, see? See how he's turned, going to the outside 'round the island? Likely he's headed home. He's way over, see? Already past the south tip a' the island."

The fog had swallowed all trace—Liza thought Crow must be reading shadows. Even the sound of the *Fighting Chance*'s engine was gone. They were as alone in the little raft as before.

She stared into nothingness, waiting for some huge shape to emerge. Now and then Crow shipped the oars to listen. The raft slipped through a flock of mergansers, its quiet passage causing only throaty protest, the birds paddling out of reach without rising. Several cormorants winged silently over their heads like a flight of arrows. Over all tolled the distant dirge of the bell. She tried to count—one-one hundred, two-one hundred—as though she could check their position by the length of the swells that rang it, then occupied her mind trying to determine the key—E flat, she thought.

Nothing appeared. Liza thought they must be going in circles. She strained every nerve to listen. Only the sound of the oars. But Crow wasn't rowing. He had shipped the oars again. They were listening to someone else rowing. The raft drifted fast enough to make a wake, the tide ebbing that fast. There was no trace of another boat, only the rhythmic shoosh of another's oars, and the slap of water on metal.

When Crow pulled forward again, the raft rammed the edge of a log boom. Crow lifted one oar slightly and gestured. In the center of the boom, barely contrasted with the raw logs, was a totem pole. All at once, Liza understood.

The totem poles were concealed in log booms. Before towing the booms to the mill, the thieves would separate the poles, leaving enough logs to disguise them, like the ones they'd seen in Red Bay. They could leave them indefinitely—salt water pickles while fresh water rots. The totem poles, which would rot in the rain forest, would last for years in salt water. At the old canneries, the buildings on land rotted and collapsed, the pilings in the sea, which supported the docks, lasted for a century.

Her train of thought was snapped by a loud report. She crouched, gripping the edge of the seat, and Crow bent low, dragging the oars to hold the raft in place. Sam stood up, his motion causing a sharp list.

"Down," Liza whispered fiercely, "down." Reluctantly he crouched, tensed to spring. Crow pulled slowly to hold the raft in place against the current. The silence was a pall deeper than the fog.

Crow's face was almost hidden beneath his cap, but Liza could see his jaw working. She knew he'd keep going if she weren't with him, but clearly he didn't know what to do with her. In a moment, he began to turn the raft away.

"No," she whispered, leaning across the space between them, trying to stay low and steady the raft. "Keep going, Crow. We can't quit now."

He looked at her, held his oars a minute, tried to look over his shoulder. "Bad. They ain't gonna give him up, eh?"

"Were they shooting at us?"

"They can't see us. We wouldn't show on their screen, see. Somebody else, must be."

"Not James—they wouldn't shoot him!"

"Naah, don't think they'd do it—not a little kid. Could be Tenney, though. He mighta tried to get over there—likely he was the one rowing. They'd pick him up on radar—he's got that metal skiff."

Crow gripped the oars and began to pull again, following the tow line from the boom. Liza watched the muscles in his jaw twitch. His eyes were slits beneath the bill of his cap.

"They better not 'a got him, is all. Not Tenney." He pulled harder, and they spun over the quiet surface.

After a few minutes he shipped his oars again and Liza could hear water slapping the hull of a boat—hear the creak of a hull bending to the tide. In another minute, the dark shape of a tug began to form, gradually lengthening as Crow pulled to starboard to pass at a distance from her stern. The tug swung on her anchor, her bow turned away in the ebb tide. Crow slacked off a bit, wanting to stay a shadow till they had a chance to size her up.

They were no more than fifty feet from the stern, now, and suddenly she could see the white letters below the port hawsehole. *Albert M. Thomas.* Ross Elliot was skipper of the *Albert M. Thomas.* No. Impossible. Ross Elliot was Andy's father. Erin and Margie's father. Willy's father. He would *never* kidnap James. But they were circling Ross Elliot's tugboat, and someone had been shooting from it.

Halfway along, Crow turned and pulled closer. Liza looked at him, wondering if he had some plan. She didn't want to ask—voices would carry like trumpets over water—but she wanted to be prepared. Sam was ready. His tongue mopped her face as she struggled to keep him down. As they got closer, Crow leaned toward her and whispered, "...saw something moving."

Liza felt Sam's hind quarters rise and begin to tremble from the tension of his half-crouch. She didn't dare even whisper, in case someone was above them on deck, but she rested one hand on his flank, hoping she could calm him enough to keep him from barking. She could feel the stiff ridge of hair rise along his neck and sense a new excitement in him, as though he planned to fling himself out of the raft at any instant, but what they desperately needed was silence. How to explain that to a dog? But he knew. Liza was sure he knew.

She would never understand how Crow knew, though. How could he have seen the slightest motion, the least suggestion of shape? His night vision must rival an owl's. Because Crow had seen what he needed to see.

Inside the seventh tire forward of the stern, someone was crouched. Liza could see knees protruding; fingers clutched the inner rim of the tire. Like Sam, she was trembling with excitement. She wanted to shout and laugh and cry as much as Sam needed to whine and bark, but they controlled themselves. Crow pulled up to the seventh tire, and in one sleek motion, James dove into Liza's arms.

Crow clung to the tire until they were settled, James between Liza's knees, Sam curled on top of him. Then Crow turned the raft out and gave a push against the tire to send it away from the tug's hull and into the fog's protective drape before they were discovered. It was his only mistake.

There was a shout from the stern, a now-familiar crack and whine. Liza pressed James down flatter on the floor under Sam. She crouched and looked back. Someone ran along the deck of the tug.

The current was carrying the raft away from the tug, but another shot struck one of the raft's air chambers. She heard the rush of air, and the tube shrank like a released balloon, throwing everyone sideways into the water.

Liza grabbed James and fought to stay afloat. When she could get her eyes open, she was looking up into a rifle barrel. Behind it a was a very familiar face. She screamed, "No! Ross, *no!*" and dove, pulling James down with her.

Chapter 43

They surfaced three times, pressed to the slimy boards of the tug's hull, as Liza tried desperately to stay hidden below the tires where no one could take aim. All she could tell from James's struggling legs, his death grip on her neck, was that he must have inhaled air the first two times. But the shock of that barely liquid water was going to finish them fast.

She couldn't dive again. James was shuddering in violent spasms against her side. If she gave up, maybe they'd take them on board, not shoot. Her mind could go no further than getting out of that ice water.

Somewhere in the distance there was splashing and shouting. Liza had a fleeting thought of Crow—was he nearby, would he find them? Then a tunnel opened in front of her tightly shut eyes, and she plunged into it.

She was being dragged by the scruff of her neck like a puppy. She struggled to keep her face out of the waves created by the forward motion. Her hands, which had been holding James, groped mindlessly, couldn't find him, searched and searched, hands frantic though her mind was empty. Her head slammed against something hard and she was dragged sideways. After a long, black, drowning time, she was thumping up a hard surface, the sound of running water loud in her ears. Water poured off something that had been fully immersed.

She was on a hard floor, a foot seemed to be jammed into her shoulder, her legs doubled painfully underneath. She nursed the pain, took strange pleasure in it, that pain of being alive. Gradually, the ringing in her ears subsided and she heard the sound of oars, and felt the rhythmic motion of the boards under her as someone rowed across the water. Her hands grew frenzied again, this time distantly connected to her own worst fears. James. Where was he? And Sam. Where was Sam?

Liza reached above her head with one hand to feel the leg attached to the foot jammed in her shoulder. Her other hand felt along the floorboards. Nothing. She cried against those oily floorboards as though her veins were filled with salt water. She had no curiosity about the rower or the destination. She cared nothing any more, for safety or future, if James and Sam were gone.

The rowing stopped, the forward motion slowed smoothly. The foot withdrew from her shoulder, and the skiff rocked as someone stood up in it. There was the sound of a line slithering across a deck, then a hand under Liza's head, forcing her up, pulling and shoving until she had to sit. Her legs were too stiff to use. She dragged herself with her arms, the hand levering her up, up, till she could grasp at the rail above her head. Familiar grip of the rail, cleat where it always was, rubber gloves wedged under the lid of the locker—the stern of the *Salmon Eye*.

The person next to Liza boosted her up till she could get her painfully stiff knees on the deck. Her tears ran uncontrollably, but hands were lifting her again, urging her up and forward into the cabin. Not hands. One hand, one metal hook. Tenney Rushmore, skipper of the *Fighting Chance*.

"James?" Endless salt water poured down her face. "Where's James?"

"Elliot grabbed him, so at least he's not in the water. We'll go after him as soon as I find Crow."

"Sam?"

"The dog? I don't know. Get your clothes off," he ordered. "Get something hot inside—I've got to go back—Crow's still out there."

Crow. She had a sudden memory of the collapsed air tube on the raft, Ross Elliot's face staring down the rifle barrel. Crow couldn't have survived the cold this long. Crow was gone.

Tenney was half-running back through the cabin, slamming out onto the deck. Liza went to the window as the skiff disappeared into the fog. She stared at the gray emptiness, then at the empty cabin. Sam. What had happened to Sam? Was he with James? With Crow? She stared around as though she'd find him under the table or asleep behind the binnacle. Sam? Knowing, denying, her breath came in deep sobs.

Everywhere Liza walked, she left pools—there seemed no end to salt water, inside or out. Her arms and legs were operating in slow motion, her thoughts sluggish and irrational. Somehow she managed to get the stove started to make some tea. While the kettle heated, she took her sopping clothes off, water spurting from cuffs and pockets till the whole cabin floor was awash. She noted dimly that she must have kicked off her boots underwater; one sock was gone, too. Maybe Sam was rescuing her boots.

Shuddering from cold and terror, she tried to stand still in the shower, but anxiety sparked along her nerves, forcing her to keep moving. She rubbed herself with a towel and put on the sweats she'd left on top of her sleeping bag. She got some dry rain gear out of the locker and dug out an old pair of leather work boots—she had to be ready when Tenney came back. They were going to get James. And Sam, please god. Sam would be there. He'd have stayed with James.

Liza went out on deck to try to hear the skiff's progress. The fog had thinned. An invisible sun was working its way through the gloom, and even as she watched, the tug began to show its red stack and white bridge. She went in and got the binoculars. There was no sign of Tenney's skiff. He must have gone around the far side under cover of the remaining fog.

Suddenly Liza caught a movement at the near end of the boom. She focused the glasses where she thought she'd seen motion. A man's head and shoulders appeared. The man pulled himself farther over the log, got one leg up, hitched himself higher, got to his knees, then his feet. For a moment he stayed in a half-crouch, gaining his balance; then he straightened, squared his shoulders and lifted his head. Crow. Like Katlian, the Tlingit warrior, swarming over the rail of the Russian warship two centuries ago, defending his nation with a hammer in his hand. Except Crow had no hammer. No weapon at all, except his pride. That he wore well.

Slowly Crow began inching forward. He leaped to another log and began to move crabwise along it. At the other end of the boom, Ross Elliot appeared and began moving toward him, both men crouched like boxers approaching the center of the ring.

Far away, Liza heard the thud of a helicopter's rotors. As she watched, the helicopter came in until it was almost overhead. Afraid to take her eyes off the two men, Liza finally looked up when the helicopter was so close its downdraft was churning the sea into a fountain around the *Salmon Eye*.

From the underside of the helicopter, a totem pole dangled. As Liza cowered, the pole descended over her head, narrowly missing the cabin top of the *Salmon Eye*. The pole was plain and smoothly polished to a crossbar. On the bar, a gleaming animal, long and narrow, arched its back, carrying in its jaws a small black bird that struggled to escape, its tongue protruding and claws bent back. Crow's ridicule pole.

The pole was fastened by log chokers and hung from the helicopter in a bridle of steel cable. Ross Elliot was waiting out there to unfasten the chokers.

She forced herself to look directly at the helicopter hovering above the boom. Was it one of Tom's? When it turns, will you see the green and orange logo of Morrison Timber Management, Liza? This is why Tom was so angry about your setting out again. He thought he could grab James right off the boat in Wrangell. And that day in the bar, he must have been talking to Ross on the phone, telling him, "James is at Tasha's—get him."

Slowly the helicopter positioned the pole above the log boom. Crow hunkered down in the fierce downdraft. The pole descended. Crow, from his crouch, launched himself upward. Grasping the crossbar, he floated above the logs like Raven fleeing with the box of Daylight.

The door of the helicopter opened, and a man's hand appeared, holding a pistol. Liza screamed, "Crow, Crow, look out," but the deafening noise of the rotors drowned all other sound. Trying to get a bead on Crow, the pilot leaned forward. She could see his other hand on the control stick. She kept shouting Crow's name as the pilot took aim.

The helicopter swerved—it had no logo and now she could see the pilot's face. It wasn't Tom.

The helicopter was still moving forward. The pilot's hand jerked suddenly, and he fell backward into the cockpit so Liza could no longer see him. He must have fired—she just couldn't hear it in all the noise. But he'd missed—the pole swung forward, still carrying Crow.

The marten dipped sharply, unbalanced by the added weight, and Ross was swept from the log boom into the sea. As the helicopter crossed the stern of the tug, Crow's end of the beam caught under the towing cable. Crow dropped off and disappeared.

With the pole caught like a sea anchor, the helicopter came to the end of its leash, nosed over, and slammed down, barely missing the tug. For an instant it churned on the surface. Through the binoculars, Liza had one last glimpse of the pilot, slumped motionless over the controls. Why wasn't he trying to get out?

Climb out, she willed, climb out. Maybe she shouted. But the helicopter filled in a rush of rotor-driven sea. In another moment, the surface of the water was calm.

It seemed an eternity before Liza could drag herself away from the rail. Her legs were full of lead, her brain switched off. Think. Think. They've got James...Crow's out there in the water...goddammit, Liza, *move*.

As she stepped out on deck to release the anchor brake, she heard the sound of an outboard very close. She looked over the side and saw a steep wake veed out behind the *Salmon Eye*. The sound of the outboard dropped abruptly and there was a thump against the planks.

Shoving the brake down again, she headed toward the stern, then stopped in her tracks. What a stupid move. They were coming after her. Get the Ruger. She swung around. No. She'd already discovered the rifle was gone. Paul Howard must have taken it. To check the bullet markings. "Gotta consider you a suspect." She turned back and James appeared, levitating over the stern rail.

She was hallucinating. She wanted him to be there so much she'd conjured him out of the sea. But he was walking toward her now, his eyes wide and fixed, his hands slowly reaching out to her. And behind him, smiling above the rail, was a wonderfully familiar face. Her knees turned to water and she sagged against the rail in relief.

Chapter 44

Paul watched the radar as Jake turned up past Point Barrie. The screen was cluttered with boats—at least three showing, plus markers on a tow, probably a log boom.

All the way across, they'd watched the boat they took to be the *Salmon Eye*. She wasn't moving anymore—she must be anchored there south of the passage that went between the islands. The boat east of the island, ahead of the boom, must be a tug, the boom in tow. Trouble Island was just long enough to conceal both.

The other boat, lying southwest of the island, was likely the boat that had jogged along just ahead of them after leaving Totem Bay. Who was that? Shit. This all looked like big trouble.

"Trouble at Trouble Island," he muttered to Jake, pointing at the cluster of boats ahead of them.

"So damn thick out here we could run 'em down if anybody's shuttlin' around. Wouldn't even pick up a skiff in this mess."

"I'm gonna get some backup. The kid must be on that tug—probably the tug that fired on the *Salmon Eye* in Stikine Strait. I hope she hasn't tried to take them on single-handed. She's got no sense—that woman was born to trouble, I can tell you."

He radioed the Manley marine operator and gave her the Wrangell Police Department number. But by the time Darnell came on, Paul had thought it over. "Forget it, this isn't even close to our jurisdiction—get the state office in Petersburg—get some uniforms out here right now."

"*Roger, Lieutenant—gimme your position again.*"

Paul repeated the coordinates and hung up. Jake was making a slow, tight circle with the *Aquila*. Paul could see a dark shape through the fog. Faint light was breaking through. He went out on deck and strained to see.

Slowly the outline of the *Salmon Eye* emerged from the fog, her crane like a giant standing on one leg. She had no lights. Paul ducked into the wheelhouse and grabbed the binoculars that hung above the chart table. He could see no movement aboard. Now they'd located her, he was reluctant to try to board. He'd only put Lizzie in more danger if they were spotted from the tug.

He went in again and told Jake to head around the west side of the island. There was a ridge on the island and it was heavily wooded. No one could see them if they were on the west side of it. "I'm gonna stay on deck," he said. "Keep off the island, but I want to get far enough up to get a look at that tug. Fog's lifting."

Jake pointed ahead. "Old double-ender anchored ahead of us. Wanna take a look?"

"Don't know who it is—better not spook him—keep clear for now."

From the deck, Paul could make out the name, *Fighting Chance*, in worn paint on the bow. Not a boat he knew. He couldn't see anyone aboard.

Now he caught the sound of a helicopter's rotors snapping along in the distance. Too soon for the uniforms. He stuck his head in and said, "Push her up a little—there's a 'copter headed this way—I wanna see that tug first." He slammed the door.

They were heading straight into something bad. He'd sworn to himself not to get Jake into anything really dangerous—they'd set out only to locate the *Salmon Eye*—now here they were going right in on armed men, assuming they were the ones who'd chased after Lizzie.

He opened the door again. "Jake, turn around. We gotta wait for backup. Rookie stuff to go in there by ourselves."

"Just lookin', just lookin'. We ain't gonna do nothin'. You already set the troopers loose. Not that they're any use. Lemme tell you about the time..."

"Listen, you got a weapon on here?"

".30-06 over the bunk. Couple boxes 'a soft-points in the drawer underneath."

"I'll load her up. I got a revolver but nothing with range. And you head out. They got some real heavy artillery over there."

"Yeah, yeah. I'm just takin' a look."

Paul plunged down the ladder and took the .30-06 off the rack, grabbed a box of cartridges, and climbed back on deck to load it. He could hear the 'copter very low now on the other side of the island. The rotor noise made his face draw tight trying to defend his eardrums. He finished loading the rifle and dropped the box of cartridges in his pocket. Then he checked his revolver.

Jake was starting the turn north of the island. Goddammit, he'd told him to head out. The tug was right there—Paul could see the whole length of it now—even the towing cable rising over the stern. The name on it was the *Albert M. Thomas*. As the *Aquila* turned across the north end of the island, he could see the log boom with two men standing on it. Over them hovered a white 'copter. Dangling from it was a totem pole with a long crossbeam—an animal, a weasel-like animal, on it.

He flung the door open. "Shit—don't go any farther," he shouted at Jake, afraid his words were lost in the tremendous noise of the rotors, but Jake nodded and pulled the throttle back till the boat stopped her forward motion.

Paul pressed his back to the side of the wheelhouse and watched. So this was how they did it. Lined up those petroglyphs at Steamer Bay the same way. Not a landing craft with a crane. A helicopter.

Suddenly the man at the far end of the logs leaped for the pole's crossbeam and hung there, trying to pull himself over the end of it. Paul stared through the glasses at the swinging pole with the man clinging to it. Black hair, face jammed against the beam so Paul couldn't make it out. The other man was much closer, at the near end of the logs, but had his back to Paul.

The helicopter dipped and the pilot's door opened. A hand appeared holding a gun—small, a pistol. The pilot was trying to get a bead on the man on the beam. Paul grabbed the rifle and sighted through it. The man on the beam raised his head.

Crow. Paul knew him instantly. Maybe he could spoil the pilot's aim. But what the hell was Crow doing?

He squinted through the sight. The helicopter had turned again, the open door directly opposite the *Aquila*'s deck. Turn, turn, goddammit. He didn't want to kill the guy. But the pistol was aimed straight down at Crow now. Hit the arm and not the chest? He could see the fingers moving on the gun—there was no more time—Paul pulled the trigger.

In a succession of slow-motion frames, the pilot slumped, the man on the boom was knocked off into the water, Crow fell from the pole, and the helicopter went down in a volcanic roar. Then nothing. Just nothing at all.

Paul stared at the vacant scene. Little by little, his numbed mind admitted the destruction. Then Jake was there next to him.

"We gotta pick those guys up," Jake said. "Come on. That was one hell of a shot, fella." He was unlashing the inflatable and winching it to the water before Paul could even get his muscles back in gear.

"No. My god, we can't just head over there. There's gotta be somebody left on that tug. They'll pick us off like a coupl'a geese."

"Those guys are in the water, man—they're cold." Jake was in the raft already, jamming oars in the oarlocks. "You comin'?"

Paul let himself heavily over the side, shuffling till his feet found the floorboards, while Jake steadied the raft with one hand on the *Aquila*'s stern.

"Head south and stay up close to the east shore of the island till we can get a look," Paul said, trying to adjust himself on the narrow board seat. He laid the rifle along the bottom of the pontoon, the barrel under Jake's feet so the grip was at Paul's fingertips. "Sheesh," he muttered. "This is not a great plan. We're just gonna be more floating meat any second."

Jake gave him a sour grin. "Yo," he said.

Jake pulled the raft along the east edge of Trouble Island, so close that at times the bottom scraped gravel. Kelp snaked off the rocks around them and Jake shoved his way through it using an oar as a battering ram. Way in the distance, drifting in and out of the fog, the *Salmon Eye* swung on her anchor. The raft moved forward quietly—the whole scene was ominously quiet to Paul's way of thinking.

They hugged the island, no more than a hundred yards off the port side of the tug. Then they were past the tug, paralleling the towing cable which dipped off the stern into the water. As they got closer to the log boom, Paul could see something floating on the surface above the submerged tow line. Something black. Black...and copper.

A metal skiff rounded the south end of the island, a man rowing. The man looked over his shoulder at them, then pulled harder. Through the glasses, Paul could see that the man had some odd metal device locked into one oar. The man looked over his shoulder again. Then he shipped his oars and turned toward Paul and Jake. With his free arm, he gestured to them to hurry.

An outboard started up and a skiff shot out from the starboard side of the tug, gathering speed till its bow was planing above the water as it passed the far side of the log boom, the person at the controls leaning forward to cover something on the floor. The black and copper object bobbed up and down in the wake.

Chapter 45

Larry stood in front of Liza, James between them. She reached out and pulled James forward, pressing his face against her.

"Thank god it's you." Her laughter burst out, painful as she gasped for air. Explanations for Larry's presence, for James's presence, were only scrambled circuits in her mind, nothing she could begin to pick apart. "So that's where it went," she said, gesturing at the gun in Larry's hand.

"You were wondering about it?" he asked. "My little Browning automatic? I never leave home without it. But you don't like guns, anyway, so you wouldn't have used it, would you? Although someone did make a rather remarkable shot from this boat recently. But it couldn't have been you. I know how you feel about firearms."

"How do you know about that shot?" Something stabbed at her mind—not fact, nothing like Truth written on a stone tablet, just some shadow of a truth long ago dismissed.

She could feel James shuddering against her. The way they were standing, Larry's gun was aimed straight at James's back. She wrenched James's hands free and pushed him behind her. The gun never quivered. Now it was aimed straight at her heart.

Her arms were heavy from holding onto James behind her. "What," she said. "What."

Larry's eyes narrowed. Pale eyes, water on a cloudy day— there had always been a peculiar absence of color in his eyes, she realized—they reflected his surroundings rather than suggesting a life behind them.

"We're going to No Name Bay," he said. "This young man knows how to find something very, very valuable near No Name Bay. We'll go over in the *Salmon Eye* and take my skiff ashore. Now. As in pronto."

He reached over and took Liza's shoulder, spinning her around and pushing her along the deck. She stumbled over James, held him as he tripped, then pressed him ahead of her. Her mind screamed questions—who was this man who'd held her in his arms, made love to her, asked her to marry him? She shuddered, trying not to scream out loud. Concentrate. Keep between the gun and James. Don't panic. Not yet.

They moved to the foredeck and Larry stood behind her while she released the brake and started the windlass. In the wheelhouse, he shoved Liza onto the captain's chair and stood James at Liza's back, holding the gun at James's head. When he pointed, she put the engine in gear.

"Past Conclusion Island," he said. "Middle of the entrance to No Name Bay is clear. Head straight in."

She pushed the throttle up slightly and the *Salmon Eye* moved forward slowly. Thoughts reeled through her head, disjointed flashes of memory—the odd sexual chemistry between them but no awakening emotion—something shallow she'd sensed— there was no tenderness, that was it. Efren had offered tenderness, gentleness, peace. This man had given her nothing but sexual exercise. Thank god she'd had nothing to give back.

But she had. She had given him James. She'd told him where James was the very day James was kidnapped. Could that have been only yesterday?

"I told you where James was, didn't I? And you went there and took him. And there never were any Japanese, were there? I mentioned them to Tom and he looked totally puzzled. What were you doing, Larry?"

"Getting rich. You turned down your chance to marry a rich man. Now you can have all that solitude you insist is best. But richer's better. Money's the standard."

"That's bullshit. Money's no standard—and even if it was, there are honest ways..."

She suddenly realized she might have been married to this man by now—might have said yes to his invitation. Hate tore through her veins. "You never intended to marry me, did you? I was going to be your moll—that was it, wasn't it?" Only the gun at James's head kept her from attack.

"There were two ways of keeping you out of my way, my dear. One much more appealing than the other. Unfortunately, you kept intruding on private business."

Why, why had she been so stubborn about getting the police? She should never have let Crow persuade her. "Crow?" she said, remembering.

"Crow's still swimming."

"He's not," she shouted, swinging on him. "He couldn't be. No one lasts in water this cold."

"Don't get excited," Larry said, raising the automatic to her face.

She stared at him in horror. "You murdered the man at the Institute, didn't you? And Goran. Now Crow." Icy rivulets shuddered down her spine.

"And more to come if you don't shut up. Look where you're going, skipper. We're getting too close to that boat."

She turned and looked forward. Dead ahead of her, the *Fighting Chance* swung on her anchor. Where was Tenney? He'd gone to look for Crow long ago—hours ago it must be—a lifetime as far as she was concerned. And certainly a lifetime for Crow. She pulled sharply to port and stared at the little fishing boat as they went by. The *Fighting Chance* rolled in the wake of the *Salmon Eye*, but no one came out on deck.

"I know this boat," Larry said. "We can make ten knots easy."

She shoved the throttle up. What difference did it make, anyway? No help was coming. "Not get to the end because of difficulties," she'd radioed to Mink and Tango. Trouble and Conclusion Islands. If they'd figured that out, at least they knew where she was.

"You've always thought the world owed you, haven't you?" she said.

"Dumpsters, remember? Benches in bus stations? Dog food for dinner?" Larry was raised by a psychotic mother who slept in bus stations and fed him out of Dumpsters. He seemed unable to get dog food out of his mind.

"So you grew up poor. But you got an education. The taxpayers paid for that, didn't they?"

"Well now, ma'am, I actually deserved it. I'm so smart I earned a free ride."

"So you're smart. You can work for a living." Her fists were clenched on top of the wheel, her fingernails digging into her palms.

"But work's not the standard. Money is. I learned that in my orange-crate bassinet. And thanks to our young friend here, we're all going to have money."

"I'm not your friend," James said. Liza could hear the tears in his voice. She could also hear, far off, the beat of another helicopter.

Larry leaned back against the windows, never lowering the gun, but twisting his head sideways to look out. He watched a moment, then moved forward and leaned across Liza's shoulder, shoving the throttle all the way up. "Gotta hurry, skipper," he said, as the packer shuddered from the force of water on the bow. He flipped the radio on and switched it to Channel 22.

"...medevac procedure—injured on board—one missing..."

"Clear to pick up from deck forward of..."

Heavy static buzzed. Larry reached up and flipped off the radio switch.

That voice. Liza knew that voice—she'd heard it recently. Tenney Rushmore. Tenney was on the tug. Was it Crow he was airlifting? Or Ross? Both? One missing. Must be the helicopter pilot. Crow, she thought, hang on. Hang on. Please.

How could she tell the helicopter she needed help? From the corner of her eye she could see Larry leaning an elbow on the door, the gun drifting between James, who was still jammed against her back, and her own head.

She could make a grab for the transmitter, but that would be suicidal. Could she do something to disable the engine? She stared at the panel of switches—battery, starter, lights—could she switch the lights on and off—try to signal? She tested his observation by dropping one hand from the wheel.

"Don't even think of touching that panel," Larry said, glancing out the window again. "Anyway, they've gone."

She could hear the helicopter noise dying away in the distance. Liza turned and looked full at Larry. "What do you want from us?"

Larry smiled and lifted the gun. "James here knows all about it."

Chapter 46

"I don't know," James said. "I don't exactly remember."

They were standing on the flat by where the creek came out in No Name Bay. The man—Larry, Liza called him—still had that gun in his hand, pointed at Liza. James hadn't seen Larry through the window of the boat that came when Goran got thrown away in the water. Maybe he was hiding. Two men he saw through the window. The man with the beard came over to the deck of the *Sarah Moon*. A horrible beard with a white worm running through it. At the Velvet Moose he'd seen the man with no beard but not this man. Not Larry.

The sun had come out and most of the fog was gone away. Only some little clouds way up there on the mountains where he thought was Listening Stone.

"I don't know where it is," he said again. "I don't remember."

"Listen, James," the man said. "You're a very smart boy. And your uncle thinks you're going to be a very great Chief. That's why he told you everything. I know you want to get back home and see him again. So all you have to..."

"Don't listen to him, James," Liza said. "He's lying. You know what happened to Goran."

The man reached across James's head and pulled Liza's arm up high behind her back, too high because she made a noise like it hurt.

"Don't," James said. "That hurts her."

"She has some lessons to learn, James. You tell me what Goran told you, and she won't get hurt anymore."

"Don't say a word," Liza said, and the man yanked her arm harder.

"All I remember," James said, "is about an ear carved on a rock. It's up high in the mountains some place. And you can only see it from where…" He stopped. He'd promised not to tell, but the man was going to hurt Liza again if he didn't.

"Go on."

"From where the white birds fly up and where ravens wait for the salmon to come back."

"From right here, in other words, this creek running into No Name Bay. I know it's close to No Name. The gulls fly up that cliff over there, and the ravens sit here on the flat."

"Well, we didn't actually see it. So I don't know if this would be the right place."

"But your uncle tried to show you where it was, didn't he?"

"Well, you can only see it the first day of spring. When day and night are the same is when the sun shines on the stone. When the sun comes up in the morning is the only time. It's only that one day. Not any time else."

"You're not answering my question, little man." Larry was looking at him with those eyes that looked like little wet stones. "Your uncle tried to show you where it is. You know he did. He pointed at it, at least. Now show me where he pointed."

"Don't tell him, James." Liza tried to jerk away, but the man hit her neck with the side of his hand and she kept trying to get her breath like she was running.

"It was raining," James said. "We couldn't see it."

"But he pointed. He said, 'Right up there—right where the…what? Right where the bare rock begins above the trees?'"

"It's up on that mountain," James said, pointing at the closest one. "But we probably can't get there. Only Chiefs know how to get there. Chiefs are the only people that know where the trail is. And anyway, there isn't anything there, just only an ear carved on a rock from when people thought everything was alive—like the wind could speak and rocks could see and hear."

"The most valuable stone in Alaska, James. You know what's buried there, too, and we're going up to get it. Right now. We have the whole day to go up. And the trip down will be easy."

The man let go of Liza's arm and gave her a push. Liza turned her head around to look at James. She looked very mad. Then the man shoved James at Liza so she had to start walking. The man, Larry, was right behind James and James could hear him breathing and once he felt the gun poke in his back.

"Follow the creek," the man said. "There's bound to be a trail up the ravine."

Liza walked pretty slow and James stayed right behind her. Sometimes he reached out his hand so he could touch her arm so she could tell he was still there.

This wasn't the way. He knew this wasn't the right way, but he wasn't saying. It wasn't on the close mountain, it was on the far back mountain with the clouds on top of it. There was a trail by the creek, and they'd walk and walk and climb high, high up. But it wasn't the right way to get to Listening Stone.

Chapter 47

She forced her mind to stay blank. As on her trip in the raft with Crow through the fog, she would concentrate on sound, on the small details of her surroundings. Behind her she could hear James's quick, shallow breathing. He wasn't yet breathing through his mouth even though the narrow trail was climbing steeply. His boots clumped and he tripped often—she'd noticed that he was wearing men's fishing boots again, as huge on him as her old ones he'd worn to Tasha's.

Tasha. Try not to think about her either. What would Tasha do when she heard about Ross? Don't think about it. Larry 's crazy. You only thought you knew him. You didn't know he was crazy, did you, Liza?

She felt as though her skin had become too tight, as though she were trapped inside it, suffocating in her own body—rising panic made her clutch at her throat. Calm down. You have to get through this for James. There's no one else to save him. Keep the panic for the last desperate move. Soon enough. It will happen—the last-ditch stand—it's going to happen.

Her head was an echoing vault. Her mother wasn't talking to her anymore. She hadn't heard that voice since she'd left the dock with Crow—since her mother had told her, *"You need help, Elizabeth."* She hadn't gotten help, so her mother had abandoned her. Like you did once before, Mother. You *died.*

She tried to listen to the water. Water singing over rock, rocks that split the creek into white slices. Ahead of their little parade, a winter wren burred a warning in the undergrowth. A dozen crows swept a noisy path through the alder along the bank. Gradually the sides grew steeper; water plummeted in a hundred-foot fall and the trail clung to the edge of a bluff the water had sheared.

The trail turned away from the gorge and plunged into dense forest, daylight all but cut out. This part of Kuiu Island was covered in old-growth forest that had somehow escaped both economics and politics. So far, at least.

Here and there a shaft of sun pointed at the first budding of red huckleberry branches and lethal-looking thorns on the devil's club. Liza's feet caught in the tangle of salal and kinni-kinnick that crisscrossed the soft layers of rotted leaves. James fell repeatedly, his breath coming now in sharp gasps. The third time he fell, Liza stopped walking.

"He's too little to hike this far."

"He's a Chief, dear. He can do it. Anyway, I think he might have done it before. Haven't you, James?"

"I didn't go so high as this. This is pretty long of a climb."

"All right, we'll take a little breather. Five minutes." Larry extended his arm and pointed to his watch.

Liza slipped down next to James and put her arm around him. It was like holding a bundle of violin strings, taut, resonating to some internal vibration. He didn't lean against her but stared off into the trees. There was nothing to say to him and she was afraid she might start to scream if she opened her mouth.

Larry, who stood a few feet from them, tapped his watch and said, "Time's up. Sooner up, the sooner we can all take it easy."

James stood up immediately. Liza used her arms to push herself up, hearing her knees crack as she finally got to her feet. She started along the trail, looking over her shoulder to see that James was close. Somebody had put him in sweats and a T-shirt that hung to his knees, and a man's black parka. Larry followed about ten feet back, a safe distance to avoid stumbling over either of them if they fell.

The trail, here nothing more than a deer track through dense undergrowth, zigzagged over their heads. As they climbed higher, at times scrambling on hands and knees, hauling themselves over ancient roots and decaying trunks, the undergrowth thinned and the trees above the trail were smaller, bent to the fierce music of winter winds.

The trail had short flat sections, a sharp angle before the next rising section, another twist, another flat one, like an ascending series of Zs. They must be several hundred feet up, now. The horizon through the treetops included the whole of No Name Bay, Conclusion Island, and a great sweep of Sumner Strait to the southeast. A few tiny boats were specks of dust on the blue surface.

The mountain dropped away below the narrow deer track in almost vertical slopes. The tops of old-growth spruce and hemlock were level with the edge of the trail now, and as they doubled back, Liza could see the line they had followed, winding through the base of the huge trunks, like risers on a flight of stairs. She could hear James's breath whistle as he exhaled. She was panting too, struggling to find handholds and a place to jam her feet into the earth at the corners before the tiny path leveled again.

She began to wonder if she could leap down on Larry and knock the gun from his hand. He was staying well back to avoid tripping over James—James slipped at the turns and had to make several attempts before he could scramble up to the next part of the trail. She could launch herself off the higher bank straight at Larry and knock that gun away.

She'd have to do it soon—she could see rocky outcroppings and alpine meadow above them, now. The trail would level out there and cross the meadow before the mountain became a rock face. A rock face? Where the carved ear was? What was there that could be worth taking such risks?

At the next turn, she tensed her body and launched herself from the edge of the bank, slamming into Larry before hitting the ground with a thud. For a second they grappled at the edge, the Browning automatic gyrating over their heads. But he never lost his grip on it. She couldn't break it loose.

Somehow he recovered his balance. He brushed himself off with one hand. "Clumsy," he said. "Not very subtle." He aimed a boot at her ribs, then reached up and hauled James down from the rocky bank.

Liza lay on her face, the mountain dropping steeply below her, treetops at eye level. "I can't go any farther," she muttered into the ground.

"Your choice, dear. Entirely up to you," Larry said, pressing the gun to her ear.

Chapter 48

Paul Howard watched from the deck of the tug as the last basket stretcher was hauled into the helicopter. Even before the hold closed, the 'copter rose and swung east. They'd hurry, but for one aboard, it wouldn't be fast enough.

Jake had already headed back to the *Aquila*—he would come alongside, pick Paul up, they'd try to find the others—the *Salmon Eye*, the *Fighting Chance*—somebody had James. At least, James wasn't on the tug—they'd searched it thoroughly.

Paul walked around the deck, staring out across the water, hoping he hadn't overlooked the boy anywhere, hadn't missed him in that kelp over there, hadn't imagined a boy to be a log. He remembered that skiff with the big outboard fleeing from the tug, the man hunched over something on the floor—could it have been James he was trying to cover?

Ahead of the tug, the top of the shame pole stuck up at an angle—the lower part submerged by the weight of the helicopter that dangled from it, perhaps sitting on the bottom now, anchoring the pole with the cable. Divers would raise it, find the pilot, see the bullet wound, and he would explain how he had made a split-second decision to save Crow. A cop's decision. He would make the same one again. But live regretting it. Paul Howard of the Wrangell Police Department didn't belong out here. Had he caused death and destruction instead of preventing it? Would he ever know?

The *Aquila* brushed the side of the tug and Jake reached over and caught the tug's rail, holding her steady while Paul climbed aboard, then pushed away and went back to the wheel.

"Where to?" Jake asked, heading south toward the open waters of Sumner Strait.

"Somebody must have the kid," Paul said. "You think that guy with the outboard coulda been covering him?"

"Didn't get a good look," Jake said. "Might, I guess. Sure in a hurry."

"See where he went?"

"Looked like he was heading for the packer, but I wasn't following after we found the fellas in the water."

"I'll try her," Paul said. He unhooked the transmitter and called, "*Salmon Eye, Salmon Eye,* this is Paul Howard, Wrangell Police, aboard *Aquila,* WYP 4577. Do you copy?"

After a minute of silence, he repeated the call. Nothing. "*Aquila,* no contact, clear," he said.

Jake reached in front of Paul and grabbed the binoculars, steadying his elbow on the chart table. "Something way up there past Conclusion Island," he said. "See it? Sun kinda pickin' out windows or poles'r somethin'." He handed Paul the glasses and turned the *Aquila* toward whatever he was seeing. "Little dot here on radar," he said, reaching out to narrow the range setting. "Carrying a radar reflector, looks like."

"Boat up there. Yeah, troller, I think." Paul went out on deck and tried to focus the glasses more precisely. It was definitely a fishing boat, smallish, trolling poles. "Might be Rushmore," he said, stepping inside. "He left the tug in a big hurry—I didn't even notice he was gone for a while—thought he'd hang around till Crow was evacuated. Maybe he saw something."

"Might be following somebody." Jake jammed the throttle up, trying to keep the smaller boat in sight.

"Lost it," he said, a few minutes later. "Went in there behind that point." He fiddled the radar and shook his head. "Must be close to shore in No Name Bay. Mess'a little islands in there plug the head—lotta hiding spots in there."

Paul nodded and rubbed his neck, which was stiffening up again. He sagged onto the seat, trying to force his eyes open, losing the battle too soon.

Then Jake was shaking him, pointing at something. Paul stood up and looked ahead. In a little pocket on the north side of No Name bay, sheltered by a forested point of land and two small knobby islands, the crane on the *Salmon Eye* was visible through the trees.

"Slow down," Paul told Jake. "Try to keep the point between us." He grabbed the 30.06 and went out on deck, crouching behind the rail.

"Ahoy, *Salmon Eye*," he shouted. "Police. We're boarding."

There was no response, not a sound or sign of movement. "*Salmon Eye,*" he shouted again. "Police."

Slowly they edged around the point, Paul keeping the rifle sighted on her foredeck. He shouted the warning once more, then waved for Jake to approach, gesturing to him to stay as low as possible over the wheel. Sliding gently alongside the old packer, they rafted the *Aquila* to her beam. There was no one aboard. Paul hadn't really expected anyone, but they searched her, stem to stern.

"Where the hell are they?" Paul said. He rotated his good shoulder and looked at Jake. "Shit. Too many losses. We're gonna sit this one out. Those uniforms'll be back pretty soon."

"You go ahead and sit," Jake said. "Me, I'm gonna cruise around a little and see what I can see."

"So where we gonna look? They're likely tramping around on shore."

"They had't've got to shore. If the fella with that big outboard boarded the packer, likely they took his skiff. You could get ashore quick with that guy."

Jake was already climbing back on the *Aquila*. Paul wondered what fueled Jake's internal engine. He himself was so tired he had to chew painfully on his tongue to keep his eyes open. He threw the lines off and climbed aboard the *Aquila*, staring back at the *Salmon Eye* as Jake pulled away.

The empty chicken crates were still there, stacked up and lashed to the crane. He could still feel those crates tilting— hear the insane cackling when he'd grabbed at the tarp. Sheesh—he was standing here mumbling like a chicken himself.

He headed for the wheelhouse, looking over the side as Jake pulled up and put the engine in reverse. He could see bottom—

silt, big rocks, weed growing up. This whole string of islands must be connected right below the surface—the passages were very shallow. Maybe they should take the raft. He went in and suggested it to Jake.

"Too slow," Jake said. "We can skirt these babies—you hang out on the bow and kinda keep an eye out. Trouble is, ain't no detail chart 'a this area—the big one don't give no depths this far in."

Paul went back on deck as Jake shoved the gears into forward. He hoped he wouldn't fall asleep again, was all. The *Aquila* inched along the east side of the small wooded knobs, her engine making a deep grumble at the slow speed. Paul could see the bottom still, shadowy, now and then a rock gleaming up. He waved his hand each time rocks were visible, pointing, back, back, keep farther off. He searched the channels beyond the islands, the shore farther in, for any trace of life or some sign of that skiff, but there was nothing but a flock of scoters traveling single file and a pair of bald eagles scowling down at them from a snag.

Past another small island, they came to a narrow channel before a high wooded point. Jake edged around the point till Paul could see into the creek mouth, a long grassy flat exposed at low tide. Lying over on her beam, high and dry in mud and eel grass, was the *Fighting Chance*.

They dropped anchor where they were. Paul insisted on rowing the raft—the pain it caused him kept him awake.

"Tenney musta come straight over here," Jake said, as Paul pulled on the oars.

"He was sure antsy to get off the tug," Paul said. "Made me kinda wonder about him. Left before the medevac—I couldn't figure him."

"Maybe he saw the packer pull out."

"Why didn't he say, then?"

"Maybe wanted us to stay. He was real upset about Crow."

"That's why I thought he'd hang around."

Paul looked over his shoulder at the *Fighting Chance*. Tenney had driven her hard onto the mud flat and the water had gone away and left her. "Must be low slack about now," he said.

"She'll float away on the next high water if he doesn't come back."

"Probably just gone ashore to look. Anyhow, he'll have his anchor out. These guys beach these old tanks all the time— paint the bottom, fix a plank. Throw the anchor out on the beach so when she floats she doesn't go anywhere."

Paul gave an extra pull on the oars and the bow of the raft ground up onto the sand. Jake swung his leg over and held the inflatable in place while Paul climbed out.

The *Fighting Chance* was heeled all the way over on her side, showing the scarred blue paint of her keel. They walked around her, trying to see into her cabin.

"Ahoy," Jake shouted, "anyone aboard? Gone up the creek," he said to Paul. "See that little path over there? Deer track. Maybe he saw something made him go along there."

Paul clomped across the flat, the mud sucking at his boots. In a small notch in the creek bank, hidden in withered grass, was a metal skiff with a big Evinrude on the stern. No doubt the one they'd seen leaving the tug. He stood over it and tried to untangle the puzzle.

The man had come over here when he left the tug. Tenney must have followed him. Lizzie followed too? But where was James? Sunk to the bottom of the sea? He held the thought away from him, but images kept leaking through the spongelike object that was now his brain.

He walked further along the flat. Above the most recent tideline, where the mud was drier, he could see tracks. He crouched over them. Boot prints, more or less the same size— couple different treads. He looked carefully—three different treads, at least—one looked like hunting boots—all going along the bank away from the water.

"Popular spot," he said to Jake. "Crowd's all headed that way." He stood up, groaning as his muscles locked up. "Might as well check it out. Those boots went some place."

They'd hiked less than half a mile when Paul heard a sharp report up the mountain. He stopped and stared back at Jake, then broke into a run, panting as the trail bent steeply up the side of the mountain.

Chapter 49

With Larry's gun at her head, Liza shoved herself to a sitting position. She dangled her legs off the trail edge and rubbed her shoulder, which had smashed the ground first. She stared down through the trees, their trunks soldiering down the mountain, thin ropes of sunlight twisting through them. Hundreds of feet below she glimpsed a flash of color like autumn leaves in the wind. Except this was the first week of spring. She tried to focus on the color but it was gone.

She put her hands on the ground to lever herself up and saw the gleam again. Pushing herself to one side, she got her knees under her. Now the bit of color had moved back to where she'd first seen it, but it seemed a tiny bit closer. By excruciatingly slow degrees, she got to her feet.

Larry held the gun on her while he walked over and lifted James to his feet. Liza tried to look over the trail edge without calling attention to what she was doing. Larry gestured at her to get ahead of James.

She took a step forward and glanced down. Nothing. Nothing. Then again a bronze flash, something moving along the trail behind them. Still far below, but coming up the trail. And all at once she knew. She knew. She stepped ahead of James and began to dig her way up the steep turn.

The trail broke out onto the meadow, a sweeping arc of tiny grasses and microscopic leaves and vines that would color the whole slope magenta and orange in the late spring and summer. Despite the low altitude of the peak—probably not more than a couple thousand feet, Liza thought, and they weren't even halfway up—pockets of snow lay in every depression, and the wind-swept rock above the meadow was etched in snow and ice.

Here above the trees the mountain seemed threatening. Despite the brilliant sun and the hard climb, Liza began to shiver. She looked back at James and pantomimed zipping the enormous men's jacket he wore.

"Stop," Larry ordered, and she halted instantly, grateful for any excuse. Delay, delay.

"James, where is it from here?"

"Well," James said, "I don't exactly know, because of we didn't ever come up here."

"But you saw it from the bay. At least, your uncle pointed at it."

"I think maybe...maybe it's up there," James said, pointing at the south edge of the rock face, a sheer rampart notched in horizontal shelves.

James's voice was thin and terrified. Liza wondered, suddenly, if he might deliberately have misled them. Or was the whole damn thing a hoax to begin with? Something Goran had invented to entertain his nephew? A myth this *creature* had gotten hold of somehow?

"We'd be able to see it from here, wouldn't we? We're close enough, we should be able to see it without the sun on it, right?"

"I...don't know." James's voice shook—Liza thought he might break down, sob, scream, vomit—but suddenly he seemed to get hold of himself. He raised his chin and looked straight at Larry. "It's around the corner," he said. "Around those rocks you can see over there. Where the rocks get straight. I remember now, that's where it is."

Larry looked at him with a little squint. "You wouldn't be lying to me, would you? You know we're going to go over there, walk right out there on that ledge that looks like it goes around the mountain? You want to do that, James? Walk out there on that ledge?"

James's glance flickered over to Liza, then back to Larry. "There's nothing there anyway," he said. "Just only a carving. Somebody made it because they thought the rock would want to hear. A long time ago."

"Yes. A long time ago, indeed. I'll tell you what it is," Larry said. "The oldest object of a lost culture. And it marks a place where all the treasures of that culture are buried."

"It isn't true. There isn't something buried there—you're telling a not-true story."

"Well, we're going to find out, aren't we? We'll find out who's right, eh? You're sure the Listening Stone's right around that corner?"

James shrugged, then nodded, once more flicking his eyes sideways at Liza. Did he hope she had some trick up her sleeve?

"Let's go," Larry said, gesturing forward with the gun.

Crossing the meadow was slow—for one thing, in the clear air, the distance to the rocks was much greater than it appeared, and then the ground was very soft from melted snow; they often had to wade through creeks that tore the thin soil away. Eventually the ground cover petered out and they trudged along a gravelly scree left by some long-vanished glacier.

Grimly, Liza held the bright bronze flash against her fear. Something moving up the trail, last seen before they'd come out onto the meadow. Her mind propelled it forward. That shiny object was still coming up the trail toward them.

Finally they walked out on the ledge. The ledge formed a level traverse across the vertical rocks. It was several feet wide, though there were places where cuts split it open and they had to step across. A scattering of stones had paused in flight and lay on the shelf, treacherous to the foot. Below, a nearly vertical wall dropped a hundred yards to the tree line. Holding her breath and trying not to look down, Liza inched along, feeling James only one step behind her now.

Gravel spattered off the cliff edge some distance behind them. All at once Liza was listening as though her head had put out antennae. Gravel, spitting out from the ledge. She scuffed her boots a little to cover the noise, whistling under her breath.

Now she could hear something else, a wheezing sound like air pumped harshly, a small stone falling off the ledge, something pounding over the gravel, close now, pounding around the chimney in the rock they'd just passed.

She swept her arms over her head and grasped one wrist with her other hand. "Get him," she screamed. "Get him!" Crushing James against the rock wall, she covered him with her body.

A gleaming copper rocket struck Larry in the back and the Browning fired at the sun. Larry careened toward her and she threw her arms out to protect herself from his fall. Her hands found his shoulder and, for a fleeting instant, she knew the cruel magic of his thigh against hers. Then she pushed.

Larry Hayden was airborne. He soared outward, a black silhouette against the sky. His cry was a shock wave to her ears. It stopped abruptly.

The mighty rocket became a whimpering, sobbing heap of legs and ears and foot-long, dripping tongue.

"Sam," James whispered, sinking down beside him. "Sam, Sam, Sam..." his whisper carried off by the sharp wind that hustled up the side of the mountain.

Chapter 50

The sun was already dropping below the ridge when Paul heard someone. Boots on a tree root, nothing loud, but someone coming down the trail. He stopped and waited, then stepped off the narrow trail into the undergrowth. He didn't know who this was, coming down, and he wasn't up for combat duty at the moment.

Jake was miles behind. For all Paul's expanding waist and lack of youth, he did keep up with the program the chief set, and something had kicked in—must be like a marathon runner's second wind or something.

Way through the trees he could see someone now, someone monstrous in height—he must be seeing things—some Bigfoot creature—no bear—a bear wouldn't be walking along on its hind legs like that. Someone behind the towering figure, now. Paul moved a little farther into the shadow, trying to quiet his labored breathing. The apparition vanished where the trail dropped into a ravine. Then a head appeared and the figure grew and grew until it reached its former enormous height. He'd really lost it—mind blown away—shit, what was it?

Now he could see the person, or whatever it was, behind the giant, and beyond that person, something shorter, an animal of some sort. What the hell? And then they were closer and he knew. He stepped back onto the trail and walked toward them. Tenney Rushmore with the kid on his shoulders. Lizzie behind them. And bringing up the rear, that dog.

How come he'd forgotten about the dog? When he and Jake and Tenney came up on the black and copper thing floating by the log boom, it'd turned out that the black thing was Crow and the copper thing was that dog still paddling its feet. They'd dragged them onto the tug's deck, and at some point he'd seen Jake rubbing the dog down with a blanket. But after that he'd been so busy trying to revive Crow and get the injured Ross evacuated he hadn't ever thought about the dog again. How the hell had he gotten over here?

They came face to face in another moment. The late afternoon light barely penetrated the forest and to Paul, their faces seemed to float detached in the darkness. They halted as he blocked the trail. Immediately Sam sank to the ground. Behind Tenney, Lizzie squatted and stroked Sam's head.

"I can take over," Paul said to Tenney, pointing at James, who raised his head to look down at him.

"I'm okay," Tenney said. "Downhill's a lot easier."

"Hard on the knees, though. Sure you don't want me to take him?"

"Nahh, we're fine—I'll get on, though, if you can stay with Liza. The dog's exhausted. Be nice if we could carry him, too, but he won't stand for it—we tried. So we've been taking it slow."

"The dog come over here with you?"

"Yeah. I just happened to see the guy go out there to the packer so I took the skiff and the dog and went after him. When the packer took off, I figured to follow, but they were outa sight by the time I got to the *Chance*. After I beached her, I brought the dog ashore because I thought he might be able to track them down. And he sure as hell did. Some dog, that one." Tenney turned around and looked at Sam lying on the trail.

"Sure he did," James said. "He even saved us of having to climb way to the top of the mountain, didn't he, Liza?"

She nodded and stood up. "He did," she said, looking up at James and trying to smile. Paul wondered if the strain could kill her—the bones in her face looked like knife blades, her eyes invisible. She seemed to be disappearing as he watched.

The dog, too. It was the world turning dark, though, the sun only a memory in an orange sky.

"Catch you at the bottom," Tenney said, and took off down the trail, James hunched on his shoulders.

Paul squatted next to Sam. The dog's coat was mud streaked and the old bullet wound in his leg was raw and messy looking. His tongue drooped from his mouth and he panted rapidly. Paul rubbed his ear and Sam's tail thumped.

"You're gonna be okay," Paul said. "We're gonna take it slow and easy and you're gonna make it fine." He stood up and faced Lizzie. "How come you didn't holler out by radio last night?" he said. "We were after you all the way from Wrangell."

"I didn't know that. Mink said something about ten cops—must have meant Tenney and cops. But Crow said, 'no cops—those guys'll kill the kid'."

"Couldn't figure what the hell you were doing."

"Me either." Something shone like rain on her shadowed face and she raised one hand and rubbed her eyes. "Lieutenant..."

"Paul."

"Paul, I don't think I can tell you about it. I mean, not right now. I...a man died. I mean, I'm sure he's dead...I didn't see him afterwards, but I think...I killed him." She reached out and gripped his arm and now he could see the light reflect in her eyes. "You have to go and look. I have to know."

Her fingers were digging into his arm, painfully gouging his bruises, and he moved involuntarily. Instantly she dropped her hand. "God, I'm so sorry. I hurt you—I didn't mean—I'm crazy, I'm crazy—it was so awful, mindless fear—I was a parent—I never understood about being a parent...you put your kid out there and you can't protect him—can't save him..."

She took another gasping breath and said, "No. Sorry. I can wait to do this—no need to crack up here. Let's go." She bent and laid her hand on the dog's neck. "Come on, Sam. Up and at 'em. Food, Sam. Dinnertime."

The dog got his hind legs under him, then pushed himself upright. He started forward, tail wagging. Paul saw that he hobbled, barely using his right front leg. "You check that leg?" Paul asked. "Maybe something caught in his paw?"

"I looked at it. The foot looks all right. I think he twisted his shoulder when he crashed on the rocks after he knocked Larry down."

Larry. Paul walked on, following Lizzie. He dug the penlight out of his jacket—so dark in here now you couldn't see where the track was. He aimed it just ahead of Lizzie's feet. Sam seemed to find his way forward on his own—in fact the dog was setting a pretty good pace for three legs. Larry, Larry, was that the guy who'd left the tug? "You said, 'Larry,'—'the dog knocked him down.' He that guy from the tug?"

Ahead of him, Lizzie raised her hands to her neck and tipped her head back. Paul wondered if she had a terrible headache— he got them—he'd grip his neck like that. If you pressed in just the right spot, for one second the pain let up till it managed to squeeze under your fingers. "Never mind," he told her. "Forget it. Plenty of time to hear about it later."

She turned on him. "Larry Hayden," she said.

He couldn't see her face at all.

"It was Larry Hayden," she shouted.

He raised the flashlight to shine on the trees beside her so it would cast a little light on her face. "Hayden? The guy that runs the charter business? That owned the *Salmon Eye?* But I thought..."

"Yes. So did I. Something happened, though. He was some kind of crazy. And a lot of people are dead because Larry Hayden believed he was a victim."

Paul thought of Crow. "...not a victim," Lizzie had told him way back there in his office, eons ago. "Crow didn't make it," he said, wanting the words back the instant he'd spoken.

He saw Lizzie raise fists to cover her mouth. Then she was on him, pounding him with those fists, shouting, "No no no no."

He grasped her arms and held her away till the rage ran out of her, then clumsily put his arms around her while she sobbed against his shoulder. "I'm sorry, I'm sorry," he said over and over, truly sorry about Crow, truly sorry he'd told her when she was on the verge of collapse.

He held her, rubbing his face against her hair. For a moment her face was pressed against his neck and he thought he heard her saying, "Paul," over and over.

Finally she pulled away. "Crow was a hero, Paul Howard," she muttered, wiping her face with her sleeve. "He proved his point." She turned back down the trail, tripping over Sam, who had thrown himself flat to wait for them.

Paul followed her, flashing the light at her feet again. What point did Crow prove, he wondered, not wanting to ask her, not wanting to quarrel with this woman anymore, with this tough, gentle, angry woman who, for one heart-wrenching moment, had fit like a piece of jigsaw puzzle in his arms.

Chapter 51

Liza stumbled out onto the tide flat ahead of Paul, shielding her eyes from the setting sun. Exhaustion was like a fever. She was having fever dreams: crying voices, someone moving away from her, too far to reach. Her arms moved restlessly. She tripped over stones and Paul caught her arm to steady her.

James and Tenney were all the way across near the bow of the *Fighting Chance*, which was almost floating now. To her amazement, she saw Jake.

"What's he doing here?" she asked Paul.

"Brought me over here. He was coming in at Shoemaker when I got down there to look for your boat."

Jake had waded out and was dragging the raft toward the flat. He waved when he saw them, looped the raft's bow line around a piece of driftwood, and clomped toward them, his boots sinking into the muck at every step.

"You okay, Skipper?" he called.

She didn't have enough energy to shout back, just nodded. She was shivering now; shock and fatigue were taking their toll. She would not think about Larry—*must* not...Later...it would all have to come later, a bomb waiting to go off in her head.

Paul still held her arm and she had a sudden urge to sink against him and bury her face. Instead, she forced herself to step away. "I'll take James home," she said. "I want to meet his grandmother. I'll take Larry's skiff."

"Yours now," Paul said. His voice still seemed very close to her ear. "To replace your raft."

"I don't want it. I never want anything he left behind."

"Not even the *Salmon Eye*?"

"He didn't leave it—I bought it. I've been making payments to him for two years now." She laughed without amusement. "Adding to his bankroll."

"Maybe you could leave the skiff for James and his family. Jake and I could pick you up."

"It's an idea. I just don't know. What I'd really like to do is sink it to the bottom of the sea. I'll ask James, though. Maybe he and his grandmother could use it to go fishing."

Coming up to stand squarely in front of Liza, Jake extended his hand. When she put hers in it, he shook it vigorously. "Did it, didn' cha? Saved the kid. Knew you would. Paul here, he wasn't sure, but I knew you'd do it."

She glanced over her shoulder at Paul. His hand was on her arm again. He turned his head away, his expression sheepish.

"Just didn't want to make a rookie error," he said. "Couldn't figure out what was going on after the boy disappeared and you went off on the boat."

"Told you she's okay," Jake said. "She's a winner, ain't she?"

Paul was looking straight at her now, his dark eyes squinted, shadowed under heavy lids. She thought suddenly how she'd imagined his eyes were like Efren's, round and black, but no, they were nothing like that. She couldn't see Efren's eyes at all anymore, only the sadness and longing in those before her. She stood there, frozen in space and time while they stared at each other. When she finally forced herself to turn away, she found that Jake had stumped off toward the *Fighting Chance* to join the others.

She wanted to leave Sam with the men while she took James home, but Sam was already in the skiff. She urged him out, noticing how his legs quivered as he sat on the seat next to James. He needed food, rest—he must be on the edge of collapse. But Sam knew his rights—salvage rights he had, and nothing would dislodge him from James's side. James pushed him down on the seat and Sam lay heavily across his lap. Liza gave up and yanked the cord on the Evinrude. It grumbled, but didn't start.

Her arm was too weary to pull again. Paul came over and started the engine for her.

"You're too tired," he said. "I'll go with you."

"I'd like to do this myself," she said. "You follow in an hour. I need some time alone with James's grandmother. She's lost her son."

She watched him till he was forced to meet her eyes. "And so have you. I know about Joe. But Joe's alive. He'll come back someday."

Paul reached for her and reeled her in. "He will," he said. "I know it."

Chapter 52

It was still a little bit light up on the mountains and James could see the rocks on top, way up above where they'd been walking. He hugged his arm tighter around Sam's neck and Sam pushed him with his nose so he'd rub his ears some more. Liza was driving the skiff very slow because of it being dark in between the islands.

The policeman said he'd take James home but Liza said no, she wanted to do it because of wanting to meet James's grandma. And she said James would show her where to go, so he was pointing when they had to go around this island or a different one.

They were going in the skiff with the big outboard that man Larry owned. The policeman said he'd pick Liza up and that way she could leave the skiff for James and his grandma. James didn't know for sure if he wanted it because it would make him think about that man. But it was a very, very fast skiff—Emerson would be pretty mad that James had such a fast boat.

James would a lot rather have Sam. But Liza said she'd come back and bring one of Simi's puppies. That will be pretty good, even though not as good as Sam. He'd rather have a boy dog, but a girl dog could be all right, actually.

He looked over Sam's head at the mountains again. Someplace up there was Listening Stone. "Where White Bird flies up and Raven waits for Salmon, high above is Listening Stone," Goran said. "First People carved the rock so the rock could hear. Every Chief must tell Listening Stone the story of what he treasures most. Then the Chief returns his treasure to Earth. But the story belongs to Listening Stone."

That man Larry told a story about a treasure that wasn't his, so the story couldn't be his, either. James told a story, too, about where was Listening Stone. To save it. So now it's James's story. No one else will ever be allowed to tell that story—it belongs to him.

Sam pushed his nose under his hand and James rubbed harder. He looked over his shoulder at Liza and waved his hand to go toward the deep part of the channel.

Pretty soon they'll see the dock and the fishing boats tied up, kind of old ones not so much like the ones in Wrangell. And they'll tie up and walk up the path till they get to his house.

His grandma will be out in front getting some wood for the fire because it's getting a little cold. She'll see him walking on the path and she'll give him a hug and tell him, 'I'm glad you're home. I missed you.' And then she'll look behind him to see Goran.

He won't cry when he tells her. But right now, just for only a minute, tears keep on coming in his eyes.

The typeface utilized for the chapter headings and the title page in *Crow in Stolen Colors* has been chosen because it so beautifully seems to complement the text. Blue Island™ was created by British designer Jeremy Tankard for Adobe Systems in 1996-1999. A ligature-based Roman typeface, Blue Island™ strives to capture the flow of of waves and the undulating beauty of the sea. For the text, itself, we have selected Adobe Garamond™ adapted by Robert Slimbach from the original Garamond typefaces in the Plantin-Moretus Museum in Antwerp, Belgium and released as the first Abobe Originals™ typeface in 1989.